TWISTED LOVE

GEORGIA LE CARRE

TWISTED LOVE

GEORGIA LE CARRE

AUTHOR'S NOTE

Whisper of Warning

Earl James Jackson is a bit of an anti-hero. So if you are looking for a man who opens doors and leaves a trail of rose petals to the bedroom for his lover, then turn away now and look elsewhere…

CHAPTER 1

EARL

https://www.youtube.com/watch?v=e3-5YC_oHjE
-I still haven't found what I'm looking for-

The lilies reek.

I fucking hate lilies.

I learned to hate them because of her. Lilies are for funerals, she used to say. Their strong sweet cloying perfume used to suffocate her and make her feel faint. And yet they seem to be the main theme of the décor of her wedding. The church looks like a glamorous winter woodland, but it doesn't fool me. Not for one second. Nothing about this charade does.

Clearly, the bride had no say in her own wedding arrangements.

But I know who did. Her new mother-in-law, the high and mighty Mrs. Evelyn Belafonte, sitting in the front pew in

her Chanel two-piece cream suit, her back ramrod straight, absolutely furious that her beloved son is marrying beneath him.

Well, I might be able to help there...

Sitting on the last pew of that cold, lovely church, farthest from the altar, I can't take my eyes off the blushing bride.

Raven Moore stands with her head bowed under a delicate veil, the soft lace spilling over her shoulders. Her dress fits her perfectly. It is elegant and understated, exactly what she dreamed about when we were dirt-poor kids living in the caravan park down the road. When she used to talk about this day like it was some kind of magical fairytale ending. Back then, fool that I was, I pictured it too.

Only in my version, I was the one standing beside her. I believed her, you see. Then, I believed we were one. No one and nothing could separate us. Not even death. Our love would last even beyond the grave.

'If I should die first, I will haunt you until you join me,' I vowed.

'Yes, you must. I wouldn't have it any other way,' she whispered back fiercely.

I stare at her now and my fists clench into blocks of hate. He lifts her veil and I want to rush forward and knock his hand away. I hate her, but she is mine forever. If I cannot have her love then I will have her hate.

Not yet, I remind myself, as I watch her get ready to say her vows to a man I'm certain she has no feelings for. How do I know?

Because she is a gold digger.

A beautiful liar.

She can always be counted on to sell herself to the highest

bidder. That is her downfall and perhaps it will be mine too. But I'm already dead inside. All that is left is my need for revenge. It eats at me, sharp and unrelenting, day and night, and follows me into my nightmares.

My gaze shifts to Charles Belafonte, the 'lucky' groom.

He stands tall and proud. He always was too smug for his own good. His handmade suit puts the finishing touch to this elaborate charade. His hand hovers close to hers, brushing against her fingers like he already owns her. His mouth is curved in that signature smirk, the one that used to make me want to wipe it off his dumb face with a fucking baseball bat.

He hasn't changed.

I haven't changed either. I still want to rip that arrogant sneer off his face and crush it beneath my heel until it becomes a howl of agony.

My jaw is clenched so hard it aches.

And Raven... She just stands there like a statue carved from some pale stone. Her head bowed as if she couldn't bear to look at him. Or maybe she's trying to hide her misery. Good, I hope she feels miserable. She deserves to.

Why shouldn't she feel as hollow and broken as I did the day I stood behind the door and heard her say the words I will never forget as long as I live?

Sure, he's a good kisser, but he has no prospects. A loser. A grease monkey. I'm only with him temporarily. As soon as I find someone with money—real money—I'm ditching him.

The words slam into me like they did back then, cutting deeper than they have any right to after all these years.

Real money. I turn my attention back to Charles. Sorry, but that won't be you, Charles, my boy. His wealth, his status —it's all gone. He's living a big fat lie. He's nothing but a fraud, senselessly and quickly blowing up even the last scraps of wealth his father left behind.

This wedding is lavish, but it's all smoke and mirrors, an illusion created on borrowed time. Charles pulled every string, cut every corner, and scraped the bottom of the barrel to make this grand wedding happen. All for her. To keep her. To fool her into thinking he's still the big cheese she thinks he is. Ha, ha, Raven is about to experience the biggest disappointment of her life.

I should allow her to walk right into her own version of a nightmare. Marry a man who can't give her the rich life he promised, and who will disappoint her every day for the rest of her life. But no. That's not enough pain for her. No, Raven Moore must suffer brutally and at my hands.

Watching her realize she traded me for a useless fool won't fill the void. I am here to wreak havoc. For Charles, it'll be the humiliation of everyone knowing he's nothing but a spoiled brat who has squandered away a great fortune. For Raven, it'll be a longer, slower revenge, and I'll have the front-row seat to every moment of it.

The priest's voice echoes through the church.

"If anyone has an objection to this union, speak now or forever hold your peace."

My chest tightens. It's time.

The priest smiles and clears his throat, the small sound amplified by the silence of the room. His voice is steady as he speaks, ready to move them another step closer to saying their vows.

"Since no one has an objection to this union…

My heart pounds, steady and deliberate. My breath slows. This is it.

I push to my feet, the pew beneath me creaking softly. All at once, the air shifts. A collective gasp ripples through the congregation. Every head swivels in my direction.

The tall, dark man in black. That's what they'll whisper

later, the stranger who stood at the back of the church and shattered a perfectly beautiful illusion.

My voice is calm, clear and deliberate. "I object."

The words hang in the air, thick and heavy, settling over the crowd. Raven's head snaps up and her spectacular gold-speckled green gaze rushes towards me. How long I've waited for this moment? They widen in shock as her lips part in a gasp of dismay.

And in that moment, for the first time in years, she sees the monster she has created.

CHAPTER 2

RAVEN

https://www.youtube.com/watch?v=qrO4YZeyl0I
-bad romance-

Until he spoke, I was trapped in a suffocating, slow-moving dream.

I stare at him in confusion, my heart racing. Unable to believe he is real. He is standing at the back of the church, tall and broad, the dark lines of his suit cutting sharply against the white-grey walls. His hair is longer, his stance still, but his dark eyes cut through the church like shards of glass, locking onto mine. Is it really him? It can't be.

But it is.

It is Earl James Jackson.

I blink with shock. I want to rush to him. Throw my arms around him and tell him since he left, I've been dead inside.

Then he moves and my breath catches. A jolt of alarm goes through me. His movements are deliberate, controlled, and somehow menacing. Like he is untouched by the chaos he's just unleashed.

He walks up the aisle, his black shoes crushing the rose petals, the sound of his footsteps echoing in the stillness. Panic and fear swirl inside me.

He's not happy to see me.

He hasn't come to claim me.

As if from far away I hear Charles mutter, "What the fuck?" The scandalized murmurs of the guests fade into a distant hum. My chest tightens, each step of his polished shoes on the hard floor hits like a hammer against my ribs. The memories flood in, unbidden. The way he used to smile, that big grin full of confidence and mischief. His eyes, so black and shiny with so much love. The delicious sound of his laugh. The wonderful feel of his touch...

This cold stranger radiating wrath and fury isn't him.

This man is physically different too. His shoulders are broader, his movements more commanding. His jaw is sharper, his gaze icy cold, the warmth I once knew swallowed whole by something dark and dangerous. There is an air of wealth about him. The suit hugs his frame like it was specially made for him, the lines crisp and unyielding.

Nobody moves. Not even Charles. Everybody is too shocked. Suddenly he's at the altar looming over me.

I can't breathe.

"Raven," he says, his voice low, almost a growl. The hairs on the back of my neck rise.

He looks at me like I'm a stranger. Like I mean nothing to him.

"Charles won't be able to keep you in the life of luxury you think he will," he says. His words are calm, deliberate, each one slicing deeper.

I feel the blood drain from my face. My lips part, but no sound comes out.

"But I will," he adds, his gaze locking on mine. "If you marry me."

The entire congregation gasps, then goes utterly silent. Every breath, every sound, every shift of fabric stops as his words leave his mouth.

The bouquet slips in my hands, nearly falling to the floor as my fingers go numb.

"Is this a joke?"

My nervous gaze sweeps the crowd, faces frozen in shock, eyes darting between me and the man standing at the altar. It can't be anything else. Who interrupts a wedding with something like this?

But Earl isn't joking.

His expression is unreadable—cold, sharp, like the cut of a blade. He doesn't move, doesn't blink, as if daring anyone to challenge the words that just set this room on fire. Slowly, deliberately, he climbs the few steps up to the altar.

He's not joking.

He's serious.

The room holds its collective breath, waiting for someone to speak, to break this unbearable tension. And then Charles, standing beside me, bursts into a strange laughter.

It's loud, abrupt, and jarring, shattering the deathly quiet like glass. I stare at him in amazement. He doesn't say, 'How dare you interrupt my wedding? Get out.' Instead, he laughs, a forced, almost guilty sound. "Oh, for a second there," he says, still laughing. "I didn't recognize you."

I glance at him, confused, but he doesn't even look my way. His focus is entirely on Earl, his smirk widening into something cruel.

"I should have known," Charles continues, his voice dripping with mockery and carrying across the room, smooth and confident like he's putting on a show for the audience. "Who else would pull something this ridiculous? Still trying to reach heights you don't deserve to be at, are you?"

Earl's eyes narrow, a flicker of something dangerous passing through them, but he doesn't respond. Not yet.

Charles doesn't stop. "I'll give you this—you clean up well. Where'd you borrow the suit?"

The air feels electric, the tension thick enough to choke on. Earl doesn't say a word, but the way he looks at Charles —sharp, cold, unrelenting—sends a chill down my spine.

Charles, oblivious or unwilling to back down, turns to the crowd, gesturing grandly. "Ladies and gentlemen," he says, his voice full of false charm, "allow me to introduce Earl Jackson. The greasy mechanic from Seagate. You know, the shop down on Maple, the one that can never quite fix anything right. You've probably met his father—the drunk who couldn't hold down a job no matter how much you paid him."

A few uneasy chuckles ripple through the crowd, but most people stay silent, their eyes locked on Earl.

Charles shrugs and there is a smirk on his face, but his voice seems nervous. "And here he is. The renegade back from the dead. The one who got himself expelled from high school and disappeared off the face of the earth."

I don't hear the rest. Charles's voice fades into the background, his words lost in the roaring in my ears. My eyes are on Earl.

I can't stop looking at him.

He's here, standing just feet from me, and it's like time is folding in on itself. Memories crash into me— he stands on the railway tracks tilting his head up to the sky shouting to the universe, "I love her. She's mine." He was the boy who made me feel like the center of creation, even though the world around us was in tatters.

But this isn't the boy I remember.

He's much broader, his presence larger, heavier, and impossible to ignore. The suit Charles mocked is immaculate, tailored to skim every inch of him, the lines crisp and unyielding. His jaw is sharper, his shoulders stronger, and those dark eyes—God, those eyes—are darker, full of bitterness and wrath.

Even so ... underneath it all, I can still see traces of him.

I can still see the wonderful soul I fell in love with when I was eleven years old. The Earl I never stopped loving, no matter how much I tried to convince myself otherwise.

My chest tightens, and tears sting my eyes. Oh, how much I've missed him and still do.

I hate that I still do, but I can't stop it.

My heart throbs painfully in my chest, the ache so deep it feels like it might swallow me whole because no matter how much I try to deny it, part of me never stopped being his.

CHAPTER 3

EARL

I don't waste another moment on Charles. The man is a joke, and his words are nothing but air. I don't need to defend myself to him. I turn my attention to Raven.

She's frozen in place, her veil half-shrouding her face, her eyes cast down. It's infuriating—how much I want to tear that delicate lace away so there's nothing between us and see her eyes, to find the truth in them.

"Raven," I say, my voice cutting through the silence.

She flinches and lifts her eyes upwards, and I feel a jolt. Like a hiss of electricity. An emotion I can't place. I tell myself it's the intensity of hate in my heart. Her trembling fingers grip the bouquet like it's her only anchor. I planned this day for so long. I will be victorious. I take a deep breath.

"Charles won't be able to keep you," I say, my tone steady and deliberate, but it cuts through the tension like a blade. "Not in the life you imagine he will."

The crowd shifts. Murmurs ripple through the room like the low hum of an approaching storm. I can already imagine the delicious gossip that will be flowing rampantly in the beauty parlors, hairdressers, and over cups of tea and muffins in living rooms tomorrow. Let them all be shocked. Let them all watch.

"Excuse me?" Charles steps forward, his voice rising in contrived indignation. "What the hell are you talking about?"

Charles grabs my shoulder as if he wants to shove me back, but I'm faster, much faster. My arm snaps up, striking his wrist with enough force to send him backwards. He yelps, his hand recoiling as he cradles his wrist with his other hand. The little coward crouches slightly as if to shield himself from further harm. All the smugness drains from his face and is replaced by shock and ... to my delight ... fear. Good. About time he knows we are not the same. The only reason I never retaliated before was because Raven was so eager to be friends with his sister. That reason is gone now, forever.

I lean in just enough for him to feel the full weight of my words. "Touch me again," I say, my voice calm but laced with venom. "And I promise, you'll regret it for the rest of your miserable life."

Charles's eyes flicker, indecision and humiliation warring in his expression, but he doesn't move, doesn't even dare to look at me directly.

I nod with satisfaction. His role today is already over.

Entirely ignoring him, I take another step towards Raven and shift my whole attention to her. My voice softens. "You deserve to know the truth," I say, and I see the flicker of something in her posture—a tremor, a hesitation.

"Charles is a fraud. He's been pretending to be rich ever since his father died and left him with huge debts. He's bankrupt, Raven." I swing my arm to encompass the interior of the church. "All of this is borrowed money and favors. His great hope is that you don't find out until it's too late."

The crowd gasps, the scandalized shock rippling outward. Raven's bouquet shakes in her hands. I see the white petals trembling. Her beautiful lost eyes stare into mine. Oh, Raven!

Charles, regaining his nerve and posture, scoffs. "That's enough. You're out of line."

I don't even glance his way. He's irrelevant.

"And the house," I say, keeping my gaze locked on hers. "The fine home you think you'll be moving into? It doesn't belong to him anymore. It belongs to me. I bought it from the bank months ago."

Her breath catches audibly this time, a faint sound that sends a rush of lovely satisfaction through me.

Finally, Charles's mask cracks. "You're lying," he cries desperately. "Raven, he's lying! Don't believe him. I love you."

But she's not looking at him. She's staring at me, the shock in her eyes unmistakable. Her lips part, but no words come out.

I lean in slightly, my voice dropping to something almost intimate, like we're the only two people in that church. "He can't give you the life he promised, Raven ... but I can."

Her shoulders stiffen, and her breathing is shallow and uneven. The room is dead silent now, the weight of my words pressing down on everyone.

The corners of my mouth twitch into a faint smile as I straighten. I cannot wait to see how my beautiful gold digger will respond.

CHAPTER 4

RAVEN

*M*y throat is dry as sandpaper and my mind is a jumbled mess. Everyone is staring, waiting for me to respond, as if there is some way to make sense of the chaos Earl has unleashed. This has to be a joke. A cruel, ridiculous prank to ruin my wedding day.

But then I turn my head, and my gaze falls on my father sitting in the front pew. His face is ashen, his hands are gripping the arm of the bench so tightly his knuckles are bone white. He looks stricken, more fragile than I've ever seen him.

Reality crashes down on me like a suffocating weight. Hell no! This isn't a dream. This is happening. To me. On my freaking wedding day.

Earl's words echo like a bell in my ears: Charles is broke. A fraud. I force myself to breathe deeply and to find something solid in the swirl of madness around me. Earl's offer to marry me still hangs in the air, bold and unrelenting, as if he didn't just flip my entire world upside down in front of the entire town.

"Raven," Charles's voice pulls me back. I turn to him slowly, my mind racing.

He's smiling, but it's forced, tight and mean. His hand touches my arm lightly, a gesture meant to comfort me, but it only adds to my disbelief and confusion.

"He's lying," Charles says, his face is white and his voice crawls with desperation. "It's not true. None of it."

Earl is not lying. My gut tells me Charles is lying.

Charles glances wildly at the crowd, his face suddenly flushing under their scrutiny. "I can explain everything. I promise to tell you everything. We'll talk about it all later," he adds, his voice dropping to an urgent whisper. "Let's finish the ceremony, get married, and then we can deal with … whatever nonsense this is."

"Nonsense?" Earl's unapologetic voice cuts through the air like a blade.

I turn back to him and my breath catches at the sheer force of his presence. He seems immovable, his dark eyes blazing with a fierce and unyielding hatred.

"You'll be making a big mistake if you marry him," he says, his gaze locking on me. "But I guess that's what you do, isn't it, Raven? Make massive, catastrophic mistakes and hurt all the people around you."

My heart feels like it is full of shards of glass, the way it felt that day when I woke up and realized my love had left forever. The pain, sharp and unrelenting, threatens to unravel me. Not here. Not in front of the whole town.

Charles steps in then, his strides hurried as he grabs my arm. His grip is too tight, bordering on painful.

"Ignore him, Raven," he mutters under his breath, his voice quivering with barely concealed panic. I've known him long enough to notice the subtle cracks in his mask, to hear the things that betray his fear.

Earl's smile becomes nasty, his dark eyes flick down to Charles's hand on my arm. That look makes the hairs on the back of my neck stand. When he speaks his voice is scathing.

"Still clinging to things that don't belong to you, Charles?"

Charles stiffens but doesn't release me. His jaw is clenched tight and his carefully constructed facade that I've only seen slip once looks in mortal danger of being completely destroyed. "You're delusional, Earl," he shouts frantically. It is almost as though he is addressing the entire congregation. "This is a desperate stunt, and everyone here knows it."

In contrast, Earl entirely ignores the congregation. They might as well not have existed for all the attention he pays them. He tilts his head slightly, the move deliberate as a slow, mocking smile stretches across his face. "Do they really?" he asks, his tone dripping with contempt.

Charles stiffens with a barely controlled temper. Earl pulls out his phone, his fingers moving purposefully over the screen.

"There it is," Earl says, turning the screen toward me. His voice is cool, steady, and somehow even more infuriating.

I stare at the glowing screen and the title deed of Thornfield Hall is right there, undeniable, glaring at me.

"This is the deed to your bridegroom's family estate," Earl says, his words cutting through the thick silence. "You might want to read it carefully."

I can't move.

"Don't take it, Raven. Please. Trust me, just this once. I promise I can explain everything," Charles implores.

My heart pounds in my chest, and my hands tremble as I take the phone from Earl. My eyes dart over the document, desperate to find something, anything that proves him wrong.

But I don't.

Charles's name isn't on it.

Earl's is.

He takes a deliberate step closer, his voice calm and cutting as he explains, "He has no money left, Raven. Isn't that what you need? Isn't that what you've always wanted? Is that not why you are marrying him? If it is, then marry me right now. And if it's not, well then, I will take my leave and you will never see me again."

My gaze stares unseeingly at the screen as my world spins, tilting wildly.

The church waits. Earl waits.

And yet I can't find the words to speak. The air feels like it's pressing in on me, a suffocating weight of silence and judgment. Every gaze in the room is glued onto me, waiting for my response. The scandalized whispers have died down, leaving an oppressive quiet that makes the pounding of my heart almost deafening.

I lift my head and force myself to look at Earl.

His eyes are fixed on mine, sharp and unyielding, daring me to speak, to humiliate myself. Is that what he wants? For me to fall into his carefully laid trap and show everyone here, including him, that I care more about the money than anything else? That I'm the gold-digging liar that he for some reason believes me to be.

I shake my head with confusion.

Why would he even think that? The question pounds in my head. Why would he come here after all these years, just to disgrace me like this? Why disappear without a word, only to reappear in the cruelest way possible?

I should shove him off the altar and spit in his face. God

knows he deserves it. But I don't move. My gaze flies over to the front pew where my father is seated. His ashen face is a stark reminder of why I'm standing here in the first place.

The town's perception of me has never mattered, and it doesn't now. Let them think what they want. I've never lied to Charles, not once. From the start, I told him exactly what I needed from this marriage—a way to take care of my father. He promised me he could do it, and in exchange, he hoped he could make me fall in love with him over time. I warned him it was unlikely to ever happen, but he was willing to take the risk.

So long as my father gets the treatment he needs, what does it matter whether it is Charles's money or Earl's money? I don't care what anyone thinks of me. For a moment I stand as still as a statue, and the whole world becomes motionless with me like a moment frozen in time ... before everything changes forever.

Then I square my shoulders and turn to Earl. My voice is steady, louder and steadier than I thought it would be. "Are you able to provide everything Charles promised me?"

Shock ripples through the crowd like an electric current, the weight of my words hanging heavy in the charged air.

Earl's smile widens maddeningly. His confidence, his arrogance—it's like he knew I would say this. He steps closer, his voice dropping low, intimate, but loud enough for everyone to hear. "I am and I will. Everyone right here, right now, is my witness."

A collective gasp echoes through the church, the murmurs swelling again. Charles's face flushes a deep, angry red, his mouth opening and closing but no sound comes out.

"You're out of your mind!" Charles finally shouts, his voice cracking. "This is insane! He's a mechanic. Someone bought the property and I'll explain it all to you later, but it is not him. It's an offshore company in the Cayman Islands. Raven, he's bluffing. You can't actually believe him."

Before I can respond, another voice rises, sharp and cutting through the tension like a blade.

"Raven Moore!"

Charles's mother's voice slices through the room, her sharp heels clicking decisively against the marble as she rises to her feet to walk towards us. Her face is a mask of disbelief and indignation, her tone dripping with condescension. "Are you about to do what I think you are?"

My stomach churns. I've always loathed her—her sneering, superior attitude, the way she looks at me as if I'm one of the hundreds of slaves her proud ancestors used to own. To her, I'm someone without any appreciable status and should be dismissed without another thought. There is nothing I could do to ever earn her respect, but to her eternal horror, her son is adamant on marrying me so she has resigned herself to subtly mocking me for the amusement of her high and mighty friends while praying he will change his mind.

Today she has her wish, but not in the way she prayed for.

I do the worst thing I could possibly do to her. I glance away from her as if she is irrelevant. Because she is and always has been. I turn my focus back to Earl. My heart is pounding, so loud it drowns out the noise around us. A steady, rhythmic thud that anchors me, pushing me onward even though my legs feel like they might give out.

His gaze has never left me. There's no hesitation in his eyes, no second thoughts, no hint of doubt. And for the first time today—hell, for the first time since this entire mess began—I feel like I'm finally present at my own wedding. No more autopilot, no more mechanical motions. I feel awake. Alive. My chest tightens with something I can't quite name.

"Okay," I say, my voice clear and unwavering. I stare

straight into Earl's dark eyes, daring him to look away. "Okay, I'll marry you."

The room erupts into chaos.

The betrayal is too much for Charles. He stands there like a lost sheep, his face twisted with disbelief and hurt until his mother marches towards him. Grabbing his hand, she storms out while muttering curses at me. Their guests follow, trailing behind, some of them murmuring insults under their breath, others are too stunned to speak.

I take a deep breath and turn towards my bridegroom.

CHAPTER 5

EARL

*T*here are over a hundred people still left in the room and their collective astonishment and faint murmurs of disapproval — there is still great respect and awe for Charles's family in this town —fade into white noise. The only thing I can focus on is my bride.

Ah, Raven.

It's not love. I deny that with every fiber of my being. It's something else entirely—maybe shock, maybe disbelief— because it has been easier, much easier than I ever dreamed of or expected. She didn't even put up a token gesture of resistance. And now I'm going to marry the woman I've sworn I hate. The reality of my revenge feels surreal. Like I've stepped into someone else's life. Or perhaps just mine. My past life.

Raven's voice pulls me back to the moment. Her words are quiet, like stones dropped into a well. "Have you changed your mind?"

"No." My voice is steady. From my pocket, I retrieve the set of gold rings I prepared in advance and turn towards the gaping priest. "You may proceed."

The priest looks at me like I've grown a second head before his gaze shifts to Raven, searching for confirmation. She nods, her expression unreadable. Disbelief ripples like a wave across the room. The priest, after a brief hesitation, clears his throat and begins to take us through our vows.

I say the words I never thought I'd speak, the ones I don't mean. Each one feels heavy, deliberate, tying me to something I can't undo and I will never let her undo.

Raven recites hers, her voice soft but unwavering. Her gaze doesn't falter. It's almost as if she means it, but obviously, she doesn't. That's something that's not up for debate. She was going to marry Charles until she found out his ass was broke. She's marrying me for my money. Nothing more.

"You may kiss the bride," the priest says and my body acts instinctively. It wants to. Damn my traitorous body! I turn away from her as if she is poison, and the ceremony ends in pure chaos. Everyone is shocked. Raven gasps at the deliberate and humiliating public snub. Her pained gasp is music to my ears. It makes my bitter heart dance. This is the beginning, my dear wife. This is the beginning of your punishment and my revenge.

People leave in droves. They don't know how to react so they file out quickly in hushed confusion. In the end, it's just me, Raven, and her parents.

Her father, pale and frail in his wheelchair, glares at me with the kind of disapproval that long ago would have made me rush to apologize and heal the relationship. Not anymore. I don't care if he disapproves. I am nothing to him. He is nothing to me.

"You should annul this marriage immediately," he says sharply.

I meet his furious gaze calmly. "Why?"

His lips press into a thin line of fury. "You can't just turn up and do this. You've ruined my daughter's wedding day and made her the laughingstock of the town. Can't you see what you have done?"

I don't respond. Partly because I don't care, and partly because he won't like my answer.

Her father's voice rises slightly, his anger bubbling to the surface. "You didn't even ask for my permission. Everything about this is wrong."

Before I can answer, Raven steps forward, her voice calm but filled with a quiet intensity. "It's not wrong, Dad. It's fine."

He shakes his head with confusion. "Why are you agreeing to this madness? You don't have to get married to either of them, sweetheart."

"Dad," she replies. "Don't worry. Everything will be okay."

Her father shakes his head, his expression a mixture of frustration and sorrow. I turn away from his impotent anger and address Raven.

"I won't be attending the reception. You may go if you wish, but I expect you to move into Thornfield Hall today. The movers are there right now to enforce the change of ownership and a car will be sent to your home in a couple of hours to pick you up."

She seems shocked, most likely because she realizes that none of this happened on a whim, but she hasn't deciphered yet why it is happening. I don't care to sate her curiosity so I turn around and step out of the church into the cool, quiet air. The world feels different now. I look down at the gold band on my finger and a smile grows on my face. I just fucking married Raven Moore. Then, still smiling, I stroll down the steps, letting the distance grow between me and the chaos I just caused.

My dove-gray Aston Martin sits like an absurd symbol of wealth in a town that feels like it's stuck in the wrong decade. It gleams under the ray of light breaking through the rain-heavy clouds, daring anyone to comment on how out of place it is. I slide into the driver's seat and wait for the engine to purr into life, smooth and steady.

I can still see her pale face as she whispered those two little words. "I do."

She doesn't know she has inalterably changed the trajectory of her life. The words loop in my mind, relentless. I shift the car into gear, letting the familiarity of the road pull me forward. My father's house isn't far. It's tucked away in the quiet outskirts of town. It's a world away from the trailer park we used to live in, a place that still feels like a scar in my memory. My knuckles tighten on the wheel as I think of him forced into his sterile box of order and recovery. My father never belonged anywhere that asked him to be anything but broken. Now, he's trying to put himself back together and, I guess, I'm supposed to be here for it.

The road blurs under the rain as my mind drifts elsewhere, pulled back to a memory of another rainy day.

It was the first week of high school.

I hadn't been in town long and Blaze High Academy had its own way of treating new arrivals from the trailer park. I'd already caught enough sullen stares to know I was unwelcome. Nobody talked to me or wanted to sit next to the trailer park trash, but that bothered me none. I was the quiet, angry kid with grease-stained hands and a chip on my shoulder the size of this entire goddamned town. I didn't need friends, didn't want them. All I wanted was to get through the day without anyone trying to test me.

That morning, I walked into class late. Heads turned, whispers followed, but I paid no mind.

Charles was already there, front and center, turning around to look mockingly at me like the smug asshole he was. His father pulled strings around town, no doubt. The family was like royalty and he was Prince Prick. The seat next to him was empty, but his bag was perched on the chair like a territorial claim. The desk in the corner was empty. I dropped my bag onto it and pulled the chair out. The scrape of the wood was loud in the awkward silence.

Then Raven sauntered in. Of course, I'd noticed her. Who wouldn't? She was smoking hot, the best-looking girl in town.

Charles pulled his bag away and grinned at her, but she walked right past him and headed straight for me. I heard the murmurs of disbelief. Charles's grin of welcome faltered, his face twisting with rejection as she passed his desk.

"What are you doing?" His voice was sharp and furious.

"Sitting where I want," she tossed back carelessly, like it was the most obvious thing in the world to reject the seat Boy Wonder had saved for her.

Charles's jaw was clenched so tight I thought it might snap. His gaze burned into her back, but she was beautifully oblivious to him. She pulled out the chair next to me and slid into it. Her bag hit the floor with a soft thud, and she pulled out her notebook and gave me a wink.

I wanted to laugh. No one had ever chosen to sit next to the boy from the wrong side of town until today, but the coolest girl in town obviously didn't give a shit about what anybody else thought. She acted like it didn't matter where I was from, or I wasn't dressed in designer gear, or what people might whisper about me behind my back. The teacher began her roll call in a monotone voice, and Raven sat next to me like it was the most natural thing in the world to do, and I fell in love.

But I didn't know it was then. I just assumed it was a mixture of curiosity, raging hormones and lust. I tried not to stare too hard at her hands, her hair, her strip of exposed skin between her pants and her white socks, the soft curve of her cheek, her mouth. By the time the last bell rang, the sky had opened up. Rain came down in heavy sheets, soaking the pavement outside the school. Most kids waited under the awning, pulling out umbrellas or calling their parents for rides.

I didn't have that luxury. My dad's truck was a piece of shit I didn't want to be caught getting into, and anyway, I wasn't about to call him for anything. I pulled my hood up and started walking, the rain quickly soaking through my jacket.

"Hey!" Her voice stopped me. I turned, and there she was, running toward me with her bag held over her head like it might do something to keep her dry.

"What?" I asked, my voice unintentionally sharp.

"Wait up. I'll walk with you."

My heart made a crazy leap inside my chest, but I wasn't about to show it. "You're gonna get soaked," I said, turning away from her.

"Already am." She fell into step beside me, her bag still held awkwardly above her head. "We live in the same park, don't we?"

I didn't answer. I was too shocked. Really? This beauty lived in the same park as me and Charles was holding a seat for her. I looked at her. And noticed that her clothes were cheap. Yet, there was something so special about her that she transcended her poverty and shone like a little star.

She stopped trying to shield herself with her bag and we walked in silence for a while, the rain pouring down on us, soaking us to the bone. By the time we reached the bus stop, we were both dripping. Two empty seats waited under the shelter. I sat next to her, leaning back and letting the sound of the rain fill the quiet.

"You look good, wet," she said with a soft laugh.

I watched her laugh and a smile tugged at the corners of my lips.

That was the start.

CHAPTER 6

RAVEN

*T*he late evening sun filters weakly through the curtains, casting long, golden streaks across the floor as I fold the last of my clothes. The closet is practically empty now—just a few hangers swinging like lonely skeletons on the rail. My hands pause over a faded hoodie, the fabric soft and worn, holding more memories than I'd like to admit. It's ridiculous how something as simple as an old sweater can feel like a thread to a past life, one that now seems impossibly far away.

Sunny, my best friend's voice crackles over the speakerphone, grounding me back in the present.

"I'm just saying," she says, her tone light but deliberate, "you have to talk to Earl. He used to be so easy to talk to. Friendly, even. He can't have changed that much."

Easy to talk to? Friendly? Not anymore. The man I married looks like Earl, but he is a stranger.

"I don't know, Sunny," I say, shaking my head as I shove the hoodie into the bag. "He's... different. Colder, harder. It's like he's carrying something, something dark, and I don't know what it is. But one thing is for sure he is very angry with me."

"With you? Why? He was the one who ghosted you and vanished off the face of the earth."

I frown. "I know."

"You have to ask him about it," Sunny says firmly. Her voice crackles slightly over the speakerphone, but her conviction is loud and clear. "I know it looks like an unsolvable mess, but you have to try. What worries me is that you're moving to Charles's former home. It's so weird. This entire thing feels like some sort of prank, and I keep waiting for the guys with the cameras to jump out."

This makes me smile despite myself. "Same here, but I'm willing to play along, as long as my father gets his treatment."

"I do think, though, that Earl came back for you. Why else would he come back to this shitty town when he is done well for himself? And why else would he snatch you away from Charles at the altar like that? There's something there. I'm convinced he's still in love with you. Just ... talk to him, okay? Find out what's going on in that thick head of his. He used to be so kind, but from all the wild talk flying around town, anyone would think you married the devil himself. For what it's worth, I think he looks even more dreamy than he did before. And he was already a ten out of ten then."

"Raven?" My mom's voice cuts into Sunny's monologue. I glance over my shoulder to see her standing in the doorway, worry etched into her face. Her hair is pulled back, and she's wearing that tired look she gets when something is weighing on her mind.

"Gotta go, Sunny," I say quickly and end the call. I turn to face my mom, brushing stray strands of hair out of my eyes.

She steps into the room, her gaze flicking to the half-packed bag on the bed. "Are you sure about this?" she asks, her voice heavy with concern. "Your father... he feels terrible about all of this. He's worried."

"Yes, I'm sure, Mom," I say, though my voice trembles under the weight of the lie. I force myself to meet her eyes, straightening my shoulders in an attempt to seem confident. "We've been... talking," I add quickly, glancing away as if that could make the lie less obvious. "Before today. I know the wedding was a bit of a scene, but things were always good between us. We understand each other and we'll work it out somehow."

The words taste sour as they leave my mouth, but I can't bring myself to admit the truth—that I am just as shocked as everyone else is.

My mom doesn't look convinced. She steps closer and lowers herself onto the edge of the bed. "And do you know why he disappeared all those years ago?" she asks gently, folding her hands in her lap.

I swallow hard and under the guise of grabbing another sweater from the closet, look away. "Issues with his dad, I think," I mumble, forcing nonchalance into my tone. "But the main thing is he's back now."

A thick unnatural silence stretches between us. When I finally look back at her, she's studying me, her expression unreadable.

"I always liked Earl, but he just seemed so different ... so furious," she says.

"It'll be okay, Mom. I promise. Earl was once my world, my anchor and nothing has changed."

She nods, stands, and places a hand briefly on my shoulder, a warm, fleeting touch. "The reason I came here is to tell you that a sleek black town car is parked outside, the kind you see in movies or TV shows, with a driver standing beside it in a crisp suit."

My eyes widen. "Thanks, Mom. Everything will be fine. You'll see."

"Just... take care of yourself, okay? And always remember, we're always here for you. No matter what happens you have a home here."

"Thanks, Mom," I blurt out before hugging her tightly.

I stand very still and watch her leave my room, but the moment she's gone, the composure I've been holding onto crumbles. My hands shake as I stuff the last few items into the bag, my mind racing.

Why did Earl leave? Why did he marry me if he hates me? And how am I supposed to make this work with someone who is convinced I'm a gold digger?

I shove the zipper closed and heave the bag off the bed, my heart pounding. There's no time to dwell on it now. I need to get to Thornfield Hall.

The rain has stopped and when I step outside, the elderly chauffeur who was leaning against the car, straightens and tips his cap in an oddly old-fashioned gesture.

"Mrs. Jackson?" he asks, his voice polite, professional.

"Uh... yes."

He opens the back door with a practiced motion. "Mr. Jackson asked me to pick you up and take you to Thornfield Hall."

I hesitate, gripping the strap of my bag tightly. The luxury, the formalities—it's all so far removed from the world we grew up in. From the trailer park. From the Earl I thought I knew.

As I slide into the car, sinking into the soft leather seat, I can't help but wonder: How did he come upon all this wealth? And what the hell happens next to us? The door closes and I'm ensconced in a gently perfumed, luxurious interior.

The journey to Charles's house feels both familiar and alien, like stepping into a memory that doesn't quite fit anymore. The town, with its tree-lined streets and weathered storefronts, hasn't changed much. The lake shimmers in the distance, surrounded by sprawling gardens, but now, everything feels surreal, like I'm watching someone else's life unfold.

I grip the handle of the car door tighter as the car turns into the driveway of the sprawling estate. My pulse has quickened and the nerves I've tried to suppress bubble up all at once as the house looms ahead. It's grand and imposing, with a pristine stone façade, wide wraparound porch, and manicured gardens that seem to stretch endlessly towards the lake. When I was a young girl living in poverty, I used to envy people living in such grandeur, but those days are gone. Now I see such massive mansions as glamorous prisons. The people who live in them are never truly happy. I wonder again how Earl came to be rich enough to buy this place.

The car comes to a smooth halt, gravel crunching softly under the tires. I hesitate for a moment, staring out at the house. Is this going to be my prison where I will never be happy? The chauffeur opens my door, his polite, "Mrs. Jackson" shaking me from my daze. The title feels strange, but foreign. Didn't I stand in front of the mirror a lifetime ago and practice saying it?

I nod and step out, clutching my purse tightly. The air smells of freshly cut grass and blooming flowers, but it does little to ease the nerves coiled tight in my stomach. None of this feels real.

I don't see Earl anywhere, and that unsettles me more than I care to admit. I glance back at the sleek black town car parked behind mine. Is that his?

Nora, the Belafonte's old housekeeper appears before I can spiral further, her warm smile a great comfort.

"Raven! Oh, my goodness, I'm so glad to see you!" she exclaims, her hands clasped in front of her as she approaches.

"Hi, Nora," I greet. I've always liked Nora. She's always been kind to me whenever I've come around. Her presence feels familiar and grounding, even as everything else feels unmoored.

"You look wonderful, Mrs. Jackson," she says, her pale blue gaze sweeping over me. There are questions in her eyes, but she's too well trained by Charles's mother to ever voice them. "I'm sure you must be exhausted with the day you've had. I've made a pot of tea for you and your favorite blueberry pie."

Nora's warm concern takes me off guard, and for a moment, I don't know how to answer. "Thank you, Nora. I don't think I can eat just yet. I'm a little nervous, I think."

"Well, that's to be expected," she says with a kind smile. "But don't you worry. The pie will keep. We'll take care of you here." She gestures toward the house, inviting me to follow her inside.

Walking through the front door feels like crossing some invisible threshold. The grand entryway is exactly as it was on my last visit, so are the gleaming hardwood floors, and the lofty ceilings, but the traditional chandelier I used to marvel at is gone. In its place hangs the most exquisitely sophisticated, massive white vine chandelier. I gasp at its ethereal beauty and once more feel a knot tightening in my chest. What did he do to get this kind of wealth? The thought doesn't sit right.

"The staff wanted to congratulate you in person," Nora says cheerfully, leading me further inside.

The other staff members stand in a polite line and convey their best wishes. They do so warmly enough, though I catch a few curious glances exchanged when they think I'm not looking. I can't blame them. What happened in the church was bizarre, to say the least and I probably seem as out of place as I feel.

The house is bustling with activity, movers hauling boxes out through the front doors as others carry Earl's things inside. The air hums with the sound of footsteps, shuffling cardboard, and muffled conversations.

Nora, noticing my distracted gaze, chuckles softly. "It's quite the scene today, isn't it? The movers are finishing up with the Belafonte's belongings. They should be out shortly." I turn towards her and she is watching me with her wise old eyes. "You belong here. You always have."

"What do you mean?"

She shrugs. "Houses are like dogs. You can never get one that is not meant for you."

"Oh."

Not knowing what to say I turn away, and through one of the long windows, watch a man carefully maneuver a box marked FRAGILE into the back of a long mover's lorry. It's surreal, to see the status symbols of Charles's family's life packed away and driven off. The house feels like it's in flux, caught between what it was and what it's about to become.

I wonder if I will see him in the house. Somehow, I don't expect to, but the thought still makes me nervous. He thinks of me as a gold digger, and my behavior today must have confirmed his opinion. I've always been clear and straight-forward with everyone; in fact, it's always been everyone else who hasn't been straight with me. I told Charles I wasn't in love with him. All I wanted from him was a loan so I could pay for my father's medical bills, instead he manipulated me into marrying him. What did he think would happen when I found out he had no means to help save my father's life?

My thoughts once again go to Earl. Once, I loved him so much that I nearly went crazy after his disappearance. Sometimes I think I have never recovered from it. That hole is still gaping in my chest. I've wondered so many times what I would do if I ever saw him again, and now that I have I cannot believe he's making me feel like I'm the one who was in the wrong. Like I'm the one who has something to be sorry for when he is the one who broke my heart into a million pieces.

Nora gestures toward the grand staircase. "Once things settle down, I'll take you on a proper tour. This house has a rich history. You'll want to get to know it."

The sound of heels clicking against the polished floors draws my attention. I look up to see Charles's mother descending the staircase, her posture as proud and regal as ever, her expression carved from stone. She looks every bit the picture of class and authority, her tailored dress immaculate, her chin tilted just high enough to make her disdain known.

When her eyes meet mine, they darken with something close to hatred. She pauses on the last step, her gaze sweeping over me. I'm an invader in her domain.

"Raven," she says, her voice clipped, each syllable dripping with venom. "Enjoying yourself, are you?"

I force myself to stay composed, even as my chest tightens. "Mrs. Belafonte," I reply, keeping my tone even. "I didn't expect to see you here."

Her lips curl into a sneer. "Well, well, well. Taken to the high life like a duck to water, I see. I always knew you would destroy my son, and you have, but be very careful, my dear. You have married a monster who detests you. I suggest you start your tour from the Music Room."

I glance at the movers coming down behind her, their arms laden with ornate lamps and hastily wrapped portraits. Her belongings. Her life. Everything she's built here is being taken away piece by piece. But I feel no pity in my heart. Not for her.

"Safe travels," I murmur and she sails past me, her expensive perfume lingering in her wake like a challenge.

I can't help but exhale a quiet breath of relief as she disappears through the front doors. The tension in the room shifts, like a storm that's finally passed.

Nora places a comforting hand on my arm, her smile warm but knowing. "Don't let her get to you, dear. The house is yours now."

I smile weakly, though the weight of her words settles heavily on my shoulders. My house. My life. No. This is not my house. It is Earl's. I desperately want to ask Nora to take me to the Music Room first, but I don't want to give any importance to her suggestion.

Nora continues the tour, her voice upbeat as she gestures toward various rooms and describes their functions. I try to focus on her words, but my thoughts are scattered. Every creak of the floorboards, every faint sound of the movers echoes too loudly in my ears. The house, with its vast hallways and ornate decor, feels both suffocating and empty. And the dread of what I will find in the Music Room hangs over me.

"I think you've probably already been in here," Nora says, her voice suddenly nervous, as she pushes open a pair of double doors, "but just in case you haven't, this is the music room."

I haven't. Charles's mother never let me go beyond the living room or the dining room. She never wanted me to feel like I belonged or was part of the family. I step inside the room. It is bathed in soft evening light slanting in through towering windows. A brand new black grand piano gleams in the almost empty room. The walls still bear the marks of all the paintings that once hung on them. But there is one painting that has recently been mounted over the fireplace. A life-size painting that stops me in my tracks. It can't be. I gasp in disbelief.

It is.

It is a portrait of me!

And yet it's not me. The crowned woman in the painting is seated on a gold throne. She is wearing a purple silk dress which exposes most of her breasts. Her posture is loose, her legs slightly open so some of the insides of her thighs are exposed, and her chin tilted in a flirtatious come-hither angle, but her eyes are hard and cold. She is decked in jewelry and gold coins drip carelessly from both her hands. She is undoubtedly a whore. A vulgar creature.

A gold digger.

My pulse pounds in my ears, and a hot flush of embarrassment spreads through me. I can't look away. Nora senses my reaction. She stands awkwardly to the side, her eyes darting between me and the lurid portrait. I can feel her unease. She is waiting for me to say something, do something.

"What... what is this?" My voice trembles.

Nora clears her throat uncomfortably. "It's... just a painting. Mr. Jackson had it commissioned. The artist is quite famous, I believe. The men moved it in earlier."

I feel my stomach twist, but I keep my expression steady, carefully neutral.

"Well, it's interesting," I say lightly and step closer to the enormous portrait as if I were admiring the brushstrokes. Inside, my thoughts are spinning, a storm I can barely contain.

"Art is never beautiful anymore. All art has to shock these days," Nora says quickly. The relief in her voice is palpable.

Who does something like this? My face stares back at me from the gold throne, cold and unrecognizable. The weight of the crown on my head in the painting seems to mock me, as though daring me to claim a role I never asked for. My jaw tightens, but I force a polite smile, nodding as if it's nothing at all.

Nora folds her hands anxiously in front of her. "Mr. Jackson told us all we could keep our jobs," she says, almost as if she's trying to reassure herself, but I catch the faintest tremor in her voice, the unease she's trying to hide. "He said nothing would change except for the ownership. It was. .. kind of him. I think he's a kind man. Underneath it all."

Kind. Her words settle awkwardly in the room. I glance at her from the corner of my eye. "That's good to hear," I reply with a small smile.

"Shall we continue with the tour, then?" she asks brightly, and I give her a small nod.

She leads me out of the music room, and I follow, my heart still pounding in my chest. The image of that cold and ugly version of myself stays lodged in my mind, impossible to shake.

We move through the rest of the house, Nora explaining its many features—the sitting room, the library, the garden view from the conservatory where breakfast will be served tomorrow morning. I make polite noises of acknowledgment, barely listening. Every corner of this house feels too large, too grand, like it belongs to someone else entirely.

Finally, she stops in front of a door near the end of the hallway on the first floor. "Mr. Jackson says this is your room," she says, pushing the door open with a small flourish.

I step inside and immediately notice what it isn't: the master bedroom. The space is lovely, with soft cream walls and a bed dressed in pale blue linens, but it's not where I imagined I'd be staying as the supposed mistress of the house. The realization lands like a quiet blow. Another humiliation. I push down the sting of it.

"Very nice," I say, my voice carefully even. "Thank you."

"You're welcome," Nora replies with a smile. "Well, I'll be downstairs. I'll send up a tray with refreshments, but please ring if you require anything else."

"Thank you, Nora."

She seems to want to say more, but instead, she nods and excuses herself, leaving me alone.

I want to call him, to confront him, to demand answers, but I don't even have his number. All I have are the old text messages on my phone, the ones I've read and reread so many times the words are seared into my memory.

I scroll through them now, my thumb lingering over the screen. Each message feels like a ghost, haunting me with fragments of who we used to be.

Then I sit on the edge of the bed, staring at the room. It's strange, feeling both relief and unease at the same time. Relief that I don't have to immediately share a room with Earl, but unease at the strangeness of my situation. He couldn't even bear to kiss me in the church. This marriage isn't meant to be real. Not in the way marriages are supposed to be.

I remind myself why I'm here. My father is getting the treatment he needs. That's what matters. Everything else is just noise. I can handle this. I have to.

Lying back against the pillows, I close my eyes, the painted image of myself on that throne flickering in the darkness behind my lids. And then I realize what this marriage is supposed to be.

It is supposed to be revenge.

CHAPTER 7

EARL

https://www.youtube.com/watch?v=bqIxCtEveG8
-beneath your beautiful-

"I'm the drunk, but sometimes you're the one who acts like you're not in your right mind," my father grumbles.

The sharp citrus scent of mandarins fills the air as I peel another one, the sticky juice coating my fingers. My father's eyes track every movement, his gaze heavy, and I can feel the weight of his unspoken thoughts pressing down on me.

"You know you caused a scandal, right?" my father asks, his voice carrying that undercurrent of sardonic humor he never seems to lose.

I glance at him, my expression unreadable. "For someone in seclusion, you seem remarkably informed."

His lips twitch into a bitter smile. "It's a small town, Earl. People talk. Especially when you do something this asinine."

I place the peeled mandarin in front of him and sit back,

leaning against the faded armrest of the chair. The room smells faintly of stale whiskey and the faint antiseptic tang that clings to places like this. His hands hover over the fruit for a moment before he picks it up and bites it like one would an apple, his eyes never leaving mine. Juices run down his chin. I'll never understand why he can't eat oranges like the rest of humanity.

"What's really going on in that head of yours?" he asks, his tone turning sharper. "What are your actual intentions? Why did you marry the girl you once told me you hated?"

My chest tightens, but I keep my expression unreadable. When I don't respond, he leans forward, his voice lowering, weighted with something between curiosity and accusation. "She came to see me, you know. After you left. Tried to find out where you were, why you disappeared."

My fingers dig into the armrest, but I keep my face blank. The memories of those days when I left this god-forsaken town feel distant, like something from another life, but the edge of it is still sharp enough to cut.

"I chased her off," he admits, a nasty chuckle escaping his throat. "Told her I didn't know where you were, and I didn't. Hell, I still don't know why you ran off like that or where you went. Supposedly, you loved her so much back then. So why'd you suddenly leave?"

The room feels stifling, the air thick with the unspoken tension hanging between us. I stare at the far wall, willing myself not to react, not to let him know how I really feel inside—just how hurt I'd been, just how much I'd loved her. Back then, I would have cut off my right arm and handed it to her on a platter if she'd asked. And to this day, it stuns me how naive I was, how completely smitten I was over someone who didn't deserve it.

"You always do this," he mutters bitterly, more to himself

than to me. "Keep everything locked up tight. Like you think no one can see what's going on in that damn head of yours. But I see it, Earl. I know a thing or two about ghosts, and seeing how impulsive you've been, I can tell they're eating you alive. Don't let them."

I finally look at him, meeting his gaze head-on. His eyes are bloodshot, but there's a clarity there that surprises me. For a moment, I wonder if he's right. Have I spent so long holding onto the hurt she caused that I've lost the ability to think rationally?

But I don't say any of that. I don't trust him. He is my father, but he's not a good man. Anything I say will be used against me one day. I stand. "I'm leaving."

He doesn't say goodbye, but I don't care. I've had a lifetime of practice. I don't look back either. I step outside into the cool night air, the quiet pressing against my ears like a living thing.

The rain has cleared the sky and made the stars shine bright. Immediately, thoughts of Raven come unbidden, so many sweet memories under the stars. I frown with frustration. I swore I wouldn't let her get to me again and keep this arrangement purely in revenge mode. But already the clear crisp edges are blurring, and I can't tell if it's her fault or mine.

I get into my car and sit quietly for a moment. My father's words settle into the silence with me. More memories flood into my head. Time passes and the chill of the night begins to creep around me. I hadn't planned on being away this long, but here I am. Unable to leave the past and go out to meet the future.

She's in the house now. I know because Ryan called to tell me he'd dropped her off. I don't have to see her to know she's probably unpacked her things, probably exploring, probably seen the portrait hanging in the music room.

I smirk as I think about that painting that she must have seen by now.

It was a spur-of-the-moment idea. I was walking past an art shop downtown and saw a caricature portrait in a similar style—gaudy, exaggerated. A mockery, and yet it was riveting. The image formed in my head before I could stop it: her, sitting on a throne like some haughty whore. Her hard, cold eyes looking down at me for the fool I had been.

But she is not a whore. She never has been. It was unfair. There is a flicker of something unwelcome—regret, maybe. It's faint, but it's there, crawling under my skin. I clench my jaw and squash it down. I'm not going to start feeling sorry for her. That way madness lies. I press harder on the gas pedal, and focus on the road ahead.

The drive back is short, the streets of town giving way to the expansive estate. The house emerges ahead, its grandeur lit softly by the glow of strategically placed lights along the driveway. It still feels foreign to me, this place. Too big, too polished, too much for me.

I park and step out into the cold air. Nora greets me at the door, her cheerful demeanor tempered with something more tentative tonight.

"Welcome back, Mr. Jackson. Dinner is ready to be served whenever you please," she says, her tone cautious.

I grunt a response and hand her my coat, my eyes scanning the polished floors and the new chandelier. It was a good decision. It looks almost magical in this setting.

I'm not hungry, but I stride toward the dining room.

The long table is set for two. Crystal chandeliers overhead cast soft light on the polished wood and velvet-lined chairs. The blood-red walls are checkered with a darker shade of rectangles and squares left by the paintings that have been removed.

"Dinner is ready," Nora says, her voice hesitant. "Should I invite Mrs. Jackson to join you? She hasn't eaten yet. Perhaps she was waiting for you."

I don't even look at her. "No," I say flatly, taking a seat at the head of the table.

With a quiet nod, she retreats, leaving me alone in the vast room. I stare out into the garden, my mind blank until the food arrives.

The silence stretches as I pick at the food, the clink of silverware against fine China the only sound. It is a feast by anyone's standards—roast shank of lamb, buttery vegetables, fresh-baked rolls, some sort of lime and chocolate dessert, fruit, cheese—but I barely taste any of it. My mind is elsewhere, circling back to her, to the painting, to the way this house feels more like a stage than a home.

Somewhere upstairs, she's probably unpacking, settling in, trying to figure out what the hell I'm playing at. Let her wonder. This is what she wanted, isn't it? To be the mistress of a grand estate, to live the life of luxury she'd always dreamed of?

I stab a piece of lamb with my fork, the force of it scraping against the plate. Let her have it. I'll make sure she enjoys every second of it.

When Nora is gone, I sit back alone with a glass of brandy and the echoes of my own thoughts. I've won. This is what winning feels like. This is how I get even.

And yet, for the briefest moment, I wonder if anyone would really call this winning.

CHAPTER 8

RAVEN

https://www.youtube.com/watch?v=OpQFFLBMEPI
-just give me a reason-

I shut my eyes and the glow of the laptop burns through my closed eyelids. Exhaustion zaps away all my energy, and hunger gnaws at my stomach. I should have eaten something earlier when Nora offered, but I stupidly refused, and then the thought of roaming the house and possibly running into him was too much to contemplate. I open my eyes and stare at the open manuscript I've been tasked with editing. It's a romance novel, the kind of story I used to dream of writing when I was younger.

Back then, it had all been so simple. Love wasn't a plot device in a novel I was editing; it was something I truly believed in, something I thought was real because I had felt it. I wrote from the heart. The words flowed easily—what I knew was raw and consuming. It left me breathless and I simply transferred it onto the pages of my novel.

But after he left, I couldn't bring myself to write a single word.

So I'm editing now. I fix other people's stories, trying to piece together happy endings when I know they don't exist. It's ironic, in a way. Here I am, making sense of fictional love while my own life is a mess I can't untangle.

I walk to the door, open it, and listen. I hear the faint sounds from far away, a chair scraping against the floor. I wonder if I'll get to eat tonight. He, on the other hand, is eating, I'm sure. I know he's back, I can feel his presence, and yet the distance between us feels insurmountable.

Should I stay here, invisible and hungry, or go down and face him? The minutes stretch. I hear the faint sound of the front door opening and closing. Then silence. This is stupid. I tell myself to shower, freshen up and go downstairs, but I can't move. My body feels frozen.

Suddenly, the sound of his voice, low and indistinct, floats up from somewhere below. Instantly, it pulls me from my thoughts and makes me recoil back into my room. I shut the door quickly and lean against it. He's here. Somewhere in this house, moving through it like a shadow.

I feel like a trapped animal.

I want to cry with sadness and frustration, but I don't. I refuse to cry. Anger rises instead, hot and fierce, because it's the only way I know how to protect myself from the ache in my chest. If I'm angry, I can win—whatever "winning" means in this strange, painful battle we're in.

The floor creaks faintly in the corridor outside, and my heart leaps into my throat. I rush to the bed and sit in front of my laptop. I don't know what to do, but I know one thing: whatever this is between us, it's far from over.

My fingers hover over the keyboard, frozen in mid-gesture, the words on the screen a meaningless blur. I tell myself to relax, to push through the fog of emotions clinging to me like smoke, but it's impossible when I hear his footsteps getting closer and closer.

They're deliberate, unhurried, and they grow louder with each passing second. My breath hitches as I instinctively hold it. The knock that follows is soft, but before I can decide whether to call out or stay silent, the door swings open.

I freeze.

He steps in. The door closes behind him with a quiet click, and I can't stop staring. Earl leans against the door-frame, his suit jacket unbuttoned, his collar open to reveal the taut line of his neck. His hair is slightly mussed, as though he's run his fingers through it a good few times. The faintest shadow of stubble lines his jaw, and despite myself, I feel the air leave my lungs sharply.

He doesn't say anything at first, just stands there, his eyes fixed on me. There's no warmth in his gaze, no hint of the man I used to know. What I see now makes my stomach twist—it's a sharp, searing dislike that I can't contest. It burns.

I sit up straighter, the sudden movement making my oversized hoodie and pleated skirt shift against my skin. I feel exposed, vulnerable, even though I know I'm completely covered. I wish I was wearing something else, something that didn't make me feel so small under his scrutiny. But it's too late for that now.

The silence stretches between us, thick and tense. My mouth opens, but no words come out. What am I supposed to say? What could I possibly say to the man who walked away from me without any explanation and then returned with this... animosity?

He steps closer, his movements slow and deliberate, like a predator sizing up its prey. The air in the room feels heavier with every inch he closes between us. My heart pounds in my chest, each beat echoing in my ears as I struggle to keep my breathing steady.

"I wasn't expecting a visit," I finally gasp. It's the only thing I can think of to break the unbearable tension.

He smiles, a cold and humorless twist that sends a shiver down my spine. "Why not?"

I swallow hard. "You seem to hate me."

"I do," he agrees.

"Why?" I whisper.

He shrugs carelessly. "Let's not rehash all that right now. I wasn't expecting you to be awake."

"I was working," I reply, gesturing to my laptop, though my words feel hollow, like they don't belong in this moment. Why does he hate me? What does he imagine I have done to him?

His gaze flickers to the screen for a fraction of a second before returning to me. "Still writing those romance novels?"

I flinch, the question striking a nerve. "Actually, I don't write anymore. I just edit other people's work now."

He pauses, his expression showing surprise. For a moment, it's as though he's genuinely curious, as though he wants to ask why. And for that brief second, it feels like all the darkness between us dissipates, like the weight we've been carrying could finally lift.

But it doesn't last. Just as quickly, his eyes shutter and the unyielding tension returns, settling back into the space between us. His face hardens, and whatever softness had surfaced vanishes like it was never there.

His smile returns, dark and mocking. Then he takes a step forward and I have to fight the urge to shrink back. His presence is overwhelming, a tangible force that fills the room and leaves no space for anything else.

"What do you want, Earl?" I ask, though my hands tremble in my lap.

"What do I want?" he echoes, his tone mocking as he tilts his head slightly, like he's considering the question. Then, without warning, he closes the distance between us entirely, towering over me as I remain frozen in place.

I tilt my head back to meet his gaze, my heart pounding so hard it feels like it might burst. He's so close I can see the bottomless wells of his eyes, the tension in his jaw, the faint lines of exhaustion etched into his face. And yet, he's never looked more imposing, more... untouchable.

"You wouldn't understand," he murmurs, his voice low, almost a growl. "You never did."

Before I can respond, he turns sharply and heads toward the window. The sudden movement jolts me, and I realize I've been holding my breath again. His back is to me now, but the tension in his shoulders is palpable, like he's barely holding something in.

I want to ask him what he means, to demand answers, but the words die in my throat. Instead, I watch him, my mind racing with all the questions left unsaid between us. The room feels unbearably small, the distance between us is a vast sea of danger.

I don't know how to bridge it.

CHAPTER 9

EARL

https://www.youtube.com/watch?v=ymPu2PdLW3I
-let me entertain you-

I want her so badly it's like an affliction, something that burns relentlessly, fueled by an immense source that refuses to acknowledge her betrayal or the wounds she left that still throb and hurt. She was going to throw me in the gutter for these useless symbols of wealth. Sacrifice my great love for sofas, beds, and chairs. Seeing her here in her dream surroundings, so calm, so composed, twists the knife further. It makes me want to break her composure, shatter her in the way she shattered me. Let her feel what I felt.

I pull off my jacket and toss it to the floor. My fingers work at the buttons of my shirt, undoing each one with deliberate slowness. I'm giving myself time to rein in the storm inside me, but every button undone feels like a step closer to the edge.

By the time I reach the last button, I turn to face her, watching the way her eyes widen slightly, the way her throat bobs as she swallows hard. Suddenly, I'm standing in my briefs. I see her take in my arms, my chest, the shift of muscle under my skin. She's seen me like this before—years ago, when we were younger, when everything between us was raw and real and terrifyingly pure. But now, I can see the tension in her, the hesitation. I know she doesn't trust me, and a cruel part of me wants to revel in that.

"Well," I say, my cold voice cutting through the silence. "What are you waiting for? Time to perform your wifely duties."

Her lips part as she stares at me in shock.

"What's wrong?" I taunt, stepping closer.

There's defiance in her eyes, a flicker of the fire I remember so well, and it's enough to set my teeth on edge.

"Don't you know there is a price to pay to fulfil your greatest dream? Weren't you going to fuck Charles for this?"

Her response, when it comes, is calmer than I expected. "I... I don't think I'm ready. We've barely spoken. Maybe in a week or two, when we've had more time together—"

The sound of my harsh and hollow laughter is like a slap in the air and cuts her off mid-sentence. She stares at me with a mixture of horror and disbelief. The laughter dies on my lips, replaced by something darker.

"I have no interest in wasting time with you. The terms of our agreement are simple. You're the mistress of this house, and when I need someone to fuck, you're supposed to look pretty and oblige."

Her sharp intake of breath is audible in the silence that follows. Then I see tears well up in her eyes, but she doesn't cry. Her lips tremble as she asks, "What is wrong with you? When did you turn into this... this monster?"

"Monster?" I repeat, letting the word hang in the air, heavy and accusing. "Is that what I am now? A monster? It does have a nice ring to it though so thank you, I guess, for the compliment."

She is flabbergasted.

"Are you going to do what's needed or not?" I ask, my tone cold and clipped, leaving no room for misunderstanding. "The consequences are simple: this marriage will be annulled immediately. You move your things back out, and we go back to having nothing to do with each other. I'll give you a minute to decide."

I step back, crossing my arms, my gaze unyielding as I wait. My words hang in the silence between us, as sharp and unyielding as the blade I feel twisting in my chest. Her eyes never leave me, but her fingers tighten painfully around the edges of her oversized hoodie.

She doesn't respond at first. She just stares at me, her wide, tear-filled eyes searching my face for something— maybe the man I used to be or the man she thinks I still am somewhere beneath all this anger and bitterness. But I'm not him anymore. He died a painful death a long time ago.

Her shoulders rise and fall with each shaky breath. Then I see the exact moment the fight drains out of her. Slowly she rises to her feet. Her movements are fluid. She takes a step forward, then another, until she's standing just inches away from me.

I can feel her warmth, smell her sweet scent, hear the soft hitch in her breath, and see the glint of unshed tears on her lashes. It hits me like a punch to the gut—this woman I've spent years trying to hate, this woman I wanted to make suffer, is still the one person who can unmake me by just standing in front of me. And I hate her for it. I hate myself even more.

But I don't let it show. I lock my jaw, keeping my face impassive. "Get on your knees," I command. My voice crackles with unspoken emotions, regrets, and a longing that I'm too proud to admit aloud, but my cock is rock-hard with anticipation.

Her gaze meets mine, defiant at first, but then her eyes soften, searching me for something—an answer, a promise, perhaps even remorse.

"Why are you making something so beautiful ugly?" she asks sadly, as she lowers herself, her enormous eyes looking up at me imploringly. In the past, there would have been no denying those eyes. They can melt a man's heart, but my heart is a tarnished stone.

I run a finger along her soft cheek and my voice is silky with hate. "Don't fool yourself, baby. What we have is raw, primitive, compulsive, wicked, and as necessary as breathing, but it is not beautiful. You are mine and you will perform for me for as long as I need you to. When I ask you to do something you will do it no matter how humiliating it is. So save the pretty words. They're wasted on me."

Her breath hitches with shock. Then she drops her head and for a while is as still as a statue, then her pale hands rise and find the waistband of my briefs. Every fiber of my being tightens under her touch. She pulls the fabric down. Her eyes widen and, for a moment, she pauses. I see her staring, her lips parted as if she's surprised by the changes to my body.

Does she remember how it used to be between us? If there's a flicker of recognition in her mind—of how we once fit together so effortlessly. Two pieces of a jigsaw puzzle. I want to ask her. I want to know if there have been others—how many others have seen her, touched her the way I have, or made her feel the way I did. But the thought of hearing the answer makes my stomach twist with jealousy. I can't bear it, so I bury it deep, where it can't hurt me.

Her hand is steady as she reaches out, hovering for a breathless moment before her fingertips graze the length of my cock. The contact is so delicate, so tentative, it sends a sharp, electric pulse through me. Her fingers brushing against my hot skin feel both foreign and achingly familiar. Heat radiates between us and my breath catches. I remember this. Oh God, I remember this. Raven. My Raven. Mine. Mine. The past comes crashing back with shocking ferocity.

The world tilts. This is going to be unbearable.

Goosebumps scatter over my body as her fingers glide over the length of my cock, her touch exploring every ridge and vein with an almost reverent curiosity. As if in awe of the changes she is seeing. Her thumb traces a deliberate path along the throbbing vein that runs down the length of me. She adjusts her grip, tightening just enough to make my breath stutter. Her thumb brushes over the tip, slow and deliberate, smearing the bead of moisture there. Then she leans forward and licks the head of my cock like a cat. Tasting me.

Then her eyes flick upwards and her gaze locks with mine. And I see everything—wonder, aching need, and something deeper, something primal and unspoken. Her eyes flicker with recognition. She sees the same thing in my eyes. That pisses me off. This is not a love-making session. She must understand that. This is just lust. Animal lust. Nothing more. She must never know how little control I have left.

"Get on with it," I snarl icily.

She flinches at my brutal tone, then obediently wraps her hand around my girth, her hand sliding carefully, as though she's holding something precious. Her other hand joins, cradling the base, her slender fingers joining together encircling the full length of me. I feel the warmth of her breath as she leans closer. Her lips stretch as her hot mouth takes me in.

She looks up at me then, her gaze locking onto mine. My chest tightens. At this moment, nothing else matters—not the years we've been apart, not the ugliness that gnaws at the edges of my mind. All that exists is her and my hard cock pushing deep into her throat.

CHAPTER 10

RAVEN

I know he is trying to make this moment as ugly as possible, but he can't because it's beautiful. He's beautiful and I'm so turned on I am dripping wet. The texture of his skin, the feel of his silky skin against my tongue—it's a mix of the familiar and the new, setting my senses ablaze. Memories rush in, unbidden and overwhelming. Of a time when we were so young and our love was innocent and full of passion. Every inch of him is burned into my memory, but experiencing it again now is almost too much to bear.

I trace him from root to tip, feeling the heat and hardness of him against my mouth. His skin is smooth, stretched tight over steel, and I savor the way he pulses, alive and raw. My hand wraps around the base of his cock, fingers tightening just enough to make him hiss through his teeth. I pump him slowly, teasing, while my tongue circles the sensitive crown.

There's salt and warmth and that taste that is uniquely

his. My hands press into his strong thighs, my fingers curling into his skin as if anchoring myself against the storm he ignites within me. A heat builds within me, raw and insistent, spreading from the pit of my stomach to every nerve ending in my body.

I close my eyes, shutting out everything but the way he feels and tastes and he lets out a ragged sound above me, and it sends a shiver down my spine. His hands hover near my face, trembling as if he's caught between holding back and surrendering. I feel his restraint, his tension, and the way he fights not to fall back into old habits.

Suddenly, his big hands grab my head and he pushes himself deeper. My eyes snap open as my lips are pulled up the pulsating length until I feel him jam the back of my throat; we are joined so tightly that we become one writhing animal.

A guttural cry escapes him from above me. That sound shocks me. It carries such terrible pain and aching need. I recognize and understand that pain. I feel it too. I have felt it all these years without him. The room around us vanishes, leaving just the two of us in this burning, consuming moment. All the anger, all the bitterness between us fades, eclipsed by something primal and undeniable. A connection that feels as ancient and unshakable as the rock faces of mountains. No amount of time or distance could ever sever it.

Even as he uses me so brutally, fucking my mouth like a man possessed, it's not ugly. I don't need to look up to know the expression in his eyes. The dam has broken. He has completely lost control. His breaths come faster, shallow and broken, each exhalation is a desperate sound that makes my thighs clench. With every involuntary thrust, his body betrays him ever more. His groans fill the room—low, guttural, feral. His hand tangles in my hair, his fingers trembling as they press against my scalp. The gesture is both commanding and pleading. All his bluster is fake. Without me, he cannot survive.

I glance up, meeting his gaze, and the raw intensity there almost shatters me. His eyes are dark, wild, a storm of need and vulnerability. I see him as he once was—the teenager who worshipped me, who offered me his heart without hesitation or reservation. He would have done anything for me. Killed for me, died for me. To watch him unraveling back to being completely mine is insanely intoxicating. A drug I can't get enough of. I start to dread the moment when he goes over the edge. What will return? The stony-eyed stranger or the old love of my life.

But at this moment, he's nothing but mine—lost in the sensations I've stirred in him.

He grips my head tightly, his fingers brutal. He's trembling as he holds me against his body, hips jerking forward with an urgency that sends shockwaves through my whole being. I feel the tension coiling in him, his body taut like a bowstring about to snap.

His release comes suddenly, my name tearing from his throat, as he spills his seed deep into my belly. But he doesn't let go, keeping me joined to him as he rides the waves, his grip unyielding. Three times he jerks against me and the sheer force of him is overwhelming.

When he finally releases my head and pulls back, my lips feel swollen and bruised, my breath shaky. I look up at him … my heart breaks.

His chest is still heaving, but only the stoney-eyed stranger remains. He looks rugged, chiseled, impossibly gorgeous and unimaginably unreachable. A man entirely in his element, and yet … he won't even look at me.

"You always were the best cocksucker in town," he murmurs cruelly.

His words sting like a whip on my skin and I stumble as I try to stand, but he doesn't move to help. The old Earl would have fallen himself rather than let me fall. But this man, he just stands there, his hands slack at his sides as if touching me would demean him. Grabbing his thighs I push myself up and I can't help the way my body brushes against his. My nipples harden instantly at the contact, even the thick fabric of my hoodie does nothing to dull the sensation.

Heat still radiates between us, but his eyes are cold as ice. How amazing. He's built up this impenetrable wall in seconds. The vulnerability I glimpsed earlier is totally gone. There's only guarded distance and dislike.

"We should talk," I say quietly, running my palm over my saliva-smeared cheeks and mouth.

It takes him a long moment to respond, his eyes lingering somewhere over my shoulder before they finally find mine. When they do, they cut me like a knife.

"What is there to talk about?" His voice is flat and dead and the rejection is complete. He is making it clear. Those unguarded moments before, that was nothing. I am nothing to him.

I swallow the lump forming in my throat. "I'm not saying we should be friends or whatever, but we can't be enemies or strangers either. There's a lot to say to clear the air. We need to talk about what happe—"

He cuts me off by stepping away, his muscles taut with tension, then turns his back to me. My words trail off, left hanging in the air like a broken thread.

I watch in amazement as he moves with detached arrogance, his gloriously naked form bathed in light. There's something brutal in the way he keeps his back to me, like I don't deserve even the courtesy of his gaze, and I hate myself for how my eyes drink him in, despite the growing knot of anger and confusion in my chest.

Every step he takes feels like a deliberate rejection, the air between us thick with unspoken words that he won't let me utter. He moves towards the bed without a word, climbing onto it with a casualness that borders on condescension. Sprawling on his back, he rests his hands behind his head and looks at me, his gaze daring me to challenge him.

"What I want out of this relationship," he says, his voice emotionless, "is blind obedience. You will do as you're told and under no circumstances do I want to 'talk' or know how you feel or what you think about anything. That's what this agreement is."

My fists clench at my sides, but before I can respond hotly, he carries on.

"For instance, right now what I want is for you to get over here and ride my dick. Ride it so hard your pussy burns and you make me forget how …" His voice trails off, and I catch the flicker of hesitation in his expression.

"Make you forget how what?" I prompt, thinking he might be about to say something real, but his lips curl into a bitter smirk.

"Your time's wasting," he says, his tone mocking, his gaze burning into me.

I want to scream at him, to demand answers, to ask him why—why he left, why he abandoned me, why he's treating me like this now. But I won't give him the satisfaction. I won't let him see how much his cruelty cuts me.

"You're an asshole," I fling at him, my chest tight with suppressed emotion. "I don't know what happened years ago to make you leave without a word and abandon me, but don't act like I'm the sinner here."

He doesn't react, just watches me with that cold, detached expression that makes me want to break something. So I keep going.

"Well, I don't care to kiss and make-up anyway," I spit. "Fine, I need the money so I'll do what you want. I'll ride your dick hard and here's hoping you forget whatever it is you want to."

I turn my back on him and push my hands up my skirt. My fingers are trembling as I hook them under the thin band of my panties and quickly slide them down, the soft, wet fabric brushing against my thighs before they fall to the floor. I leave my skirt on. My face burns, but I hold my head high, refusing to let him see the war raging inside me.

I'm about to climb onto the bed when his voice slices through the tense air.

"I didn't pay for a half show," he says coldly, his eyes narrowing. "Strip. Then touch your boobs. Squeeze them. Show me what I'm paying for. Convince me it's worth it."

My breath catches. He is determined to get his pound of flesh. With gritted teeth, I force my hands to move. The hoodie catches briefly on my hair before I tug it free, letting it fall carelessly to the floor. I stand there, chest rising and falling with shallow breaths, refusing to let my vulnerability show. My eyes meet his, daring him to look away—but he doesn't. His gaze is locked on me, piercing and unrelenting.

My hands slide up to cup my breasts, the weight of them heavy in my palms. My fingers tremble slightly, but I dig my nails into my resolve, refusing to falter.

I squeeze them gently at first, my thumbs grazing over my nipples, hard against the chill of the room. His gaze darkens, eyes fixed on every movement like a predator locked onto its prey.

"More," he commands, his voice low and edged with impatience. "Don't make me wait."

My stomach twists, but I do as he says, rolling my nipples between my fingers, a reluctant heat pooling in my belly. His breathing grows heavier, the tension between us thick enough to choke on.

"Good girl," he murmurs, his lips curling into a smirk that makes my skin crawl and ignite all at once. "This is what you're made for. Now keep going."

His words make me freeze. Humiliation wells up, sharp and suffocating. I feel like a piece of meat on display, but I force myself to breathe. He won't see me crack. He won't get the satisfaction I want to see skin."

My hands move to the hem of my hoodie, gripping the fabric tightly to still the slight tremor in my fingers. I lift it slowly, peeling it away from my body, the cool air brushing against my skin as it rises.

He leans back against the headboard, his eyes roaming over me with a mixture of hunger and something darker, something colder. His jaw tightens, and I can see the way he fights against his own desire. The tension between us is electric, charged, and I hate the way it makes me feel.

I unclasp my bra, letting it fall. My breasts feel heavy under his gaze, my nipples hardening against the cool air. His eyes darken, and for a moment, he seems lost in the sight of me.

"Happy now?" I ask, my voice sharp, cutting through the silence.

"Not yet," he says, his smirk returning. "But I'm getting there."

His words linger in the air, sharp and cutting, as if daring me to push back.

"Cup them," he commands, motioning lazily with his

hand, his voice low and edged with impatience. "Squeeze them. Take that skirt off as well. Finger yourself."

My breath catches. Heat rushes to my face, but I force myself not to hesitate.

"I'm getting bored," he taunts. "Don't forget, at any point, this agreement can end. I'm afraid you'll have to work for the money you want, honey."

My jaw tightens as a storm of emotions churns inside me —humiliation, defiance, and something I can't fully name. I do as he says, but make sure my movements are mechanical and deliberately unsexy. Even so, his eyes darken with a hunger that's barely restrained. As I take my skirt off, I notice my fingers trembling slightly so I clench my teeth to steady them.

"Take off your skirt, sit on that chair, open your legs wide, and finger yourself," he commands.

I should have felt a mix of hate, anger and shame, but infuriatingly, I feel unbelievably excited and turned on as I pull my skirt down, the fabric brushing my thighs. The silence is broken only by the sound of my own shallow breathing and the rustle of my skirt pooling on the floor.

"Do go on," he approves, a wolfish grin appearing on his face.

My heart is pounding in my chest. I can feel his eyes on me, unrelenting, watching every movement I make. But what is worse is the heat pooling in my stomach. I hate the way my body betrays me even now. Even put to this unthinkable humiliation I can't seem to stop my body from responding to him.

"Look at you," he taunts. "You're getting off on this, aren't you?"

"No," I snap, the word almost a growl. But the way my body shakes betrays me. I can feel the flush spreading across my skin, the tightening in my chest as I fight to maintain control.

"You can't even lie properly," he mutters, his mockery vanishing. "Take a seat and get on with the show, I haven't got all night."

I perch at the end of the chair and slowly open my legs.

"Damn! How wet your little cunt is. It's dripping," he notes interestedly.

I glare at him, but say nothing. What can I say? It is the truth. I am so aroused my sex is wet and throbbing wildly.

"Lean back," he orders, "and raise your legs up in a V shape."

I obey, exposing my pink flesh completely to him.

He draws in a sharp breath and his voice is harsh. "Masturbate. Play with yourself."

My fingertips delicately brush my swollen sensitive clit then circle it. My movements are hesitant to start with, but they quickly become frantic as the tension inside me builds. I hate how easily he's broken me down, how powerless I feel under his gaze. And yet, I can't stop.

I shudder, unable to hold back the soft, involuntary moan that escapes my lips. It's humiliating, the sound echoing in the suffocating silence of the room. My left fist clenches as I will myself to stay calm, but it's no use. My body is no longer mine, consumed by something I can't control.

"Now finger fuck yourself," he commands. His voice seems far away and strange.

My fingers slide deep inside me. In, out. In, out. Relentless. It's a show. For him. For money. Tears sting the backs of my eyes.

"That's enough," he says abruptly, his voice low and commanding. "Come over here. Crawl towards me."

I freeze.

Crawl?

My mind is screaming at me to walk away from this degradation, to do anything but obey his sick command, but my body doesn't want to stop. It can't. It remembers too well the deep pleasures of being with him and it wants it now. And it won't be denied. He owns my body. He always has. And he always will.

I get down on the ground, and on my hands and feet, I crawl towards him like an animal. The carpet is rough against my palms and there is a fire between my legs as I move myself closer and closer to him. As I reach the side of the bed he reaches down and hauls me effortlessly into the air and plops me on top of him. The sheets are cool against my heated skin. My soaking pussy is pressed onto his thigh and I have to resist the desire to rub myself against it.

He watches me intently, his expression unreadable, his mocking smirk gone. "Are you on birth control?"

I nod slowly.

"Good. We don't deserve to be parents."

I gasp with shock.

And he smiles silkily. "I think I'm going to really enjoy being married to you. Now fucking ride my cock."

CHAPTER 11

EARL

*S*he recoils at my deliberately cruel words.

But silently she raises herself and sits astride me. Her soft wet pussy squelches on my thigh and I feel how it throbs for my cock. So ... she wants me with every fiber in her body, but she absolutely loathes wanting me. I see it in the way she glares at me, her clenched hands, her pert breasts rising and falling with sharp breaths. And I savor it. Her anger is my feast, feeding that dark, twisted part of me that thrives on knowing I've gotten under her skin. And hurt her.

And yet, something in me stirs, an old, buried instinct that flinches at treating her like this. It pricks at the edges of my resolve, threatening to soften me, but I shove it away quickly.

My eyes trail over her body, taking in every detail.

She was beautiful before—achingly so—but now, she's something else entirely. Time has honed her into a vision so impossibly breathtaking, it's almost painful. Her curves, her lips, the slight flush coloring her cheeks—I can't stop look-ing, can't stop remembering how utterly consumed I used to be by her.

Even knowing what a shallow creature she is, I can't fight it. The desire coils low in my stomach, a visceral, demanding force I can't ignore. It's maddening.

"Do that thing you used to do," I say, my voice low and rough.

A sigh escapes her lips—soft, resigned—and she rises up on her knees and repositions herself over my rock-hard cock. Then she lowers the lips of her sex onto the head of my cock and squeezes, then massages it with her inner muscles. I exhale slowly. Only she, only she knows how to do this prop-erly. Her hips move in a slow snake-like dance, teasing, torturing. My control is hanging by a thread. She's so wet, so warm, so delicious.

Her moans start soft, stifled, as if she's trying to hold back, but they break free despite her efforts. That sound—God, that sound—it's been years, but it undoes me, just like it used to.

The way she moves against me is pure memory and instinct, like we've fallen back into the rhythm of who we once were. She's riding me now, and the rush of sensation and sweetness is incredible.

But it's not sweet. Not really. It's selfish, raw, a desperate grasp for everything we've both lost. Every movement is a demand, a silent plea to take more, to give more, until there's nothing left of either of us.

For a brief moment, my mind drifts to Charles— she was planning to do all this with him. The thought sets something dark and primal loose inside me.

I grab her hips and impale her fully on my thick cock, savoring the way her eyes widen with the sudden stretch as her body yields and her tight warmth wraps around me. She takes all of me. I meet her gaze, and for a moment, we're locked there, staring into each other's eyes, the pleasures of the past and the fire of the present mingling.

Her hazel eyes are almost all pupils with the same hunger clawing at my chest. It's like she's daring me to break, daring me to give in completely. I grip her hips tighter, dragging her up and down slowly, inch by inch, and the soft gasp that escapes her lips sends a shiver through me.

She clenches her muscles around me and I feel every inch of her, every pulse and quiver, and the intensity is unbearable, a mix of pleasure and torment.

"You feel … incredible," I murmur, the words slipping out unbidden, raw and unfiltered.

She leans closer, her silky hair brushing against my chest, her breaths mingling with mine. Her lips part, but no words come, only a soft, broken moan that sends heat rushing through me. I thrust upward again, the motion forcing her to take me deeper into her slick heat, to feel every inch of me stretching her, filling her. Her nails bite into my shoulders. I welcome the sting, the grounding pain amidst the storm of sensation.

Her head falls back, exposing the tender curve of her throat. I can't resist. I lean forward, pressing my lips to her skin, tasting the salt and warmth of her. My teeth graze her neck, as I suck her neck hard, enough to leave a mark, to claim her as mine. Her moan is loud and uninhibited, and it sends a thrill through me, a primal satisfaction.

"Look at me when you fuck me," I demand, my voice rough.

Her eyes snap open and lock onto mine, and it's like the world tilts, narrowing down to just us.

She looks at me as if I'm the only thing that matters in the world as she moves above me, her hips rocking and circling, and her walls squeezing me with every motion. I drown in her. My thrusts meet hers, harder, more demanding, each one driving us closer to the edge, closer to losing ourselves completely.

Fucking her feels unreal—it's everything I've ever wanted.

She kisses me and her breath mingles with mine, soft and sweet, carrying a hint of something that's purely her. The taste of her floods my senses, familiar and maddening. I can't fight it anymore. The memories ... they come rushing back with a force that almost knocks the breath out of me.

The way we used to be ... reckless, unrestrained, consumed by each other.

Her lips move against mine, urgent, persuasive, passionate, intoxicating, but beneath it lies something else—a bittersweet ache, a reminder of everything we once had and everything we lost. I can taste our teenage years, the laughter, the stolen moments, the promises we made when we thought we'd have forever.

And then it hits me. The betrayal. The knife she drove into my back when she thought I wasn't there, the words that burned the world I built around her into ashes. The pain cuts through the sweetness like a blade.

A choked sound escapes me, part groan, part growl. My fingers dig into her arms as I push her away, breaking the kiss with a sharp, ragged breath. Her lips are swollen, her chest is heaving, her hazel eyes wide and shimmering with confusion.

I stare into her eyes, and for a moment, all I can feel is rage—rage at her for breaking me, at myself for still wanting her, for still craving her even after everything.

"You don't get to do this," I snarl.

She looks at me, perplexed. "You don't want me to kiss you? I'm your wife."

"And it doesn't mean what you think it means. It means what I fucking say it means."

Her lips part, but no words come. The silence stretches between us. I roll her onto the mattress and look down at her. Her hair splayed out like a dark halo, her body trembling.

How could she look so angelic and be such a cheap whore?

My hands open her legs, rough and demanding. She gasps, but there's no protest—only the soft, desperate sound of her surrender. I push into her tight heat again. She arches beneath me, her body welcoming me in a way that makes my head spin and my resolve shatter.

There's no tenderness left.

All the softness we shared only moments ago has vanished. All that is left is something raw, frantic, a clash of need and anger that neither of us can control. I thrust into her mercilessly, relentlessly, my movements unrelenting, driven by a dark fury inside me. Her moans fill the room and they only spur me on, dragging me further into the madness of her.

The sight of her—flushed, trembling, completely undone —makes my chest ache with something I can't name, something I can't bear. I squeeze my eyes shut instead, letting the old memory of her burn into my mind.

But that memory is worse. It drags me back to another time, another place. When I believed she was everything to me. When I was totally convinced that she was the love of my life. She and only she would do. The sweetness of her, the way she used to whisper my name like a prayer—it all crashes into me now making me feel bitter.

I hate her for making me feel this way. For breaking me and still holding the pieces in her hands.

I open my eyes and pretend she is a street whore I paid for the night. Her belly is full of my cum and now I'm going to fill her pussy with it. I'll fill her ass with my seed too. I don't last long. The intensity, the heat, it's too much. When I come, it's with a force that leaves me trembling, my hands gripping her hips as though letting go will destroy me.

She's not far behind. Her body tightens around me, her cries turning into broken, gasping sobs as she thrashes beneath me, clutching at my arms as though I'm the only thing anchoring her to the world. She calls out my name—or rather my middle name. She used to call me that all the time. A soft and sweet sound I haven't heard in years.

"James," she calls, her voice thick with emotion, and it's like a punch to the gut.

I nearly choke on the flood of feelings that surge through me. It's too easy to fall, to forgive, to let myself believe for even a second that we could go back. I hate how weak she makes me feel, how easily she strips away the walls I've built.

Her arms wrap around me, holding me close as she tries to steady her breaths. I should pull away. I know I should, but I can't. Just for a moment, I let myself savor the way she clings to me, the way her perfume lingers in the air, and the way her body trembles against mine.

But I can't stay. I won't let her have that power over me again.

It takes everything I have to pull away and get off the bed. My chest feels tight as I move to grab my clothes.

I want to walk out without looking back. I look over my shoulder. She's splayed out on the bed, her skin flushed, her hair wild, her chest rising and, between her open legs, her glistening just fucked, swollen pussy. She looks beautiful.

Ravaged. And the best part is, I know I'm the one who made her feel this way. I know now. She will always be the wound that refuses to close.

I dig into the pocket of my pants and my fingers curl around my wallet. I pull out five one-hundred-dollar bills and place them on the side tab.

When I lift my gaze, she's watching me, her hazel eyes wide with confusion and hurt.

I give her a dry smile, one that doesn't reach my eyes, and turn away. I shut the door behind me and stand in the corridor for a second. Then I make my way back to my own bedroom.

CHAPTER 12

RAVEN

I can't move at first. My breath is caught somewhere between my chest and throat, shallow and shaky. My shocked gaze returns to the crisp bills lying there on the side table, their edges too sharp, too neat.

Did he just …?

I sit bolt upright. I can't believe it. The money stares back at me, loud and vulgar against the polished surface of the wood. My heart pounds as sheer disbelief floods me, a hot, nauseating wave that leaves me utterly bewildered.

I glance toward the door he exited out of, then back to the money, my vision blurring as tears threaten to spill. Slowly, I lift my gaze to the ceiling, as if the answer might be there, etched into the plaster. But it's not.

I can't think. My mind is a jumbled mess of questions, anger, and hurt. The significance of what he's just done settles over me. He didn't just leave—he left me like .. like …

A prostitute.

The word claws at my chest, tearing through whatever composure I thought I had left. My throat tightens as I stand on shaky legs, my eyes darting around the room. The nearest thing within reach is the blanket sprawled across the bed. It's disheveled and warm from where we'd been on it. I grab it and huddle into it, as if it could shield me from the sting of what he's done.

The fabric is soft and heavy, holding the faintest trace of our shared heat. It doesn't comfort me. It doesn't numb the hurt. Instead, it weighs on me, reminding me of him, of his hands, his voice, the way he looked at me before he walked out.

I need to move. I need to do something—anything—to escape the smothering thoughts in my head. I shove my hair out of my face and make my way hastily to the bathroom. I throw off the blanket and step into the shower. The freezing water shocks my system. I turn it almost all the way up until the water becomes almost scalding hot. The water pounds against my skin as I scrub myself with a desperation that borders on madness. My hands shake as they move over my body, trying to erase the way he touched me. He made me feel so alive, so wanted, only to leave me hollow and raw.

But no matter how hard I scrub I can't rid myself of him. His touch lingers, searing and cruel, a brand I can't escape.

By the time I step out, my skin is red and stinging, but it's nothing compared to the ache in my chest. I wrap a towel around myself and stare at my reflection in the mirror. At the large love bite he's left on my neck. My hair is wet and clinging to my cheeks and my eyes are swollen and glassy. I don't recognize the woman in the mirror—She looks like someone broken.

I glance back at the bedroom, the crumpled sheets, and the side table where those bills still sit, mocking me. My breath hitches, and I feel like screaming, tearing the room apart, and erasing every trace of him. But I can't. I have my father to think about. That is what this marriage is about. Saving my father. That money will go into the little kitty that holds all the money I've saved up so far for Dad's medical expenses. Mom remortgaged their home, but that money is almost all gone, and soon I'll have to start dipping into my fund.

I get on the bed and close my eyes, but find I can't fall asleep. No matter how hard I try, images of me crawling towards him play in my mind. Then I think of the portrait depicting me as a gold-digging whore downstairs and my entire body burns with shame.

Why? Why does he hate me so much?

CHAPTER 13

RAVEN

*B*y the next afternoon, I make my way to Sunny's little bakery.

I slip inside, the bell over the door chiming softly. The bakery is warm and bustling, the scent of sugar and vanilla filling the air. Sunlight streams through the windows, glinting off the glass cases filled with pastries and macarons. It is a little early so there are no customers yet. Sunny is in her usual spot behind the counter, piping delicate swirls of buttercream onto a cake. I make my way over to her. She looks up, her brown eyes sharp and perceptive, and immediately sets the piping bag down.

"Raven," she says in a concerned voice. "What's wrong? What did that man do to you? You look terrible."

The bakery is warm, the faint hum of the ovens in the background, but it does nothing to soothe the cold knot in my chest. I smile, but it feels hollow.

"Thanks for the confidence boost," I say with forced humor.

She frowns, reaching for a stool and motioning for me to sit. "Your eyes are sunken. You didn't sleep last night, did you? What happened?"

I sink onto the stool Sunny set out for me and answer her, but I don't tell her the most humiliating stuff. I do tell her that he left the money on the side table after sex.

Her jaw drops with astonishment. "What? How dare he?" she gasps furiously. "Did you return the money?"

"No." My fingers grip the edges of the counter as I take a deep breath.

"Why?" she demands. "You should have thrown it back in his stupid face."

"I put the money into the kitty, Sunny."

"Oh, Raven," she whispers.

Her compassion makes me feel tearful. I push myself up and move toward the counter where the coffee pot sits. The action is mechanical, a small reprieve to keep my hands busy. I pour a cup, the dark liquid steaming as I cup it in my palms, letting the heat seep into my skin.

When I return, Sunny is back at work, her focus trained on icing a cake with deliberate precision. I pause, watching her for a moment. The rhythm of her hands is steady and confident, something I envy in this moment of chaos.

"Give me something to do. I need to feel useful. What can I do?" I ask.

Sunny nods toward a bowl of sugar pearls sitting nearby. "You can handle those, right?"

I set my coffee down, rolling up my sleeves as I step closer. "Yeah," I murmur, heading to the sink to wash my hands. When I return, I pick up the tray of pearls and settle into the task. One by one, I place them along the edge of the frosted cake, matching Sunny's earlier pattern. We work in silence, the occasional sound of clinking tools and quiet movements filling the space. It's what I need. The quiet, the simplicity, the chance to escape the chaos in my head.

"You're a fighter. You'll be fine," Sunny says suddenly, cutting through the quiet.

"I don't know if I will. It hurts too much because I still love him, you know." I don't look up from my work, but I know Sunny is listening. "I don't know if I can bear the cold-ness, the disrespect. I'm sure now that I must have done something to hurt him ... to make him leave. But no matter how hard I try to rack my brain I have no idea what it is."

"Why can't you just ask him?"

I shake my head, biting the inside of my cheek. "I did, but he just refuses to talk about the past."

"He didn't use to be like this. What's his problem?" she says, irritation evident in her voice.

"No, he didn't," I admit. "He could be short-tempered with other people, sure. But never with me. He was always so tolerant. Once I drew on his face with a permanent marker pen and even then, he just laughed. He didn't care that he had to walk around with my drawing on his face for days. But now, he's just so incredibly mad at me. It's like he hates me and he hates himself even more that he still wants to have sex with me."

"Any idea how he got rich so fast?"

"No. He refuses to talk to me, remember?"

"Well, gossip has it he invested in companies... or rather, the companies he invested in turned out to be good bets, but no clue how a dirt-poor kid actually got the initial funds to invest in these companies though."

"These are things I'd like to talk to him about. Despite the wall of antagonism between us, I am immensely impressed by him and all he has achieved."

Sunny sets down her piping bag, brushing her hands on her apron as she turns to me. "Do you want me to talk to him? Maybe I can get through to him."

I glance up at her, startled. "No," I say quickly, shaking my head. "I don't think he would appreciate you getting involved. He isn't the old Earl. You saw what he was like in the church. Anyway, this is a very delicate situation. Between us. Until I've exhausted every option, I don't want you getting involved."

"It's so bizarre. He used to be so freaking crazy about you. I was sure back then he'd give up his life for you. I guess it's true what they say about hate being the other side of the love coin."

She glances at the work I've done so far. "Looks good," she says, offering me a thumbs-up and a warm smile.

I smile back.

CHAPTER 14

EARL

The tires crunch over the gravel as we pull into the lot. The place is nothing fancy—just a commercial property tucked between two weather-beaten buildings—but it has potential. My agent, Olivia Pierce, sits beside me, flipping through her notes with the efficiency of someone who thrives on control. She's a sharp, no-nonsense operator, and she's been relentless about finding me the right investments.

"This is a solid option," she says, not looking up. "Prime location. Good foot traffic. You could do a lot with it."

My focus is on the building as I step out of the car. The late afternoon sun casts long shadows across the lot, and there's a faint smell of asphalt and fresh paint in the air.

I can immediately see that it's a decent investment. The door of the property opens before Olivia and I can reach it, and I groan inwardly.

For fucks sake. Not him.

Daniel Grayson steps out, a practiced smile plastered

across his face, the kind of smile that makes you want to wipe it off with your fist. He's dressed sharp—too sharp for someone showing a property in a town like this—but that's Grayson for you. Always playing the part.

"Mr. Jackson, welcome," he says smoothly, his voice sliding over my name like oil on water. The bastard doesn't even flinch. It's like high school never happened. Like he and his crew didn't spend years making my life hell.

I stop dead in my tracks and his smile falters for the briefest moment, tightening at the edges—a crack in the facade he's desperate to maintain. It's not confidence; it's nerves. He wants me to acknowledge him, to brush the past aside and play nice, but I see the tension in his shoulders, the way his fingers twitch slightly at his sides.

He needs this.

I feel his desperation radiating off him. I'm a very wealthy investor now, and he's just a man trying to close a deal. He's probably ready to lick my boots if it means securing this sale. He's praying I won't drag our history into the open.

Olivia, blissfully unaware of the tension coiled between us, steps forward, her heels clicking on the concrete ground.

I follow them inside, my shoulders stiff. The air between us crackles, unspoken tension filling the space as Grayson launches into his sales pitch.

"This is a fantastic opportunity," he says, gesturing toward the open floor plan. His tone is slick and professional, but there's a glint in his eye that wasn't there before. "Perfect for the kind of business you are thinking of, Mr. Jackson."

The way he says my name makes my teeth clench. He knows exactly who I am.

Olivia hums in approval, scribbling something on her clipboard as Grayson leads us to the windows. "You'll notice the whole area is filled with natural light," he says, all charm and polish. "It's one of the property's best features."

Olivia's phone buzzes, cutting through the tension. She glances at the screen. "So sorry, I need to take this. Carry on without me. Be back in a moment."

She steps out, and the air in the room shifts instantly.

A heavy silence stretches between us, thick and uncomfortable. Daniel stands awkwardly, his smile faltering but not entirely disappearing. He shifts his weight from one foot to the other, clasping his hands in front of him like he's trying to hold on to some semblance of professionalism.

"So," he starts, his voice a touch higher than before, "do you have any questions about the property? Issues, history … anything at all? I want to be one hundred percent honest with you. I want to make sure you're confident in your decision."

I raise an eyebrow, amused by the way he's squirming. "You don't remember me?" I ask, my tone calm but pointed. "Or are you just putting on an act?"

His face freezes for a fraction of a second, and then he laughs—a nervous, breathy sound that's almost convincing. "Oh, wait—Earl? Earl Jackson?" He snaps his fingers as if the recognition has just dawned on him. "Man, it's been forever! I didn't even recognize you at first. You look great!"

He thrusts his hand out for a handshake, his grin widening in what I can only describe as forced excitement.

I don't take it.

Instead, I fold my arms across my chest and stare at him, letting the silence drag on just long enough to make him uncomfortable. "Nice to see you again, man. It really has been forever," I say, my voice flat.

Daniel pulls his hand back, his smile flickering. "Yeah, yeah, it's crazy running into you like this. Small world, huh? I heard you were back in town for a bit. Uh, I got married a little while ago. Uh, we've got a baby on the way."

"Congratulations," I say, my lips curling into a faint smirk. I can tell he's trying to shift the conversation, to keep things light, but it's not working.

The tension between us is a living thing now, and he knows it.

Before he can dig himself into a deeper hole, Olivia walks back into the room. She looks between us, her brow furrowing slightly at the atmosphere. "Everything okay here?"

I don't take my eyes off Daniel. "I like this property," I say, my voice cutting through the air. "I'll take it—if Daniel here can explain, in gorgeous detail, how we know each other."

Olivia blinks, confused, her gaze darting between us. "I'm sorry, what?"

Daniel stiffens, his shoulders drawing up as he tries to keep his composure. "Earl, come on," he says, his tone tight. "That was a long time ago. We were kids. It was just a prank."

My smirk vanishes. I take a step closer, and his breath hitches. "The part where you mocked me and my father?" I say quietly, my voice low and dangerous. "Or the part where you and your loser friends got me expelled?"

The room feels like it's shrinking. Olivia's eyes widen as she looks at Daniel, waiting for him to respond.

"I'm—" He stammers, his hands lifting in a gesture of surrender. "I'm sorry. Really, I am. It was stupid, okay? We were just kids. We didn't mean for things to go that far."

"Save it," I snap, cutting him off. My voice is cold now, sharper than the shards of glass I'd like to grind under my heel.

I turn to Olivia, my decision already made. "I have no interest in this property. Let's go."

She hesitates, clearly caught off guard, but then quickly follows me out. Behind us, Daniel doesn't say a word, his silence and disappointment heavier than any revenge I could have planned.

Olivia and I see a few more properties before I head home. It's almost evening, and there is a high chance I'd see Raven. The flicker of anticipation irritates me, but I can't stop it.

The moment I step through the door, the first thing I notice is the massive glass vase of roses sitting in the entryway foyer. Its size alone makes it impossible to ignore, the blood-red blooms spilling over like some gaudy center-piece at a wedding.

I freeze, narrowing my eyes. Where the hell did that come from?

"It's definitely not from the garden," I mutter striding past. Even the thought is absurd—the arrangement is too professional, too ... obnoxious. Only one person would think of something so ostentatious.

"Nora," I call out, and she appears almost instantly, her smile warm as always. "Mr. Jackson," she greets with a small nod.

I glance at the arrangement again. "Where did that come from?" I ask sharply.

Nora tilts her head, her brow furrowing. "It came for the Mrs., Sir."

"Who sent it?" My voice is clipped and throbbing with fury.

Nora hesitates, glancing back at the roses before stepping forward to retrieve something tucked beneath the glass jar. It's a small white card, and she offers it to me with hesitant fingers, clearly picking up on the tension radiating off me.

I snatch it from her hand, flipping it open.

Yours always.

The words are bold, scrawled in familiar handwriting and the heart and sad face—that make my blood boil even.

Fuck Charles.

The words sear through any semblance of control I have left. Before I can stop myself, my fist swings out, smashing into the glass jar.

The roses explode across the floor and shards of glass scatter like shrapnel. The crash is deafening, a violent symphony that echoes through the foyer.

Nora screams, startled by the outburst. "Sir!" she exclaims, moving back, her hands flying to her mouth as she takes in the carnage.

I glare down at the mess I've made. The once-pristine roses are crushed, their ruined deep red petals stark against the pale marble. Drops of water slide down the wall where the vase had smashed, tracing slow, mocking lines.

Nora takes a tentative step forward, then backwards, her wide eyes fixed on the wreckage. Her voice trembles. "I'll I'll clean this up, Sir."

She hurries away and disappears in the direction of the kitchen.

With my fists clenched I stare at the remains of Charles's pathetic attempt to stake a claim. He's playing games, and it's fucking working—every nerve in my body is on fire.

The only thing worse than his audacity is the fact that I can't shake the question of whether Raven would be happy that he sent them. Maybe she is expecting them and just hasn't come down to collect them and take them up to her bedroom.

Maybe they are still texting in private. Even after marrying me, she would still be in contact with him. In my eyes, she's a consummate liar and a gold digger. The more I think about it the more furious I become. At the same time, I'm startled by the intensity of my reaction. Jealousy burns and rages inside my chest. I want to kill that bastard.

I hear hurried footsteps. I look up and there she is at the top of the stairs: the gold digger I married.

CHAPTER 15

RAVEN

I stand frozen at the top of the stairs, my feet rooted to the cold wooden floor. My pulse is pounding in my ears as I stare down at the mess below. Scattered across the entryway are shards of glass that glitter under the light from the chandeliers like broken stars. Amongst them, gorgeous, blood-red roses lay dying.

And over it all, like avenging God, he stands.

His chest heaving, his fists clenched at his sides. His face is a mask of fury, his eyes like embers that burn right through me when they lock onto mine. My heart stutters, an involuntary rush of fear coursing through me. I've seen him angry before, but this … this is different.

I grip the banister to steady myself. I don't dare move, my mind racing to make sense of the scene below. Why would he destroy those beautiful roses?

"Is something wrong?" I call down, my voice thin, tentative.

He doesn't answer immediately, his jaw working as he glares up at me. The silence stretches. Then, without a word, he begins closing the distance between us, each step slow and deliberate. His anger fills the space between us, making it hard to breathe.

By the time he reaches me, my nerves are shot to pieces, though I force myself to stand my ground. He stops just a step away, his height and intensity overwhelming me.

"Follow me," he says, his voice low and cold.

I hesitate, searching his face for a hint of something—anything—that might explain what's happening. But all I see is black, barely controlled fury. Reluctantly, I trail behind him when he turns and heads down the hall toward the library.

The library is quiet, the heavy wooden door silent as I shut it behind me. He strides to the window, and with his back to me, he stares out over the estate. The lake glistens in the fading sunlight, and the orchard beyond it is bathed in the soft golden glow of the setting sun. It's breathtakingly serene, a stark contrast to the storm raging in this room.

I hover near the door, unsure what to do, what to say. The silence is unbearable, stretching out like a taut wire ready to snap.

"Earl?" I venture cautiously. "What's wrong? Did something happen? Did the roses … fall?"

He turns then, slowly, and the look in his eyes makes my stomach twist. There's no softness there, no trace of the man a part of me still swears I know. His gaze is piercing, and it pins me in place.

"Did you leave them out there for me to see?" he asks, his tone venomous. "Were you trying to send a message?"

I blink, confused. "What? What are you talking about?" I

stop, shaking my head. "I don't understand. Why would I do that?"

His eyes narrow, and he takes a step closer, the tension between us crackling like a live wire. "Don't play dumb, Raven. Was this some kind of stunt? Something to irritate me?"

I feel the blood drain from my face, the accusation cutting deeper than I thought possible. "Irritate you? Earl, I have no idea what you're talking about!" My voice rises, tinged with desperation. "Those roses—I didn't send them!"

"You didn't send them?" he interrupts, his laugh bitter, humorless. "Do you take me for a fool, Raven? I never took you for a liar."

I take a step back, my hands trembling. "I'm not lying," I whisper, my throat tight. "Why would I lie about this?"

His gaze bores into me, searching for something I can't give him. His mistrust is crushing and it leaves me gasping for air.

"I can't take it anymore. "Earl," I say, my voice breaking, "just tell me what's going on. Please."

He exhales sharply, dragging a hand through his hair as he looks away, his jaw tight. "They're from Charles," he mutters finally, the name like poison on his tongue. "He sent them to you. Are you really trying to tell me that you're unaware? That you weren't expecting them? That you didn't see the card? That you're not still talking to him?"

I'm taken aback by his accusations, his relentless questions that jab at me like daggers. My nails bite into my palms as I struggle to maintain some semblance of composure. "No to all of them, Earl." ·

His frown deepens, his jaw tightening until I can see the pulse tick furiously at his temple. "Are you playing with me?" he snaps, his voice sharp and cutting.

I shake my head. "I don't know who the hell would think of sending me roses when I'm already—" My words falter, catching in my throat like a shard of glass.

His face twists, a bitter smirk curling at his lips as he cuts in. "What?" he sneers. "Married to me? Has commitment ever stopped you before? From doing whatever you want?"

I can't respond. My mouth opens, but no sound escapes. His words hit harder than I expected, slicing through any defenses I thought I had left. The man who once made me feel like I was the only girl in the world now stands before me and every syllable he utters makes me feel smaller and smaller, as if I could disappear under the weight of his disdain.

"I … I need to leave," I say, my voice barely audible. I turn on my heel, heading for the door, my heart pounding in my chest. Tears threaten to spill over, but I will myself to hold them back. I won't cry in front of him. I won't give him the satisfaction.

"I'm not finished with you. Don't you dare take another step," he says, his voice cold and commanding.

But I don't stop, my only focus is on escaping, not letting him see me cry, but just as I reach for the handle, the door slams shut with a force that makes my heart leap into my throat. The sound reverberates through the room.

Before I can react, he spins me around and catches both my arms. His strength overwhelms mine with ease as he holds me against the door. I meet his eyes, dark and blazing with emotions I can't decipher—anger, frustration, something deeper, something that terrifies me.

I struggle against him, but it's futile. His grip doesn't loosen, and I'm trapped, caught between the door and the storm of emotions radiating off him. All I can hear is the erratic pounding of my own heart.

The sharp rise and fall of my chest pressing against his hardness. His eyes bore into mine, dark and unrelenting, and I can feel the heat radiating from his body, suffocating me further.

"Now what?" I finally bite out, my voice trembling with defiance. "Is this it? Do you want to hurt me? Hit me? What?"

His lips twitch into a bitter smile, and it's the most chilling thing I've ever seen. "Why would I damage something I've already paid for?" he murmurs, his tone low and dangerous, sending a shiver straight down my spine. "There are other ways to make you sorry if you betray me again. So, here's your last warning—stop talking to Charles."

"I'm not talking to him!" I yell. Now I'm angry too.

"You better not be lying to me, Raven. I'm not seventeen and stupidly in love anymore. I know who you are. I know what you are. And I've accepted it." He leans in closer, his breath hot against my cheek. "But for your own sake, don't make the mistake of underestimating me. You have no idea what I'll do if you betray me again."

Betray him? The word rattles around in my mind, an unwelcome echo. My throat tightens, and I search his face, desperate for answers. "Betray you again?" I manage to whisper, my voice barely audible. "What are you even talking about? I've never—"

"Shut up," he growls, cutting me off before I can finish.

Then his hand moves to my chin, his fingers firm as they tilt my face up to his. Before I can react, his lips crush mine, but it's not a kiss. It's an invasion, hard and bruising and filled with anger. My hands come up to push him away, to resist, but the moment his tongue brushes against mine, I feel something deep inside me unravel.

The taste of him— his heat, his fury—sinks into me, winding its way down my throat and settling in my belly like a fire I can't extinguish. My knees feel like jelly and my legs buckle beneath me, and I cling frantically to him, my hands fisting in his shirt as though I'll fall apart if I let go.

The press of his body against mine is pure pleasure. Every inch of him, solid and unyielding, traps me against the door, his heat searing through the thin fabric of my dress. I can't breathe. All I want is him, at this moment, even though it terrifies me.

His lips move over mine, unrelenting, demanding, and I meet his intensity with my own, my tears breaking free and rolling down my cheeks as the tension in me crumbles. I hate him for making me feel this way. For turning me into this shaking, vulnerable mess.

And yet, I love it.

Then I hate myself for loving it.

When he finally pulls back, I gasp for air, my chest heaving as I look up at him, my vision blurred with unshed tears. His eyes are darker than I've ever seen them. It sends a shiver of indescribable longing through me.

I don't know what to say. I don't think I can say anything.

CHAPTER 16

EARL

I was going to take her against the door, empty every last ounce of anger and lust into her, but the moment I see her eyes well up with tears, the raging inferno in me cools, and something inside me breaks. I stare at her in shock.

I've hurt her.

I've actually hurt her.

In a flash, I put her away from me, swing open the door and walk through it.

"Don't walk away from me. I want to talk to you," she calls, chasing me as I stride down the corridor. Her bare feet are light on the hardwood. I ignore her and keep walking until I reach the sanctuary of my bedroom. I turn to close the door and she is standing right there.

Her eyelashes are still wet. I turn away from her, shrug off my jacket, and start on the buttons of my shirt. My fingers move fast, fueled by irritation at myself. The sound of the door clicking shut behind her stops me. I glance over my shoulder, and there she is, standing just inside the doorway, her arms crossed like she's holding herself together.

"What do you want?" I ask, my voice sharp. She followed me—this is on her.

"I … uh …" She hesitates, her hands twisting together in front of her. "I wanted to talk to you about one of the reasons I agreed to this marriage."

I arch a brow, pulling my shirt free of my shoulders and tossing it onto the bed. "Oh?" My voice drips with sarcasm. "I thought it was because you want a lavish lifestyle."

Her expression tightens, her fists clenched by her sides as if she's physically holding herself together. "My father is ill," she says, her eyes boldly holding mine. "He has thyroid cancer."

I stare at her. What new scam is this?

She continues, her tone brittle, "We caught it late. He knew something was wrong for months, maybe longer, but he didn't have the money to see a doctor. He thought he could manage until he couldn't anymore. He collapsed at home one evening. That's when we finally found out. By then the cancer had progressed, and there were other complications. They told us his time is limited unless we start treatment immediately. My mother remortgaged the house, but almost all of that money is gone now."

I can see it—her father, proud and stubborn, brushing off every warning sign until his body gave out on him.

She takes a shaky breath, but her jaw sets, her chin lifting defiantly as if daring me to dismiss her pain.

Her voice cracks, but she keeps going. "I want to get his next lot of treatments scheduled as soon as possible, but I don't have enough. All I'm asking for is help to pay his medical bills, Earl. I don't want your pity. I don't want a lavish lifestyle. I just want enough to make sure he gets the help he needs."

I listen in silence. She's not lying. I know that. I know her father—knew him when we were young, living in that crammed trailer park. He was the kind of man who'd give you the shirt off his back if you needed it, always with a kind word, always working himself to the bone for his family. I remember seeing him at the wedding. He looked sickly — pale, thin, like the life had been drained out of him—but I was so consumed with Raven I hadn't thought much of it at the time.

My first reaction is to go to her and hug her and tell her everything is going to be fine. I'll take care of it all, but then another part of me feels like a fool for falling for her shit again. I push the sentimental fool away, back into the darkness and look at her with cold eyes. She's asking for more —again.

"So you don't want the lavish lifestyle?" I ask derisively.

Her head tilts slightly, her brow furrowing. "No," she says, shaking her head. "This is all I want. Handle this for me, and you can banish me to the maid's quarters, make me a servant in this house if that's what you want. I'll gladly accept."

Her words confuse me. Is this another plot to manipulate me? I don't understand her. How could she be standing here, offering to live as nothing more than a shadow in this house just to save her father? It doesn't make sense. Is it because she is far more cunning than I gave her credit for? She knows very well I will never allow her to do that.

I feel the anger bubbling up again, unbidden and wild. "So you don't care?" I snap. "You don't care for this life, the money, the power—all the things you seemed so eager to acquire for all the time I've known you? You just want money for your father?"

"Yes, of course, I wanted to live a good life when I was a young girl. Any person growing up as poor as I did wants that, but I don't know where you got the idea that I'm a gold digger. I love my father, Earl, and the deal I had with Charles was that he would take care of Dad's medical expenses. And I married you because he lied and you promised to take over that obligation from Charles."

I stare at her in disbelief. This is the Raven I loved, the Raven I trusted, but I can't reconcile it. I can't reconcile the woman in front of me with the one who said those damning words all those years ago. Is she telling the truth? Her words circle like a noose around my neck. A raw, confused mess of emotions fills me. Have I been wrong about her? Is there some other explanation for what I heard?

And then it hits me. What the fuck am I doing? Falling at the first hurdle. Of course, she knows me—knows exactly how to play me, how to twist my emotions until I'm caught up in her web again. She's done it before and I fell for it hook line and sinker. Even so, there's something in the way she speaks now, something in her trembling voice and those pleading eyes that feels... different.

Maybe even her cold heart has the ability to love. Maybe she does care for her father.

I don't trust myself to look at her, so I turn away and head toward a painting hanging on a wall. It opens to reveal the embedded safe. My fingers work the combination out, the clicks loud in the stillness between us.

The door swings open. Any normal man would simply transfer the amount she needed, but I am not a normal man. I have been driven mad with hate and jealousy. I pull out two thick stacks of cash—fifty thousand each. The crisp notes are bound in neat wrappers. This should be enough to start off her father's treatment.

"You want this?" I ask, turning around. "Fine. Take it."

But I don't hand it to her like a normal man. Instead, the twisted monster in me tears the wrappers off the stack and flings the loose bills up into the air. One thousand one-hundred-dollar bills sail through the air, rain down on her, and scatter all around her like leaves after a storm.

She stares at the money, wide-eyed and stunned, and for a moment, I wonder if she'll snap—if she'll finally fight back and scream at me, call me the monster I've become. A part of me wants her to.

But she doesn't.

Instead, she lowers her head, her shoulders hunching slightly as she murmurs, "Thank you." Her voice is so soft, so broken, it feels like a punch to the gut.

Then she sinks to the floor.

My chest tightens painfully as I watch her gather the scattered bills. Her fingers tremble as she picks up the notes one by one. She doesn't look at me—not even once.

I wanted this, didn't I? Wanted to see her humbled, humiliated, crawling around on the floor picking up my dirty money while I stood above her. I thought it would feel good, like justice, like revenge.

It doesn't.

Instead, it feels like someone's taken a blade to my chest, carving out pieces of me with every move she makes. I wanted her to hurt, but seeing her like this—so small, so defeated—only makes me feel worse. The sight of her crouched on the floor, surrounded by money, is unbearable. It makes me want to grab her, to pull her to her feet, to tell her I'm sorry for every cruel thing I've done.

But I don't.

I can't see her like this though. Scurrying around for grubby money. The sight sickens me. I made her do this. The guilt is terrible. I can't stay in this house. I turn on my heel, grab my coat with a jerky movement, and stride out of the room.

But the rustle of her fingers picking up cash trails after me like a ghost.

CHAPTER 17

RAVEN

*T*he air smells of grease and gasoline as I step into the mechanic's shop, the sounds of clanging tools and a distant radio filling the space. My heart races in my chest. I've spent the entire morning building up the courage to come here. I don't even know if he'll recognize me—or worse, if he'll care.

I spot him under the hood of an old pickup truck, his body half-hidden. His father isn't in sight, but Earl is here, his jeans low on his hips, grease smeared along his forearm. Then he rolls out from beneath the truck, his shirtless body glistening with sweat. Sitting up, he reaches for a rag to wipe his hands.

My eyes widen.

I've never seen him like this. The sunlight streaming through the open garage doors catches the sheen of sweat on his chest, the lean muscles of his shoulders. There is a faint smudge of grease on his jaw that I itch to wipe off. My face burns, and for a moment, I feel like I should turn around and leave. But I can't.

He glances up, and his dark eyes lock onto mine. There's a

flicker of something—curiosity, maybe—but his expression remains guarded. He's so different from the boys at school. Much more mature, much more regal.

"Do you need something?" he asks coldly, like he's embarrassed I'm seeing him unwashed in these greasy surroundings.

I swallow hard, gripping the handles of my bike tighter. "Um, my chain," I say, stumbling over my words. "It—it's broken. I thought maybe ... you could help."

He raises an eyebrow. "We fix cars, not bikes."

"I know," I say quickly. "But you're good with tools, right? It shouldn't be that different."

"Fine," he says gruffly. "Bring it here."

I wheel the bike over, feeling both triumphant and stupid that my fairly transparent stunt worked. He crouches down, inspecting the chain with a practiced hand, and I catch a better view of his face—a sharp jawline, a stray strand of dark hair falling into his eyes. God, he's beautiful.

He doesn't say much as he works, his hands deftly repairing the chain while I stand awkwardly beside him. I'm mesmerized by the precision of his movements. My heart beats erratically as I watch him, every tilt of his head, every flex of his fingers sending a spark through me. I try to keep my gaze neutral, but it's impossible not to admire the way his body moves—fluid, efficient, strong.

For once, I do not get bored. I soak in every passing second as I watch his body move. Eventually, he's done.

"There." He stands. "It's fixed."

I beam at him. "Thanks! How much do I owe you?"

His brow furrows. "Forget it."

"Okay then, how about a game of Monopoly?" I offer quickly.

He looks at me like I've lost my mind. "Monopoly?"

"Yeah, I'm the best there is. If you can beat me, I'll buy you an extra-large burger, chips, and the biggest sundae at Tim & Marty's."

He crosses his arms. "Okay."

"Great," I flush all over. "I have it right here."

I reach into the basket and retrieve the box. I'd known when I'd destroyed my bike chain that I'd need an excuse to spend some time with him.

He stares at me.

Does he suspect that I came here intentionally with the flimsiest plan ever just so I can see him again? My pulse quickens under his gaze, every second stretching endlessly. His dark eyes are sharp, penetrating, and entirely unreadable and I feel like I might disintegrate under his gaze. Is he trying to figure me out? I shift nervously on my feet, gripping the Monopoly set tighter in my hands, but I don't look away.

Finally, he exhales and pulls a stool next to the wall with one hand, setting it down near the workbench. "Fine," he mutters. "Let's play your game."

I can't help but grin as I pull up a stool across from him, setting the board on the workbench between us. My heart pounds with excitement, but I force myself to keep it together. He agreed. He's actually going along with this.

"Okay, rules are simple," I say, opening the box and pulling out the pieces. "No cheating, no backing out, and no crying when I destroy you."

He snorts, leaning back slightly. "You've got a lot of confidence for someone who brought a board game to a mechanic's shop."

"And you've got a lot of attitude for someone who's about to lose," I fire back, handing him the Banker's tray.

His lips twitch as if he's holding back a smile. "We'll see."

As we start to set up the game, I can't help but steal glances at him. He's not like no one I know. There's a weight to him, a gravity that makes him seem older, more serious. I roll first, landing on a property. "Hah, Park Lane," I declare proudly, placing my token on the space. "Of course, I'm buying. One hotel, please."

"Spending all your money already?" he drawls, handing me the deed. "Bold move."

"Bold is my middle name," I reply, grinning as I hand over the cash.

He shakes his head, rolling the dice and landing on Chance. He picks up the card and he reads it aloud. "Advance to Go. Collect $200." For the first time, I see him smile. It's small, fleeting, but it lights up his whole face. My heart flutters in my chest, and I have to remind myself to breathe. This is why I came here. To see this side of him. To make him laugh, even if just a little.

"Lucky," I mutter, but I'm secretly thrilled that he's started to enjoy the game.

Slowly, the tension between us vanishes. I crack jokes whenever he lands on my properties, charging him exorbitant rent with exaggerated glee. He groans every time but pays up without complaint, his lips quirking in amusement despite himself.

"You're enjoying this way too much," he says at one point, after narrowly avoiding my three hotels on Boardwalk.

By the time the game is nearing its end, I've built an empire of properties, and he's barely hanging on.

"Game over," I announce triumphantly, counting my stack of cash with a dramatic flourish. "You've been thoroughly defeated."

He leans back, arms crossed, watching me with an unreadable expression. "I thought your intention with this was to make me feel better. I can assure you that right now I do not feel better."

"Womp womp," I mock, grinning as I hold up the wad of fake cash. "I do, however, have compassion, and I'm such a generous winner, so I'll let you have this as a consolation prize."

"You're giving me fake money?" he asks, his tone dry.

"It's the thought that counts," I reply, laughing happily ...

"MRS. JACKSON. WE'RE HERE."

At the sudden announcement, I jerk back to the present and realize that we've arrived at my parents' house. I lean back against the seat for a moment, my fingers tightening around the strap of my bag as the memory fades. It feels like a lifetime ago.

Only the memory of those wads of cash flying through the air is still sharp enough to cut. The contrast between the young man I knew and the man he's become is almost too much to bear. My heart twists painfully and I will the tears brimming in my eyes to stay put. There's no time for this sentimentality—not now. Now I have to stop thinking of myself and save my father.

I draw in a deep breath, straighten my posture and wipe away the single tear that managed to escape. My face smooths into something bright, something cheerful, though it feels like I'm wearing a mask made of fragile glass. My parents can't see me breaking—they need to believe I'm happy, that this marriage, strange as it is, hasn't broken me.

"Mrs. Jackson?" the driver calls again.

"Yes," I nod, forcing a smile. "Thank you."

With steady hands, I push the car door open and step out, letting the cool air wash over me. The sight of my parents' home brings a fleeting sense of comfort. I helped them buy this house with my wages. I clutch onto the feeling with everything I have. All that matters is that I make them happy and show them I'm okay—even if I'm not.

Inside, the smell of something delicious wafts through the air—a comforting mix of meat, onions, and herbs. My mom is in the kitchen, her apron dusted with flour, humming as she stirs a pot on the stove. Her face lights up when she sees me.

"There's my girl!" she says, wiping her hands on a dish towel and pulling me into a hug. Her embrace is warm and smells faintly of the lavender talcum powder she always uses. "I've missed you."

"I've missed you too, Mom," I say, squeezing her tightly. "What's cooking? Smells amazing."

"Just meatloaf, soup, and your favorite cookies," she replies, her eyes twinkling. "Thought you could use a good home-cooked meal."

I laugh softly, following her into the kitchen and setting my bag on the counter. "Thank you, I do."

"Now, tell me everything. How's the house? And how does it feel to have staff serving you?"

I smile and am about to lie through my teeth when the sound of my father shifting in his recliner catches my attention.

"Hang on a sec, Mom," I say softly and make my way over to him. He's in his usual spot, his chair tilted back for a nap, but his face looks pale, drawn, even as he sits up at my approach and smiles warmly.

"Hi, Dad," I say gently, bending down to wrap my arms around him. He pulls me into a bear hug, but his embrace is weaker than I remember.

"Ah! you're home," he says, his voice raspy with sleep. "How are you doing, kiddo? Everything okay?"

I nod, pressing a quick kiss to his cheek. "I'm fine, Dad." The words feel heavy, but I force them out with a smile. "You get some rest. Mom and I will catch up in the kitchen and we'll have lunch together, okay?"

He nods, though his eyes linger on me with the kind of worry only a parent can carry. I give his shoulder a reassuring squeeze before heading back to my mother, who's already bustling around the stove.

As soon as I rejoin her, she's ready, questions spilling out like steam from a pot.

"So," she begins, her voice light but probing, as she glances at me out of the corner of her eye. "How's the marriage? What about you and Earl? Is he treating you well? Do you ... see him much?"

The rhythm of her chopping slows slightly, a subtle cue that she's paying close attention to. With a soft laugh, I pull out a chair and collapse into it. I lean my elbows on the kitchen table. "You can stop worrying, Mom, I'm fine. Really. The house is beautiful—absolutely gorgeous. It's lovely having staff. And Earl and I are slowly working our issues out." I force my tone to sound lighter. "And once Dad is well, you'll both have to come up to the house. Maybe in summer. It's beautiful. A dream, really. There's a lake too and I know Dad will love it."

Mom sets down the spoon and leans against the counter, tilting her head with a knowing look. "And what about Mrs. Belafonte's staff? How are they treating you? Are they polite to you?"

I chuckle softly and tuck a loose strand of hair behind my ear. "Oh, Mom, they're wonderful. Honestly, I couldn't have asked for better people. They're so kind and helpful. They ... they actually make me feel at home."

Her eyebrows lift with surprise. "That's good to hear. I've heard stories about Mrs. Belafonte and how she used to treat her staff, so I thought they might be a bit difficult or stand-offish with you."

I shake my head, smiling. "Not at all. They've been nothing but welcoming. I guess they much prefer me to their old mistress. Apparently, she was a real tyrant."

"Yes, I heard that too," my mom confirms. "Apparently, she used to make their lives miserable."

"Well, I certainly don't. Obviously, they do their jobs, but

I treat them with respect. I didn't grow up rich, so I think they see me as no different than them."

"Good. That is how your father and I brought you up to be. To be kind. Never change, Raven," she says, her voice thick with pride.

I nod, the words sinking into me with a quiet comfort. "I try to be kind, but they've made it so easy. Nora and I talk, we laugh… It's nice. I don't feel lonely at all."

Mom's eyes crinkle with joy and her shoulders relax. She turns back to stir the pot of soup on the stove. "Good. You deserve to be surrounded by people who care about you."

"I am," I reply.

"And what about your husband?" she asks. "I really wonder if I'm ever going to get used to that. Have you gotten used to saying it?"

"Not at all," I smile. "And he's alright. We're working things out slowly. No issues there."

I can tell something in my voice or expression must have given the game away and she doesn't really believe me, but thankfully she doesn't press and instead shifts the focus of the conversation.

"Your clothes look new. Did he buy them for you?" she probes.

I glance down at the simple outfit I'd thrown on that morning—a blouse I bought a long time ago and never wore, and jeans. "No," I say, brushing off invisible lint from my sleeve. "These are just some old things I dug out of my closet."

Her eyes linger on me for a moment longer, as though trying to read between the lines of what I'm not saying. Then she picks up the knife again and continues.

"I'm glad you're here," she murmurs, almost to herself. "It was too strange and sad when you moved out so suddenly."

Tears fill my eyes at her words. I rush up to her and hug her hard. I need the warmth and love more than she will ever know.

"It's good to be back," I whisper tearfully.

Soon lunch is ready. Mom wipes her hands on her apron and calls out to Dad. I follow her into the small dining room, where he's already sitting at the table that has been set for three.

I help Mom bring all the food to the table, making sure everything looks perfect. The aroma of warm soup and freshly baked meatloaf fills the room. The weight on my chest feels lighter. We start eating and the conversation flows easily at first, focusing on little things—the neighbor's dog, a new series Mom has started watching, and the state of Dad's vegetable patch.

But as the meal progresses, the inevitable topic surfaces: Dad's health.

"How are you feeling, Dad?" I ask gently, my gaze settling on him. "Any changes since last week?"

He shifts in his chair, his shoulders slumping slightly as he exhales. "About the same," he says, his voice low. "Tired, mostly. And the cough's been worse at night."

Mom glances over at him, her lips pressed into a thin line. "It's been hard," she admits softly, her fingers tightening around her napkin. "I'm trying to get him to rest more, but … you know how stubborn he is."

Dad gives a weak chuckle, though it doesn't quite reach his eyes. "Resting doesn't fix much," he says. "But I'm good."

I nod, biting back the urge to argue. "Well," I say, folding my hands in front of me, "we don't have to wait anymore. I've made arrangements, and we can start treatment as soon as Monday."

Their heads snap toward me, and for a moment, neither

of them speaks. Mom's eyes fill with emotion as she places her hand over her mouth. Dad blinks, his expression a mixture of shock and disbelief. "This Monday?" he asks, his voice barely audible.

"Yes," I say firmly. "Earl was very generous. He's already given me the first instalment for Dad's medical procedures and I've already contacted the hospital and made an appointment for next week. So everything is ready. The doctors can start the process immediately."

Mom sets down her fork, her brow furrowed in the way it always does when she's worried. "We're so grateful, sweetheart," she says softly. "But ... it just feels so fast. Are you sure about all this? About asking Earl for the money?"

I smile, keeping my tone light, even teasing. "Mom, he's my husband. It's his job to help with things like this. Honestly, he didn't even hesitate. He wanted to come along today to say hello, but he's busy during work hours. But he'll try to come next time."

They exchange a glance—one of those quiet exchanges that speak volumes without words. Dad clears his throat, leaning back in his chair. He looks tired and pale, but there's a flicker of hope in his eyes. "It's not just the money, though," he says, his voice rough. "We're worried about you, kiddo. This whole situation ... it wasn't what you wanted, was it?"

"Dad," I say firmly, reaching across the table to squeeze his hand. "This is exactly what I always wanted. I've wanted Earl from the first moment I set eyes on him. No more discussions about my marriage. You're going to start your treatment on Monday, and everything's going to be okay. That's all that matters for now."

"You've always been stubborn, but thank you, Raven. I couldn't ask for a better daughter than you," Dad mutters gruffly.

But my mother refuses to let it lie. "It's just ... Earl is such a mystery. How did he get so wealthy so quickly? Why did he disappear for all those years?"

I laugh lightly and lean back against my chair. "You know, I asked him the very same thing. He told me it wasn't overnight—it just looks that way. He got lucky and put everything into the right opportunities. He's smart, Mom. And determined. I promise I'll tell you more about it, but another time, okay?"

Mom nods, but there's a flicker of unease in her eyes. "Well, if he's taking good care of you, that's all we can ask for."

"He is," I say brightly, forcing my voice to bubble with enthusiasm. "He's been amazing, really. And once things settle down, he's going to come by and visit you both. I promise."

They don't push further, though I can feel their worries lingering in the room like an uninvited guest. I take a deep breath, determined to shift the mood. "Anyway," I say, standing and stacking the plates to bring to the sink, "let's not dwell on all that. The important thing is that we can schedule Dad's treatment starting Monday. Isn't that amazing?"

Dad's lips tremble slightly as he nods. "It's more than amazing, kid. It's a miracle."

"We'll get through this," I tell him firmly. "Together."

The conversation lightens after that, and we finish the meal with Mom's famous cookies. We laugh and share old stories, and for a little while, it almost feels normal. I cling to that feeling.

For now, I'll keep doing what I do best—pretending everything is fine.

CHAPTER 18

EARL

I hardly ever drink. I've seen what it's done to my father, how he sought it out as refuge through every failure in his life. Failed businesses. Failed marriages.

But now, here I am, seated in the music room, staring out at the storm raging across the night sky, a tumbler of whiskey in my hand. It burns down my throat. I've been sipping it steadily—not drunk, but I know it's almost time to stop. And yet, I don't, because I'm waiting. Not consciously, but the storm holds my gaze. I know what I'm waiting for.

Raven isn't back yet.

Irritation coils in my chest, tightening with every crack of thunder. She said she was visiting her parents, but so many hours have passed. And the thought gnaws at me: Is she really? Or is she with Charles? My stomach twists at the possibility, and I grit my teeth, hating myself for being so obsessed with someone who already betrayed me once. No matter how much I want to believe her, doubt clings to me like a second skin.

The headlights of the car I assigned for her use finally slice through the rain. She's back. A flicker of relief settles in my chest as I straighten. I watch her figure dart through the downpour, her movements unhurried and graceful. And I remember she likes walking in the rain. I see Nora rushing out with an umbrella to meet her and shield her. I can make out the older woman's voice, scolding her for not waiting in the car a moment longer.

I've left instructions for her to come see me the moment she returns and they have been dutifully passed on. I hear her footsteps on the hardwood floor and there is no urgency in them. I grip my glass tightly as I listen, my pulse quickening with every approaching step.

And then, there she is.

Her hair clings to her face, damp and wild, her blouse plastered to her skin from the rain. It clings in all the right places. A shaft of lightning lights up her face and figure. My eyes roam over her before I can stop myself, taking in the curve of her body, the delicate outline of her bra beneath the soaked fabric. My blood heats, and I hate how instantly and thoroughly she affects me.

"You wanted to see me," she says softly, stepping into the room. Her lips are slightly parted, and I can see the faint tremor in her shoulders, whether from the coldness of the rain or nerves, I don't know.

I lean back in the chair, forcing my expression into something impassive, detached. "You took your time."

Her eyes flicker with defiance. She shifts her weight, her wet hair sliding over her shoulder. "The rain slowed me down," she replies, her voice even, though I catch the hint of an edge. "And my parents wanted me to stay for dinner."

I swirl the amber liquid in my glass, watching her closely. "Convenient."

Her brows knit together, and she crosses her arms, though it only makes the wet fabric of her blouse pull tighter. "What's that supposed to mean?"

The tension between us becomes electric, the storm outside nothing compared to the one brewing here. I lift my gaze to meet hers, hating how easily she stirs every part of me—anger, doubt, desire.

"You know exactly what it means," I say sharply.

Her eyes lock onto mine, daring me to push her further. The rain beats against the windows, the sound filling the heavy silence between us. Then, with a sigh, she brushes a damp strand of hair from her face and takes a cautious step closer.

"I'm not doing this with you tonight," she says. "I went to see my parents. That's it. If you don't believe me, that's your problem."

My mind is torn between wanting to believe her and knowing better. Trusting doesn't come easily for me anymore. Maybe it never will again. But as she stands there, rain-soaked and defiant, there's something in her eyes that almost makes me falter. Almost.

I down the rest of the whiskey in one long swallow. "You're right," I agree, setting the empty glass down with a decisive clink. "It is my problem."

Her shoulders tense at my words, but she doesn't look away. Neither do I. And in the charged silence that follows, I wonder if we'll ever find our way back to something real—or if our relationship will always be like this storm.

"Didn't your parents pay for you to learn to play the piano?" I ask, nodding toward the grand instrument, its dark lacquer glinting faintly in the dim light.

"Yes," she says simply.

"Play something to make me feel good," I hear myself say.

I expect her to protest. She's always been fiery, full of opinions and ready to argue every point to exhaustion. My blood hums with anticipation, already bracing for her defiance, for her biting retort that'll make me feel alive, even in irritation. But once again, she surprises me. She smiles softly —a kind, gentle curve of her lips that cuts deeper than anger ever could. It's the same smile that made me fall for her, and I hate how it disarms me even now. Without a word, she moves toward the piano.

I watch intently as she lifts the lid and looks down at the gleaming keys. Then she takes her seat on the piano stool.

Her fingers hover over the keys before she starts to play. At first, it's just a few hesitant notes, soft and uncertain, like she's testing whether she still remembers how to. But then, without warning, her fingers explode into movement. Vivaldi's Four Seasons, the piece from our school play—a piece that rushes back into my memory as if it never left.

I used to sit in on her practices. I'd been there for every single one, watching her. She was the sun. Every note she played, every smile she gave—it lit me up in ways I hadn't thought possible.

And now, hearing the music again, it's like a chokehold on my chest. The warmth spreads through me. Old emotions hit me hard, so fast. The arousal, the heat, the raw desire—they all rush back, as strong as they ever were.

The final note lingers in the air like a whisper of the past. She turns to look at me and our gazes lock. There is such sadness in her eyes that it disarms me.

"Tell me more about your dad's condition," I say, my voice cutting through the haze of nostalgia and longing.

She sighs softly. "He has thyroid cancer." Her eyes glisten

with unshed tears under the soft light and to hide her vulnerability she turns back to face the piano. "We found out a few months ago. At first, he thought it was just some swelling, maybe a nodule or something harmless, but the tests confirmed it. Stage two."

I lean forward slightly, my elbows on my knees as I listen.

"They went through all the treatment options—surgery, radiation, even targeted therapies. The doctors think his prognosis is good as long as we move quickly, but it's been... hard, you know? Adjusting to it all."

Her fingers brush lightly over the piano keys as she speaks, almost absentmindedly, like she's grounding herself in the feel of the instrument. "I've scheduled his first treatment on Monday morning," she says, her voice softer now. "It's... a relief, honestly. Knowing we're finally doing something about it." She glances at me warily. "Thanks to you."

I study her, the way her shoulders are slumped as she talks, the way her voice carries that faint tremor of hope mixed with weariness. And for the first time in what feels like forever, I wonder if she's the only person who I have ever loved and has ever made me feel loved.

That's probably why the betrayal stung so much. She was my sun, moon, and stars, and after her treachery, it was as though my entire being was plunged into darkness. I hate that I gave her that much power. I hate even more that once again I've given her just as much power—maybe even more —by marrying her. At the time, I told myself it was to torture her. To make her pay for what she did. But why does it feel as if I'm the one who is being tortured? Why is it that I'm not having any fun at all?

"Do you like your portrait?" I ask, my voice smooth.

Her eyes flick to the massive canvas hanging above the fireplace. The shift in her expression is immediate. Her shoulders stiffen, her earlier ease evaporates into tension. Perfect. Just what I wanted, I tell myself.

Her gaze lingers on the portrait as though she's trying to make sense of it, to find something polite to say about the woman staring back at her from the golden throne. I watch her intently, savoring the discomfort that radiates from her like heat from a flame.

Finally, she speaks, her voice soft and neutral. "It's an interesting painting."

"That's all you have to say? Interesting?"

She tears her eyes away from the painting and looks at me. There's no anger in her gaze, no defiance—just exhaustion, like she's too tired to fight. "What do you want me to say, Earl? That I hate it? That I very clearly get your message with it? Would that make you happy?"

I lean back in my chair, studying her. "I just thought you'd appreciate the artistry," I say coolly. "I had it commissioned specially for you. To capture the essence of who you are."

Her lips press into a thin line, and for a moment, I think she might explode. Instead, she takes a deep breath and nods.

"Well, thank you for going to such trouble. It's nice of you. It's ... unforgettable."

One thing I can't take from her mockery. I didn't marry her for that. I rise from my seat and move closer to the painting. "Unforgettable," I repeat, tasting the word. "That's exactly what I was going for."

She looks away, her fingers tightening around the edge of the piano stool. "Why?" she asks quietly, almost to herself. "Why did you do it?"

The question hangs in the air between us, unanswered. I know why I did it. To remind her—and myself—that I'm the one in control now. That she doesn't get to rewrite the past or pretend it didn't happen. No matter how much she smiles, how pitiful she looks, or how much she wants to move forward and forget the past, I'll always be here to drag her back.

I refill my glass again and swirl the amber liquid gently. I don't want to spend any more time with her tonight. I want to be alone. To drown in the quiet and let the storm outside mirror the one inside me.

"It's late," I say, my tone dismissive. "You should get to bed."

She shakes her head in defeat and without another word, she rises and heads for the door. I watch her go, the faint scent of rain clinging to her as she moves. The outline of her silhouette against the dim light of the hallway makes something twist deep inside me—something I wish I didn't feel.

The door clicks shut behind her, and for a long while, I just stand there, staring at the empty space where she had been. Then I turn back to the painting, my gaze locking onto those cold, unrecognizable eyes.

Unforgettable. Yes, that's exactly what I wanted. But that creature is a lie. That is not her. Even I know it.

I stare out of the window and can't stop thinking about her. How wet she was from the rain, her clothes clinging to her curves, the way her hair dripped in dark rivulets down her back.

The liquor burns through me, igniting a fire I can't extinguish. It fuels a raw, untamed need—an aching desperation to silence my thoughts the only way I know how. I need her. I need to lose myself in her. To drown in her until there's nothing left of this restless, raging heat. I need to fuck her. Hard.

Before I know it, I'm on my feet. My steps are quick and decisive. I catch up to her just as she reaches the top of the stairs. Her hand is on the banister, and she's mid-turn when I grab her arm and tug her toward me.

"Earl!" she exclaims, startled, her voice a mix of confusion and astonishment. "What are you—?"

"Come on," I cut her off, my tone rough and uncaring. I don't give her a chance to argue as I pull her along, her footsteps stumbling slightly to keep up with mine.

"Ow," she mutters, her tone sharp. Her free hand goes to my wrist, trying to ease my grip, but I don't let go. I can't. My pulse is pounding too hard, and the feel of her skin against mine only stokes the fire.

I lead her straight to my bedroom, the door swinging shut behind us with a finality that makes the air in the room feel heavier. She looks at me, her brows furrowed, her lips parting as if to speak, but I don't give her the chance.

"Strip," I say, my voice low, roughened by desire and whiskey.

Her eyes widen slightly, a flicker of hesitation crossing her face. But I don't wait to see if she'll obey. I reach for my own shirt, tugging it over my head in one swift motion. The fabric falls to the floor, followed quickly by the rest of my clothes, each piece stripped away with a sense of urgency I can't control.

I turn toward the bathroom, my hands pushing the door open. "Don't make me wait," I call over my shoulder, the words coming out sharper than I intended. "You'll be sorry if you do."

The water runs cold at first, biting against my skin and making me shiver as I step under the spray. Gradually, it warms, the heat seeping into my muscles. It feels good—too good—but it doesn't quell the fire burning inside me. The anticipation is a steady thrum in my veins, an ache that no amount of steam or scalding heat can erase.

I stand there for a few minutes, letting the water cascade over me, my head tilted forward, eyes closed, trying to focus on the steady rhythm of the droplets against my shoulders. I'm burning. Burning for her.

Then I feel it—a cold burst of air sweeping in as the bathroom door opens. I don't have to turn around to know she's entered. The sound of the door clicking shut behind her sends a shiver down my spine, though the heat of the water keeps my skin aflame. The anticipation is unbearable.

When I finally turn, the sight of her hits me like a physical force. She stands just a few feet away, her damp hair falling in dark waves around her face, completely naked.

In the yellow light of the bathroom, her skin glistens still with droplets of rain. She's breathtaking—every inch of her. On her pert, high breasts, her nipples have hardened into delicious peaks, their soft pink hue practically begging for my touch. My gaze travels down, over the elegant curve of her slender arms and the taut lines of her toned stomach, down to the gentle flare of her hips.

My mind is a swirling storm of raw desire. I tell myself to look away, to pull back before I fall too far, but I can't. My eyes are locked on her, tracing every detail, committing every inch of her to memory as though I'll never see her like this again.

Her gaze is unwavering, fearless. There's something in her eyes that shakes me—a quiet strength, a vulnerability she doesn't attempt to hide, and an intensity that mirrors my own. The way she looks at me makes my blood roar, makes every muscle in my body tense with need and my chest ache. My mouth dries and my hands clench at my sides, resisting the overwhelming urge to reach for her, to feel the softness of her skin under my palms, to claim her.

She tilts her head slightly, her lips curving into a small,

knowing smile. I don't know how she does it—how she manages to unravel me with a single look. It's infuriating and intoxicating all at once. It's shocking how much power she has over me.

Her eyes move over me, slow and deliberate, like she's taking her time to commit every detail to memory. Her gaze trails downward, over the hard planes of my chest, the muscles slick and glistening under the water, down to the sharp line of my hips and lower. Her eyes linger there. My cock hardens even more till it is curved and leaning towards my navel.

"Like what you see?" I ask, my voice low and rough.

Her eyes snap back to mine. "I do," she says simply.

CHAPTER 19

RAVEN

*W*ater cascades over Earl's taut shoulders, dripping down his chest and along the lean lines of his body. He doesn't move, but his eyes devour me from afar. It's as though he's daring me to come closer, to break the barrier he's so carefully erected between us.

The heat of the shower wraps around us, steam curling in the sizable stall.

I'm trembling—partly from the desire that's been simmering under my skin all day long, partly from the emotions twisting inside me. My mind is full of the memory of the ravenous desperation with which he kissed me earlier —God, he kissed me like a starving man. It made me breathless and filled my heart with hope. But he stopped suddenly, as though terrified of what might happen if he let it go any further.

Now, as he watches me, I see that war inside him again. The way he loathes me, yet can't seem to stay away. It's that obvious hesitation, that struggle, that is what gives me courage. Maybe one day he'll break and tell me why he pushes me away so vehemently. Why is he so furious at me?

But right now, all I want is him. To feel him. To let this tension between us snap.

I take a step forward, and the water streams over me. I'm close enough to feel the heat radiating from his body. His chest rises and falls sharply and his jaw is tight. Still, he says nothing.

Brushing my fingers against his wet skin, I gently push him so he is leaning against the tiled wall. He doesn't stop me, just keeps watching as if I'm not quite real, a phantom that could vanish at any second.

Without a word, I lean forward, pressing my lips to his chest. His skin is warm and wet, the faint taste of him still not washed away by the water. I hear his sharp intake of breath, and feel the way his body stiffens under my touch. My lips trail lower, slow and deliberate, savoring every inch of him. I kiss the dip of his collarbone, the curve of his pectoral, the hardness of his abdomen. Each kiss feels like a small victory, a crack in the armor he is desperately trying to keep intact.

When my lips brush against his nipple, his head tilts back slightly, a low, guttural sound escaping him. It's a sound I've heard from him before, one that never fails to make my knees weak. Emboldened, I swirl my tongue over the hardened peak, and his hands fly to my shoulders, gripping me tightly as though trying to anchor himself.

I glance up, meeting his gaze, and the sheer vulnerability in his eyes almost undoes me. But I don't stop. I kiss my way lower, sliding to my knees on the wet tiles. The water droplets clinging to him glisten like tiny diamonds, and I'm struck by how utterly beautiful he is. He's watching me, his chest heaving, his lips parted slightly as though he wants to say something but can't find the words.

My hands trail along his thighs, trembling slightly as I take his gorgeous cock in my grasp. He's heavy and hard, and I can feel the pulse of his arousal against my palm. I look up at him again, searching his face for any sign of protest. There's none. Just a desperate, raw hunger that mirrors my own.

Slowly, I take him into my mouth, my tongue swirling over the sensitive tip. He groans, his head falling forward as his fingers tangle in my hair. The sound sends a thrill through me, and I take him deeper, savoring the way he fills me, the way his control begins to slip.

"Raven," he rasps, his voice strained and thick with need. His hands tighten in my hair, guiding me, urging me to take more. I obey, letting him press deeper, letting myself become intoxicated with his taste and smell. He's completely in control now, and I love it. I love that he's letting himself go, even if just for this moment.

His hips begin to move, shallow thrusts that he tries to hold back but can't. I relax my throat, letting him in further, and the sound he makes is almost feral. His hands grip my hair tighter, and I can feel him trembling, his restraint hanging by a thread.

"Look at me," he commands, his voice low and breathless. I do, my gaze locking with his as I take him as deeply as I can. His eyes darken, his jaw tightening as he watches me, the intensity between us crackling like a live wire.

The feel of him overwhelms me—the smoothness of his skin, the pulsing heat against my tongue. Every inch of him seems to demand my attention, his arousal filling my senses. The faint saltiness of his seed, the musky scent of him in the steamy air—it intoxicates me, leaves me craving more. I can't get enough, as though every part of him is designed to draw me further under his spell, to make me lose myself completely.

I pull back just slightly, wrapping my hand around his length to stroke him slowly, deliberately. My fingers glide from the base to the tip, slick and firm as I keep my lips and tongue working on him. I savor every reaction, the way his body jerks against me, how his breathing falters. Then I trace my tongue down the elegant line of his shaft, tasting every inch, letting it glide lower until my lips reach the heavy weight of him.

I press kisses there first, soft and reverent, before taking one of his balls into my mouth. The new sensation makes him groan, low and guttural, and I can feel his hand tremble in my hair. His reactions send a thrill through me, a wave of triumph, a surge of pride. I'm unraveling him. I'm making him come undone.

I suck harder.

When he finally spills into me, his release is shuddering and violent, his whole body tensing as he emits a strangled groan. I swallow every last drop, my own body humming with a strange mix of ecstasy and gratitude. Without his help, I wouldn't have been able to schedule my father's treatment. It had been the greatest source of pain and worry in my life; that I would lose my beloved father simply because I couldn't afford his medical bills. But Earl made that terrible burden magically disappear. No matter how difficult he made things for me, I won't forget this amazing thing he did for me and my father.

As I rise to my feet, my legs shaky, I meet with his gaze once more. There's something different in his eyes now, something softer, more vulnerable. He reaches out, his hand brushing against my cheek, and for a moment, I think he might say something. But he doesn't. Instead, he pulls away, retreating behind his walls once more.

"Turn around," he murmurs, his voice low, barely audible over the sound of our ragged breaths.

I hesitate, my heart pounding so hard I can feel it in my throat. But there's no mistaking the command in his tone. Slowly, I turn, my palms finding the cool, slick tiles of the wall. My breath hitches as I feel his hands on my hips, firm and grounding, guiding me into place. His touch sends a shiver down my spine, anticipation coiling in my belly like a spring about to snap.

"Hands on the wall," he says, his voice rougher now, more urgent.

I do as he says, bracing myself as the heat of his body presses against me. The angle bends me slightly forward, and I can feel the weight of his gaze burning into my skin. My breath comes in shallow gasps, the tension between us almost unbearable.

I reach back and my fingers wrap around his length. He's so hard and so impossibly smooth. The way he throbs under my touch makes my knees tremble. The sound of his sharp inhale is a reward in itself, spurring me on. I stroke him slowly at first, teasing, savoring the way his hips twitch toward me, the way his breath hitches with each deliberate movement.

"Don't stop," he growls.

I don't.

I trace my fingers along his shaft, down to the base, and then lower still, my lips curling into a smile as I hear the low, guttural noise he makes. The air was thick with steam and the raw scent of desire. His hips jerk, his control slipping further with every touch.

His fingers slide down my body and brush against the

slick, swollen folds of my sex. I gasp, my body arching into his touch as he strokes me with a precision that leaves me trembling. The wet heat of his fingers sends sparks shooting up my spine, and I can barely keep my balance as he teases me, pushing me to the brink. His fingers slip into me.

"You're so silky," he murmurs, almost to himself, and I hear the awe in his voice.

"Please," I whisper, my voice trembling with need. I don't care how desperate I sound. I just need him—now, completely, without reservation.

He answers without words, his fingers withdrawing only to be replaced by something much larger, much harder. The head of his cock presses against me, its size stretching me even before he fully enters. Slowly, deliberately, he sinks in, his hands gripping my hips tightly.

He's so thick and seems to go so impossibly deep. I can feel every inch of him as he fills me completely. I brace myself against the wall, my breath coming in shallow, broken gasps. He doesn't move at first, just holds himself there, buried inside me as though savoring the moment.

"Fuck," he groans, his voice raw.

"Fuck me, Earl. Fuck me," I beg, my voice barely audible.

That's all it takes. His hips pull back, and then he thrusts in, slow and deliberate at first, as though testing how much I can take. But there's no need—my body welcomes him, drawing him in with a hunger that matches his own. The rhythm he sets is almost tender, a stark contrast to the raw, animalistic need that burns between us.

Eventually, the tenderness gives way to urgency and his thrusts become faster and harder, each one driving me closer to the edge. The sound of water and our bodies colliding fills the stall. I cry out, unable to hold back the sounds of pleasure that spill from my lips, and his hand moves to cover my mouth, muffling my cries as though reminding me of the danger of being overheard. It's an act of habit, something we'd had to do in our younger years so as not to get caught. There's no need for it now, but it warms me either way. It's almost like he's lost in that time. It's too easy to remember, impossible to forget, just how good it was—just how good we both felt to the other.

Fucking like this completely dissolves the antagonism between us, making it seem as though no time has passed at all and we are still the other's soulmates. I melt into him on one particularly brutal thrust, my eyes rolling back, my back arching. He glues his body to mine, his hard hand curving around my waist like a vice as he keeps me from sliding down to the floor, like the pool of wax my entire body mass seems to have melted into.

His body rocks against mine, each thrust sending ripples of wonderful sensation through me. I cling to the wall for support, my fingers splayed against the slick tiles as he drives deeper, harder, until the world narrows to just us—him and me.

"Earl," I gasp, his name spilling from my lips like a prayer. I feel as if I'm drowning in him and he must feel it too because his hands grip my hips like he's afraid I'll disappear. The tension coils tighter and tighter until it's unbearable. He leans forward, his breath hot against my ear.

"You feel so fucking good," he mutters, his voice hoarse, almost broken.

That takes me over the edge. My head falls back against his shoulder as my climax crashes through me, violent and unrelenting. It pulls his name from my throat in a desperate cry.

His arms wrap around me, one hand cupping my breast as his thumb brushes over the hardened peak, the other splayed across my belly, holding me against him. I feel him everywhere, his strength, his heat, the steady rhythm of his thrusts as he chases his own release. His fingers tighten on me, grounding me as I spiral in the aftershocks of my pleasure, my body trembling uncontrollably.

"Raven," he growls, his pace quickening, more erratic now, and I feel it building in him, the way his body tenses, his breaths coming faster and rougher. I reach back, my hand finding his cheek, and he turns his head to press his lips to my palm, the gesture so tender it steals my breath.

When he finally comes, it's with a force that makes him shudder against me, his grip on me unyielding as he spills inside me. The heat of him, the way he buries his face in the curve of my neck, the relentless spray of water falling on us as he groans my name feels like coming home.

As the last tremors fade, he doesn't pull away. Instead, he holds me, his chest heaving against my back, his lips brushing over my wet skin in a way that feels almost reverent. I close my eyes and for the first time in what feels like forever, I feel whole.

CHAPTER 20

EARL

I'm not done with her. I'm never done with her. I push the stall door and grab a towel. I wrap her in it.

"Follow me," I say, and grabbing another towel head straight to the bed. I finish towelling myself, drop the towel to the floor and sit at its edge. Dampness still clings to my hair and skin. Moments later, she appears, her own towel wrapped loosely around her, the sight of her steals the air from my lungs. She pauses in the doorway briefly, a flicker of hesitation in her eyes, but when she meets my gaze, something unspoken passes between us. She crosses the room slowly, her steps light and careful and comes to stand in front of me.

I reach out and take her wrist, and gently pull her onto the bed. She comes willingly and I position her on the bed. Her legs fall open under my hands, and I settle between them, my gaze never leaving hers. She looks at me like I'm the only thing tethering her to reality, like she might shatter if I so much as blink.

"Stay still," I murmur. Then I lean down and lick her sex. It's what I wanted to do from the first moment I saw her in the church, but I was afraid her taste would break me.

The first touch of my tongue against her makes her cry out, a sound that sends a jolt of heat through me. She trembles under me, her hands gripping the sheets as though they're her only anchor. I go slow at first, savoring her, but her taste is intoxicating, and I lose myself in her, in the softness of her thighs, the warmth of her skin, the electricity that sparks between us with every movement.

Her body arches off the bed as I deepen my attention, my tongue moving in slow, deliberate strokes that leave her writhing. Her hands find my hair and her fingers tangle in it, pulling hard as if she's trying to drag me deeper into her. And I let her. I'd let her rip me apart if it meant staying here, like this … with her.

Her hips move against me, uncontrollable now, desperate, and I grip them, holding her steady as I take her higher and higher. Her moans turn to pleas, incoherent and breathless, and I can feel the tension building in her, a coiled spring ready to snap. I suck harder, faster, the pressure driving her to the edge until she shatters beneath me, crying out as her body trembles violently.

Her release is everything—raw, unrestrained, and utterly consuming. She's spilling into my mouth, and I drink every bit of her, my tongue working to prolong her pleasure, to draw out every last shudder.

When she finally stills and lays limp, my lips press gentle kisses to her skin, feeling her pulse race beneath me. Her breath comes in shallow, ragged gasps, and her body glistens with a sheen of sweat and satisfaction. I watch her struggle to regain herself, her chest rising and falling rapidly, her lips parted, her hair splayed wildly across the bed. She looks wrecked and radiant all at once, and the sight of her like this—undone, beautiful, mine—burns itself into my memory.

For a long moment, neither of us speaks, the room filled only with the sound of her breathing and the lingering echoes of what we've just shared. I lean forward, resting my forehead against the softness of her thigh, and close my eyes, savoring the warmth of her.

My lips move over her skin, reverent and unhurried, trailing along the curve of her thighs, over the softness of her sex, up the line of her abdomen. She gasps when my tongue dips into the shallow hollow of her belly button, and the sound shoots through me like a live current. I linger, savoring the way her muscles tense beneath my mouth, the way her breath catches as though she's completely at my mercy.

Next is her breasts. I take my time, cupping their fullness in my hands, feeling their delicious roundness, their warmth. My lips brush against one taut peak, then the other, my tongue teasing in soft, flicking strokes. Her nipples harden against my tongue, and I can feel myself responding in kind, the ache inside me building, building. She cries out, her back arching off the bed, her hands gripping my arms as though she wants to pull me closer.

Her gasps turn to pleas as I take her nipple fully into my mouth, sucking gently at first, then harder. Her cries are high and breathless, her hands now clawing at my shoulders, her legs shifting restlessly beneath me. She tries to twist away, overwhelmed, it's all too much for her, but I hold her steady, my mouth devouring her, savoring her, drowning in the sweetness of her taste and the sheer intoxicating feel of her.

It's endless, this kiss, this moment, this connection I can't let go of.

Unwilling to stop, I trail back down her body, my lips tracing the same path they took moments ago, but this time slower, deeper, as though I'm memorizing every inch of her. I reach between us, my hand guiding myself to her, and with deliberate care, I position the tip of my cock against her entrance. She's so wet, so ready, her slick heat coating me as I thrust into her until she takes all of me.

Her body welcomes me, enveloping me in a way that makes my head spin. I take my time, moving gently at first, rocking into her with an excruciating slowness that has her trembling beneath me. Her hands clutch at my arms, her nails digging into my skin as though she can't handle the unbearable tension building between us. Her moans are soft and breathless, every sound she makes adding fuel to the fire raging inside me.

I change my rhythm, my movements turning deep and deliberate, every thrust designed to stretch the moment, to draw out every ounce of pleasure. Her legs wrap around me, her heels pressing into my back, urging me to go harder, deeper. I oblige, my pace quickening, the force of my thrusts causing the bed to creak beneath us. Her cries grow louder, more desperate, and I cover her mouth with mine, swallowing her sounds as though I can't bear the thought of losing even one of them.

"Earl," she cries against my lips, her voice breaking when I shift my angle and drive into her with a newfound intensity. Her body arches beneath me, her hands tangling in my hair, pulling hard enough to make me groan. I grip her hips, holding her steady as I lose myself in the rhythm of us, the way we fit together, the way every thrust, every movement sends her closer to the edge.

Her release comes suddenly, violently, her body clenching around me as she cries out my name, her voice wrecked with the force of her orgasm. The sight of her coming undone beneath me—her head craned back, throat exposed, lips parted, eyes fluttering shut—is enough to send me over the edge. I follow her, my release hitting me like a tidal wave, pulling me under, leaving me shaking and breathless as I collapse against her.

For a moment, neither of us moves, the room filled with the sound of our ragged breathing, the scent of sex and sweat hanging heavy in the air. I press a kiss to her shoulder, then her neck, and finally her lips, the taste of her grounding me, reminding me that she's here, that this is real.

She reaches up, her fingers brushing against my cheek, her touch soft, tentative, as though she's afraid this moment might shatter if she holds on too tightly. I cover her hand with mine, pressing it to my face, and for just this moment, I let myself believe that maybe, just maybe, we could have this again.

CHAPTER 21

RAVEN

I'm well aware that in the long term, sex changes very little, but at this moment, as he presses my hand to his face and kisses the middle of my palm, I am liable to believe anything. That we have a chance. All we need to do is talk it out.

Especially when he doesn't get up to leave, but collapses against me, his face buried in my neck. This is not an opportunity to be missed. His guard is down, and it might not remain this way once this moment passes and the bliss gives way to reality.

I steel myself, my voice soft. "You're going to tell me to leave, aren't you? To go back to my room?"

He shifts slightly, pulling away just enough to look at me, his expression cautious. "You want to stay?"

My heart is pounding so loud I'm sure he can hear it. "Yes, I want to stay, but if you're going to kick me out, anyway, then I, at least, want to have my say."

Almost instantly, his gaze sharpens. In real time I see reality seeping back in, its cold edges slicing through the warmth of the moment. "And what is it you want to say?"

I take a deep breath, steadying myself. "I want to know why you're so angry with me. Why you left so suddenly back then, out of the blue, without a call or even a text. There was no way to reach you. Your phone number was dead. I was blindsided, Earl. We didn't even argue or anything. I didn't understand, and it was maddening, but I can see clearly now that it had something to do with me, but I have no idea what. Please, tell me why. Help me understand."

The air between us grows oppressive. His jaw tightens and his eyes burn into mine. The intolerable silence stretches. Swallowing hard, I wait.

Then he pulls away, swinging his legs over the edge of the bed. One hard word drops out of him.

"No."

I reach out, grasping his arm, desperate to hold onto whatever fragile thread still connects us. "Earl, you need to talk to me. If I did something wrong, you need to tell me. Why punish me this way?"

"Punish you?" he snaps, his voice low and biting. He jerks his arm free from my grasp and stands. "I haven't even started, my darling wife."

"I never forgot about you," I say, my voice trembling but firm. "I never stopped thinking about you—not even for a moment. I was hurt, furious that you left, that you disappeared without a word. And now, I want to be angry. I want to scream at you for breaking my heart into a million pieces. But I can't even do that, because right now …" My throat tightens, the words catching, but I push through. "Right now, you seem more hurt and angry than I am. And I can't help but wonder if something happened, if there was some kind of misunderstanding. Please, Earl. Talk to me. I'm sure we can resolve this."

His eyes stay on me, unreadable, until I see cold anger spread across his face like a storm and his expression becomes hard. "Get out," he says, his voice sharp, final. "You've overstayed your welcome."

My body goes cold. I want to defy him, force him to tell me what I have done, but the sting of his total rejection cuts too deep. I force myself to stand, my movements stiff, every step away from him is like dragging weights behind me. "Fine," I say, my voice brittle. "Keep tearing at me until you destroy me if that's what you enjoy so much."

I reach the door, but as my fingers brush the handle, his words stop me in my tracks.

"You're not going to take your payment?"

Slowly, I turn, my gaze locking onto his. He is like a stranger. Not an ounce of the lover he was only a few moments ago remains.

"This is the second time," I say, my voice steely. "I'm not a prostitute. I'm your wife."

His lips curl into a smirk, cold and cruel. "You really want to act like this is a genuine marriage? I thought it was a transaction based on who had the most money. Isn't that why you dumped Charles at the altar for me? Isn't money all you've ever wanted? Isn't it all you care about? So why pretend now?"

"I'm not pretending," I say, turning around to face him.

"I get it. I'd do the same in your shoes. You want to find a way to be civil with me so your life will be easier. So you can have your cake and eat it. But no, darling, you don't get to do that. Sure, I'm gonna be generous, in fact, outrageously generous. You'll have everything you ever wanted. Clothes, shoes, designer bags. You'll have it all. But in return, I want my pound of flesh. I want to see you live in your gilded cage and suffer. I want to see you rue the day you thought money could buy you happiness."

"Seeing me suffer will give you pleasure?" I ask incredulously.

He doesn't miss a beat. "Yes."

I stare at him in shock. I cannot believe that this is the man I have just given all of myself to, but the worst part is no matter how hard I try, I cannot find it in myself to regret it. Maybe it's because a part of me is hoping this cannot go on and he will come to his senses someday. Or maybe it's because he hasn't done anything unforgivable yet. Despite the complete hostility, he's still ensured that my father has been taken care of. He's kept his side of the bargain. I take in a deep breath and release it. For my father, I will bear everything, and so I even manage to work up the sliver of a smile.

"Okay," I reply. "We'll do as you wish. I will not remind you of the past again."

He pulls open the drawer on the bedside table and it is stuffed full with money. Disdainfully, he grabs a handful of bills and holds them out to me. His eyes dare me not to disobey him.

Clearly, he wants a reaction, and I decide that I am going to give it to him. Perhaps the only way to make him just as miserable as he is making me is to ensure that I don't give him the satisfaction of seeing me cower. I walk up to him.

Somehow I manage to work up a smile as I reach for the money. "Thank you. This is generous, but I hope you can do better next time."

I turn around to leave. I expect him to call me back and stop me and make me pay for the way I have just spoken, but he doesn't. It's pure silence behind me as I make my way out. I know he's watching my every move.

Once the door closes behind me, my shoulders slump. I return to my room and tuck the bills carefully into my kitty. I do not know what I will do yet, but someday, somehow I'll make him understand that I am innocent of whatever he thinks I have done and I will make him apologize to me for this terrible injustice he is doing to me. For now, I need more than ever to make myself devoid of emotions and feelings because this is the only way I will be able to find my way through this nightmare.

"Just until Dad is well," I console myself as I head to the bathroom. I need to wash him, us, the passion, the sweetness … the pain.

CHAPTER 22

EARL

I stand there, fists clenched at my sides, watching her leave, head held high and clutching her towel like some kind of armor. The air in the room shifts and it feels like she's stealing something I can't name. She doesn't glance back, and somehow that makes it worse.

And as the door clicks shut behind her, the sound final and hollow, I realize I don't feel the triumph I should. Instead, there's a gnawing ache in my chest, a void that only seems to grow the longer I stand here.

She's beautiful. God, she's beautiful in a way that makes me want to rip her apart just to see the flaws I am so sure that she is so cleverly hiding deep inside her. And that thought makes me want to lash out, to hurt her before she can hurt me again. And I know exactly why it is like this. Why every time she makes me feel good, I have to tear it down. Why every time she softens the edges of my anger, I sharpen it against her. Why then does it hurt me to hurt her?

139

When I know with every fiber of my being that she deserves it. That I am getting the revenge that I wanted.

I hate her. Don't I?

But the truth? The truth is I don't know anymore.

She makes me question everything. My anger. My hatred. Myself. And the worst part? She doesn't even realize she's doing it.

I drag a hand down my face, trying to shake the weight of it all. My legs feel heavy as I move toward the bed, the sheets still carrying her scent, her warmth.

All I can think about is the vulnerability in her eyes, the way her lips trembled before she forced that defiant smile. The rain outside doesn't let up, hammering against the windows in a steady, unrelenting rhythm, matching the chaos in my head and heart. As I sink onto the bed, still reeling from the sweetness of her body against mine, I feel unmoored, like I'm digging myself into a hole I'll never climb out of.

The memory of her surrounds me—her scent, her taste, the way her body yielded to mine, soft and urgent. I can still feel her, every part of her, as if she's left an imprint on my skin. My chest tightens as I sink deeper into the bed, her warmth still clinging to the sheets like a ghost I can't shake.

I press my palms against my face.

It was just sex. I tell myself that, over and over, as if the repetition can make it true or false. It was just physical. It was just her body beneath mine, her thighs wrapped around me, her nails digging into my back as she gasped my name.

Her voice still lingers in my ears—those soft, breathless sounds she made, as if I was the only thing tethering her to the world.

I hated it. I loved it. I hated how much I loved it.

The rain continues to fall, unrelenting, as I lie there

staring at the ceiling. My body still aches for her. I don't know if this is victory or defeat, but I know one thing for certain.

I cannot stop. I cannot put away my anger just because of the way her pussy smells. She will not make a fool of me again. I need to continue with this torture until she breaks or I do. This is the only way that there will ever be an end to this relationship.

With this resolve in my mind, I shut my eyes and try to find some sleep.

But sleep does not come.

As the morning light creeps through the curtains, faint and reluctant, casting the room in muted gold, the perfect plan forms in my head. I lie still for a moment, staring at the ceiling. Then I throw the covers off with a sharp motion, determined to push her out of my head, at least for now. The cool air bites at me as I stand, and I call the housekeeper. My voice is calm and measured, as I issue the command. My wife will join me for breakfast. I'll make her sit across from me in silence, let her feel the distance between us—both literal and figurative.

When I enter the dining room, the table is already set for two. The rain has stopped, but the air is still heavy with the moisture. I take my seat at the far end, picking up my phone, going through my emails and checking my stocks.

She appears a few minutes later, led in by the house-keeper. Her steps are sure and her head is held high. The blanket from last night has been replaced by a simple robe tied at the waist. Her hair is still damp, strands clinging to her neck, and the sight makes something twist in my chest.

She takes her seat without a word, her eyes briefly meeting mine before darting away. I let the silence stretch, filling the space between us like a living thing. I know it bothers her. I can see it in the way her hands fidget with the napkin on the table, the way her gaze flickers to the food but she doesn't eat.

She used to talk endlessly during meals when we were young. Banter, laughter, questions—she'd chatter so much I'd have to feed her myself just to make sure she ate. The memory sneaks in unbidden, and I shove it away, focusing instead on this quiet sullen version of her. I want her to feel it, to remember that we're not those people anymore.

The clink of utensils against plates is the only sound, each bite calculated, each swallow deliberate. Her presence across from me is aloof and electrifying all at once. When our eyes meet again, I don't bother hiding the scowl that forms. She looks back at me with defiance. Or hurt? It doesn't matter.

When I'm done eating, I wipe my mouth with a napkin. She glances at me warily. The air grows heavier with antici- pation, her tension so palpable it's almost stifling. I push back my chair, the screech of wood against the floor breaking the fragile quiet.

"Go get dressed. I'm flying you to New York to do some shopping."

She blinks, clearly taken aback. "New York? Shopping?"

"Yes." My tone is cold and calculated, each word laced with intent. The words flow out, cruel and deliberate, each one designed to cut deeper than the last. "I've realized I've been doing things halfway. If this is purely transactional, as it should be, then I might as well treat you the way you've always wanted to be treated. You should be rewarded gener- ously for fucking me. A whore would be if she were in your shoes, so why not you? And let's be honest, there's not much of a difference either, is there?"

Her face tightens, but I don't stop.

"You can buy whatever your heart desires." I lean forward

slightly, my gaze locking onto hers. "Isn't this what you've always wanted? Isn't this the only quality you've ever cared about in a man? Someone to spoil you? Someone to give you everything you ever dreamed of?"

Her lips part as if she's about to say something, but no words come. Her hands grip the edge of the table, her knuckles white, and for a moment, I think she might snap. But she doesn't. Instead, she nods, her voice steady but icy when she finally speaks.

"Okay."

The single word hangs in the air, heavy and final, and I stand, signaling the end of the conversation. I don't give her a chance to linger. "You have thirty minutes. Don't make me wait a second longer."

With that, I turn and walk away, a gnawing ache in my chest, each step pulling me further away from her.

CHAPTER 23

RAVEN

I stare at the open closet, almost dizzy with disbelief. Is he planning to take me shopping? The old Earl never cared for clothes. Just like me. I have no real interest in clothes and I'm not even a shopping kind of girl. All I ever wanted to do was write and build my life with Earl. I thought he knew that, but I guess this is another sick game he wants to play to torment me. I have no choice but to play along.

The hangers clink together as I push them aside. A simple cream dress catches my eye. It is everything this situation isn't. I hesitate before pulling it off the rack. It's a strange kind of rebellion—choosing something so unassuming and dull when I know he expects me to dress to impress. Let him be annoyed. Let him hate it. Let him hate me. I have no energy left for anything else.

When I slip it on and glance at my reflection again. I look... ordinary. The realization makes me wonder why he came back for me. He could have had any beauty from wherever he had disappeared to all these years. Was it just all revenge and hate for whatever he imagines I have done to him ... or is there something more?

I slip on a pair of comfortable flats and hurry out of the room. The sharp, impatient blare of the car horn echoes through the house. He's already annoyed. Good.

The rain from last night has left the ground damp and the air thick with the scent of wet earth as I walk unhurriedly toward the car. He's seated in the driver's seat, his leather jacket gleaming under the overcast sky. He looks effortlessly good—too good—and I hate myself for noticing.

Sliding into the passenger seat, I make a point not to look at him, though I can feel his gaze on me. The engine hums as he pulls away from the house, the silence between us heavy.

We're not shopping locally it would seem as the town passes by in a blur of color and bustle. I guess we must be heading to the mall in the next town two hours away. He doesn't speak and neither do I. About half an hour later his phone rings and he talks on the speaker with someone called Olivia about some property he is acquiring. I notice he is friendly and almost flirtatious and that makes my stomach tighten with jealousy.

I turn my head away and look out at the countryside. The call ends and still he says nothing. My thoughts drift, unbidden, to the department store we're headed to. The last time we were there together was so long ago it feels like another lifetime.

Back then, it was never for shopping. We went on Earl's motorbike to eat slices of Mario's extra-large, thick-crust pepperoni pizza and share ice cream sundaes like they were delicacies. I didn't care about the high-end brands lining the food halls, and neither did he. It was simple. It was us.

The last time we were there it was my birthday. Earl and I were sitting in one of the rickety booths near the edge. The smell of fried food and the distant hum of chatter filled the air, mixing with the faint sounds of people talking and the clatter of trays. Then Charles showed up, flanked by his usual crowd of loud, arrogant friends. I noticed them before they noticed us, their expensive sneakers and designer gear making them stand out from the casual crowd. Charles's laugh carried across the space. He always behaved as if he owned whatever space he was in.

When he spotted us, his eyes changed into that familiar, predatory gleam. He hated Earl. Hands stuffed casually into his trouser pockets, and his friends trailing behind him like a pack of hyenas, he sauntered over. Earl stiffened beside me, his hand tightening around the flimsy plastic spoon he was holding. I could feel the tension radiating off him. His jaw was clenched tight by the time Charles's shadow loomed over our table.

"Well, well, Raven," Charles drawled, his smile dripping with false charm. "Celebrating your birthday in style with pizza and ice cream, I see. Really? Is that the best your greasy boyfriend could do?" He let his gaze slide over to Earl, his eyes assessing, mocking. Then he shook his head with disgust. "What a loser."

The flimsy plastic spoon snapped in half, but Earl didn't say a word. He didn't even look up, but I could see the way his knuckles whitened. Charles leaned in closer, his voice dropping to a conspiratorial whisper that was loud enough for everyone to hear. "You know, if you were with me, I'd show you what a real birthday looks like. I'd take you some-where special. Buy you a meal fit for a princess because that's what you are. A right princess."

The words hung in the air, heavy and cutting, and I felt

the burn of anger rise in my chest. I looked at Earl then, at the way he sat so still, his shoulders rigid, his eyes fixed on the table like he was trying to will himself not to react, make a scene and ruin my birthday. It broke something in me to see him like that.

"No, thank you," I said sharply. "This is *exactly* what I wanted on my birthday and I'm celebrating it with the person who matters."

Charles's smirk faltered, just for a second, before he recovered, laughing like I'd just told the world's funniest joke. "Come on, Raven. Be serious. What could he possibly offer you? Maybe his drunkard father begging for change in the parking lot outside the liquor store? Oh, wait, didn't that already happen last week?"

His friends erupted into laughter, the sound grating and cruel. I felt my hands ball into fists at my sides, the heat of my fury threatening to spill over. "You're pathetic," I said quietly. Then I stood abruptly, my chair screeching against the floor, and shoved past Charles, my shoulder deliberately colliding with his in a way that made him stumble.

"Come on," I said to Earl, grabbing his hand. "Let's get out of here."

"Oh, come on," Charles had called after us. "I'm not lying. His father was on his knees before mine begging to borrow some money. Tell her, Earl!"

"Ignore him." I'd rubbed Earl's arm. "He's an asshole." Earl followed without a word, his hand hot and tense in mine. We walked away, leaving Charles and his pack behind, their laughter fading into the distance. I didn't let go of Earl's hand until we were outside, the cool air biting at my skin, the noise of the food court replaced by the distant hum of traffic.

I looked at him then, at the way his head was bowed, his eyes fixed on the ground. "Are you okay?" I asked softly.

"Of course I am," he replied. "And he's right, my father did do that. We might lose the workshop."

"I'm sorry," I'd replied, worried on his behalf.

"Hey, It's not your fault, you know," he'd smiled in the way that made my heart stop.

"And it's not yours either," I'd told him.

"Yeah," he smiled and kissed me and I felt so in love it made me dizzy.

Now, the memory burns like acid in my chest and I can't help but steal a glance at him. His jaw is tight, his focus unyielding on the road ahead. The same guy, but not the same at all.

"How did you do it?" I ask before I can stop myself, my voice breaking the silence.

He doesn't look at me, doesn't even flinch. "Do what?"

"All of this." I gesture vaguely at the car, at him, at the life we're both pretending to live. "The money. Where did it come from? And so quickly at that."

There's a pause, thick and deliberate, before he finally answers. "Every cent of it is dirty."

Something in me recoils with horror, and I turn to face him fully, searching his expression for any hint of hesitation, any sign he's lying. But his face is a mask, his tone devoid of anything but cold truth.

"All of it," he continues, his gaze fixed ahead. "Every last cent. But there's a lot of it, and you'll be able to shop until you drop."

His words are flippant, but they leave a bitter taste in my mouth. A part of me wants to push, to demand answers, but the other part—the part that still cares, that still worries—hesitates. What happened to him? Was it Charles's humiliation that pushed him to this? Was it something worse?

The questions swirl in my mind, unanswered and relentless, as the car pulls up to the entrance of the department store. The glass façade gleams like a promise I don't trust.

As I slide out, I realize my hands are trembling. Earl rounds the car, his expression unreadable, and for a moment, our eyes meet. There's something there, something fleeting, but before I can place it, he looks away.

"Let's go," he says, his voice sharp and detached, and I follow him inside, my heart heavy with the weight of everything left unsaid.

CHAPTER 24

EARL

*T*he gleaming floors and carefully curated displays in the most expensive boutique in the mall reek of excess. Raven hesitates at the threshold, her hands tightening around the strap of her bag.

"After you," I say, gesturing grandly. She shoots me a look but steps inside.

A sales associate appears almost immediately, her smile practiced and polished. "How can I assist you today?"

"She's living out her pretty-woman fantasy," I say, my voice cold and clipped. Raven stiffens beside me, but I don't stop. "Show her the best of what you've got. The more extravagant, the better. I plan to spend an indecent amount of money."

The woman blinks, her smile faltering for a split second before she recovers and goes into overdrive. "Of course, Sir. Right this way, Madam," she chirps, ushering us toward a section filled with shimmering gowns that scream old money.

Raven does me proud, her head tilts up slightly, her posture straightens, and she strides forward like she owns the place. I trail behind them, my eyes narrowing. We're playing a game, and I can't tell if I'm the one setting the rules or if she is.

Raven runs her fingers over the fabric of a silver dress, her expression unreadable. "This one's nice," she says lightly, her voice calm and detached, like she's picking out groceries instead of something worth more than most people's rent.

"Try it on," I order, my arms crossed.

She doesn't hesitate, doesn't argue. She walks to the fitting room with the poise of someone who's used to getting what she wants and the assistant follows meekly behind carrying the dress.

When she comes out, the dress clings to her curves in a way that makes my throat tighten. The diamantes catch the light, and I almost hate how perfect she looks. How impossible it is not to want her. She twirls once, her lips curving into a smile that's almost mocking.

"Well?" she asks robotically. "Do I look like your queen yet?"

"Not yet. Try the next one," I mutter.

She disappears again, and I lean against the plush sofa and watch the changing room curtain like a hawk. Each dress she tries is more breathtaking than the last, but she never lets me see anything beyond cool indifference. It's infuriating. She's supposed to love this. This is the pinnacle of everything she has dreamed of all her life. Instead, she's turning this into a performance, almost an ordeal. This bothers me because if she is the gold-digging bitch I believe her to be, then why does she not seem to be enjoying this shopping experience. Unless this too is an act. I know from experience she is a consummate and highly skilled actress. I certainly fell for her act.

"Stunning," I say dryly when she emerges in a pale gold gown that makes her look almost untouchable. I take a sip of the iced lemon tea one of the sales assistants served me. "We'll take them all."

"Of course," she replies smoothly, her smile never wavering. "Thank you, Earl. I've always wanted these."

I frown.

"Where next?" she asks, and the way she emphasizes the last word sets my teeth on edge. She's mocking me. I know she is, but I can't call her out without sounding ridiculous. Instead, I nod to the sales assistant who has now been joined by others who can't seem to do enough to keep me happy. They rush off to wrap up the purchase.

When we move to the next boutique and the game continues, I pick the most extravagant pieces I can find—a gown with intricate beadwork, a fur-lined coat, a pair of shoes that could pay someone's mortgage. Raven tries them all without complaint, each time stepping out of the fitting room with a brilliant smile that never reaches her eyes.

"Do I meet your standards now?" she asks as she poses in a red velvet dress.

"Not yet, but you're getting there," I reply, my voice clipped.

She laughs softly, the sound grating. "Well, then. Let's not stop now. I wouldn't want to disappoint."

By the time we're halfway through the next high-end boutique, I can feel the tension mounting. I know she's tired, and I know she hates it, but she won't give me the satisfaction of seeing it. She walks with her head held high, her movements graceful. She's winning, and I hate it. Somehow she has beaten me at my own game. Frustration boils under my skin.

"Living the dream, aren't you?" I say as the associate hands her another piece. "All this—everything you've ever wanted."

She turns to me. "Exactly," she says sweetly. "And you're so generous for making it happen."

She turns away before I can respond, and heads toward the fitting room, but I don't miss the way her shoulders stiffen. She's holding it together, but I'm wearing her down.

Or so I think.

The moment she returns, dressed in her own clothes, she hands the sales assistant the last gown without a word and walks towards the till, I catch a glimpse of her reflection in the mirror as she passes—her face pale, her lips pressed into a thin line. She's not okay.

By the time I join her she looks composed again, like nothing's happened. But I see the strain in her eyes, the exhaustion she's trying so hard to hide.

I hand the smiling assistant my card, my voice colder than ice. "Bag everything. Deliver it to my wife at the address associated with the credit card."

"Of course, Sir," she replies.

I slip my hand proprietarily on the small of Raven's back and lead her out of the premises.

CHAPTER 25

RAVEN

*W*e walk through the gleaming halls of the mall and people turn to look at us. Mostly at Earl, but perhaps we seem like the perfect couple. If only they knew. My face aches from smiling.

Bag after bag, thousands upon thousands of dollars spent, and yet not a single thing we bought feels like mine. Every dress, every pair of shoes, every gilded piece of jewelry feels like a chain, tethering me to this nightmare. I already know I won't wear most of it. In fact I want to return it all. One day, I swear I will. Maybe I'll even give him back the money. Maybe I won't. Maybe I'll use it to ensure my father's treatment continues when Earl inevitably tires of this game, of me.

The thought makes my throat tighten. I blink hard, refusing to let the tears that sting my eyes escape. I've done so well today—holding it together, deflecting his barbs, standing tall. But the truth is, I'm breaking inside. The realization that his unprovoked hatred for me is real, sinks deeper with every step. And yet, the hurt I feel only fuels my resolve. He won't see me falter. Not now. Not ever.

But as we near the exit, defiance flickers to life inside me like a flame, small but steady. I stop abruptly, forcing him to halt too. He looks down at me, his expression a mixture of suspicion and query.

"I'm hungry," I say. "I want some pizza. Care to join me? Since you've been so generous today, I'll buy."

His eyes narrow, and I can see the wheels turning in his mind, trying to figure out my angle. For a moment, I think he'll refuse, but then he nods curtly, and gestures for me to lead the way.

My heart pounds as I turn and head back toward Mario's corner. The old memories bubble up unbidden—all of them heart-wrenchingly sweet and innocent. It was never about the food for us. It was about being together. All those small moments that felt like they belonged only to us. And now, I'm leading him back there, unsure if I'm trying to rekindle something or drive a dagger into the memory.

The scent of grilling cheese and baking dough hits me as we approach. I force myself to take a steadying breath. He walks beside me, his presence a storm cloud, dark and brooding, but I can feel his eyes on me, assessing, questioning.

I don't look at him. Not yet.

We reach the counter, and I order a pepperoni cheese pizza with gherkins on the side. "Just like we used to," I say lightly, offering him a small smile.

He pulls out his wallet, but I stop him. "I said I'll buy. Don't worry, I can handle it."

The cashier rings me up, and I pay quickly, my hands trembling slightly as I swipe my card. Earl doesn't say a word, but I can feel the tension radiating off him as I move towards 'our' table by the window, overlooking the bustling floor below. I take my seat and he follows, sitting across from me, his posture rigid.

The pizza arrives quickly, and I push a slice without gherkins onto his plate before taking one for myself. For a moment, we eat in silence. I glance at him, and his eyes are dark and unreadable. I love his eyes. It's the first thing that I noticed about him. It's like staring into a storm. The noise of the food court fades into the background. It's just the two of us, locked in a battle of wills, each daring the other to break first.

"Do you remember?" I ask softly. "We used to come here all the time. Pizza, ice cream, sundaes, the works."

"No," he lies abruptly.

"Okay," I say easily and carry on eating until the last bite of pizza on my plate is gone. Earl wipes his hands with the damp towel the food court provided and rises to his feet.

"Let's go," he says coldly, his tone leaving no room for argument. "I have work to do."

I see now that there is nothing I can do to bring the old Earl back. I follow him silently as we weave through the bustling food court.

The ride back to the house is even quieter than the ride away from it. I keep my gaze fixed on the view outside the window, watching the world blur past, trying to hold onto the faint flicker of hope that one day, one day I will prove to him that I am not what he thinks I am. But it's hard.

When we arrive at Thornfield Hall, Earl steps out without a backward glance. I have a feeling the trip is not what he had expected it to be. Back in my room, I close the door and lean against it. All the purchases are like a monument to everything wrong between us, now I'm the owner of things I don't need or want and what I want is moving further and further away from me.

I try to lie down, to sleep, but it's impossible. The day replays in my mind. I roll onto my side, staring at the faint patterns of light on the ceiling, and decide I can't just lie here. I need something to occupy my mind. I slip outside and the house is quiet and still.

The library feels like a safe haven as I step inside, the scent of old books and polished wood a balm to my frayed nerves. I run my fingers along the leather spines until I touch a 1987 first-edition European copy of Bram Stoker's Dracula. My finger stops and I smile slowly. "Wow," I marvel. I pull it out and carefully open it. The old pages smell of ashes.

To my friend, Hommy-beg, the dedication reads and above it is Bram Stoker's signature.

I shake my head in wonder. "He did it. He got himself the signed first-edition." I settle into a chair, switch on the table lamp, and start reading. How strange, but the old book is like a magic cloak pulled over me. I read for hours and when I finish, I creep upstairs and my laptop waiting is like an old friend.

The screen glows to life, and for the first time in what feels like forever, I begin to write. The words pour out of me —a story of a woman trapped in a castle with a man who loathes her, their lives tangled in a web of hatred and longing. It feels cathartic, giving shape to the emotions I can't express aloud.

When I finally pause for a break, the light streaming in through the window has shifted to a soft amber, painting the walls in the hues of a late autumn gold morning. I had not realized how much time has slipped away. The gardens outside catch my eye, vibrant and serene, their beauty made richer by the new light. A gentle breeze stirs the trees, their leaves shimmering. It's the kind of gentle morning that beckons for reflection, for escape.

I close the laptop, stretching as I stand. I grab a cardigan from the back of the chair and drape it over my shoulders. Its soft fabric will be a comforting shield against the crisp morning air.

Stepping outside, I let the coolness envelop me. The compound is breathtaking in this light, the kind of beauty that feels almost surreal. The manicured paths wind through beds of late-blooming roses whose rich colors seem to drink in the morning sun. The lake in the distance glistens like liquid gold, its surface rippling gently as soft breezes skim across it. I walk toward it savoring the peace this place seems to offer despite my difficult situation.

The scent of roses wafts through the air, mingling with the earthy aroma of the damp soil. I trail my fingers along the tops of the hedges, the leaves cool and dewy against my skin. The property stretches endlessly, each corner revealing some new piece of its charm—a small wooden bench nestled beneath a willow tree, a stone fountain with water that sparkles like diamonds in the first rays of sunlight.

I pause near the lake, the chill of the morning seeping through the thin fabric of my cardigan. The water reflects the sky above. It's stunning, a moment of perfect stillness.

Sooner or later, you will leave this place.

The thought rises unbidden, clear and certain. This life, this mansion, this game—it's all temporary. It has to be. I can't imagine spending my days in a world where beauty hides cruelty and every gift feels like a shackle. But for now, I walk, soaking in the fragile serenity.

The path leads me towards a small gazebo overlooking the lake. I sit down on its stone bench. The world around me is so quiet, so calm, so peaceful until I spot the tree at the edge of the lake.

It stands tall and weathered, its roots twisting into the earth like the veins of some ancient creature. There's something about it, something achingly familiar. Then I remember.

It is *the* tree.

Memories come flooding back. Earl and I, years ago, sneaking across the tall walls that bordered this estate. The air had been warm, heavy with the scent of summer blooms, and the laughter from the party had drifted to us like forbidden music. We'd climbed this tree, our hands brushing against rough bark as we found a perch high enough to spy on the glittering world below.

Charles's garden party. His house. His world.

Earl didn't want to come here, but I had talked him into it. 'Please,' I begged. 'I just want to see how the other half live. No one will see us. We'll just climb into one of the trees, spy on them and leave. No one will know.'

He could never say no to me, and even though it would mean a terrible humiliation for him if he had been caught on Charles's grounds, he came with me.

My chest tightens as the details come rushing back.

The dazzling lights strung across the lawn, the elegant music, the finely dressed guests drinking champagne and fluttering like butterflies from one group to another. While Earl muttered about their empty grandeur, I remember laughing, the kind of laugh that makes you feel invincible, as if the world could never touch me so long as we were together. I agreed with him. Their world was indeed meaningless.

Before I can even arrange the idea, my legs are already moving toward the tree. My hands tremble as they reach for the lowest branch. The bark scrapes against my palm, rough and unyielding, but I don't stop. I can't. I need to find something. It's proof. Proof of who we used to be because, at that moment, I'm unconvinced we ever had a relationship or I called him the love of my life.

The climb is awkward and graceless, my movements hindered by my sandals. My foot slips once, and a gasp escapes me as the bark scrapes against my shin. It stings, but I press on. The branches groan under my weight, but I don't care.

My hands grope along the trunk, searching. We left our mark. A carving, something to prove we were here. I reach higher, my fingers brushing frantically against rough edges, searching and searching around the place where we had been perched on, our bodies touching.

I find nothing.

The tears come before I can stop them. Hot and unrelenting, they blur my vision as I clutch the tree, my forehead resting against the bark. "Why can't I find it?" I whisper to no one, my voice breaking. "Why isn't it here?"

The tears fall freely, each one carrying all my frustrations, my sense of helplessness, and my grief for a version of myself that was lost long ago. For a while, the world is a silent witness to my quiet sobs among the gently rustling of leaves.

Then a harsh voice cuts suddenly through the stillness, furious and cold.

"What the hell are you doing up there? Are you trying to break your neck?"

My heart lurches. Startled, I look down and find Earl standing beneath the tree, his arms crossed, his dark eyes fixed on me with a mixture of anger and something I can't quite place. The sight of him, standing there like an avenging god, sends a shiver down my spine.

"Get down," he orders, his tone clipped and hard.

For a moment, I can't move. My hands grip the branch tighter, tears still cling to my lashes. I stare down at him. All the anger, the pain, the longing I've tried so hard to bury swirls inside me like a hurricane.

"No," I say defiantly. "Not unless you come up here and help me find it."

CHAPTER 26

EARL

"Find what?" I ask sharply, staring up at her. She's perched on a branch like some stubborn bird refusing to come down. "Come down before you hurt yourself."

She shakes her head. "What do you care?" she throws back at me and leans back against the tree trunk.

"Fuck this," I mutter. What an infuriating brat she has turned out to be. I turn on my heel and start walking away. Let her stay up there. Let her stew in her own ridiculousness. But as I take a few steps, a knot tightens in my chest. One slip, one misstep, and she'll fall. She'll break something. Worse.

I curse under my breath and spin around on my heel. Damn her. And damn me for caring.

When I reach the base of the tree again, I grab onto the nearest branch and hoist myself up.

"Right. What the fuck are you looking for, Raven? Are

you insane?" My voice rises as I climb higher, each word laced with exasperation.

She doesn't even look at me. Her focus is fixed on something near the tree trunk, her gaze wide and filled with wonder? It stops me in my tracks, mid-climb. For a moment, the morning sunlight catches her face, illuminating an expression I haven't seen in years—pure, unfiltered joy.

"Look," she whispers, her voice trembling but full of something I can't quite place. "I found it. I found us."

I follow her gaze, and there it is. Carved into the bark, weathered but unmistakable—our names, enclosed in a heart. The memory crashes into me like a wave. I can still feel the knife in my hand, the bark giving way as I carved it out for her all those years ago. Back then, it had felt permanent, unbreakable. Back then, I had believed in forever.

Now? Now it feels like a sick joke.

Before I can stop myself, I reach into my pocket and pull out the penknife I always carry. I flick it open, and slash the gleaming blade across the carving of my name. The letters splinter, the grooves disappearing into jagged scratches.

"What are you doing?" she cries with shock.

But I keep hacking, the motion mechanical, driven by something I can't control. Her protests blur together, and it's not until I hear her scream that I finally stop.

"Stop!" she yells, her voice shaking with fury and something deeper. "What the hell is wrong with you?"

She lunges towards me, almost loses her balance, and has to grip the branch she is sitting on so tightly her knuckles show white. Tears glisten in her eyes, and I realize just how close she was to falling. The craziness of what I've done sinks in. Christ. I'm going mad. She's driven me insane.

"You're going to fall," I snap, reaching out to catch her.

But she jerks away from my touch, her body swaying

precariously. "You're the one doing this!" she shouts, her voice raw. "You're the one ruining everything!"

"Raven," I say, my tone low but firm. "Stop before you fall and break your neck."

She glares at me, her chest heaving, her eyes blazing with anger. For a moment, it's a standoff—her defiance against my frustration and anxiety. But then, she shifts her weight, her movements careful and fearful. She starts climbing down the other side of the trunk. I don't move at all so I don't spook her. Every muscle of my body is tense with worry. Only when her feet finally touch the ground do I climb down myself.

I step onto solid ground and see that she's already storming off, her shoulders squared, her stride quick and purposeful.

"Raven," I call after her, but she doesn't stop. She doesn't even look back.

With a sigh I close the penknife and shove it back into my pocket. I don't know whether to feel regret or relief at this moment, but one thing I do know is that I feel immense sadness. I don't even recognize myself anymore. I've become a monster. Worse than Charles. I start walking towards the house.

Suddenly, she stops mid-stomp and then turns around to glare at me. I wait, wondering what kind of lunacy she is going to exhibit this time around. Angrily, she marches back toward me, and then with both of her hands against my chest, she pushes hard at me. Her strength is pathetic, so it barely moves me, but it does, however, alleviate some of my annoyance.

"What is your problem?" she demands, her voice trembling with fury. "Why do you hate me so much?"

The familiar burn of anger is instant. It is far greater than hers ."Why do I hate you?" I echo, my voice cold. "You really want to know?"

"Yes, I do," she yells.

"I hate you," I begin, "because I see you clearly now. For what you really are."

Her breath hitches, but she doesn't look away, doesn't interrupt. Good. Let her hear this. Let her feel it.

"Before, before I was blind—blinded by infatuation, by whatever the hell I thought we had. But now? Now I see the truth. You're just like Charles and his ilk. All you've ever wanted was this," I gesture broadly at the estate around us, my voice growing louder. "The big house, the wealth, the status. Isn't this what you dreamed of, Raven? Well, congratulations. You got it. So what the fuck are you so mad about?"

The silence that follows feels like it could shatter under its own weight. Her lips part, but no sound escapes. For a moment, I think she might cry, but instead, she draws herself up, her frame trembling with barely contained rage.

"Go to hell, Earl," she spits, her voice low but venomous. Then, without another word, she turns and begins running back toward the house.

I stand there, rooted to the spot, watching her go. Her movements are jerky, almost frantic, as though she's trying to run away from the words I just threw at her. And for a fleeting moment, something unfamiliar stirs in my chest.

Regret? Guilt? I don't know, but I push it away as quickly as it comes.

CHAPTER 27

RAVEN

*M*y breath comes in short, shallow bursts as I storm into the kitchen, my vision blurred with unshed tears. He is killing my love for him. Every day bit by bit he is making me hate him. It is unbearable. The warmth of the house and the faint aroma of food and mulled wine being made waft through the air. It feels cozy, almost festive, like Christmas came early and entirely at odds with the chaos churning inside me.

Nora appears, her face lighting up when she spots me. She holds out a steaming mug. "Raven! You must try this. I've been perfecting the recipe—"

"I'm so sorry, Nora," I interrupt, my voice cracking. "But not right now."

I skirt around her, desperate to avoid her kind eyes, her questions, and the realization of how wrecked I am. My eyes are stinging, but I refuse to break down here, in front of her. The gossip will definitely reach my mother if I do.

I don't stop moving, my legs race me up the stairs, through the corridor and into the room that has never felt like mine. My mind races. I can't stay here. I really can't. I can't endure this house, that man, this life for another second.

I know if I stay, I will freaking lose my mind and I am one hundred percent sure of that. How long will I be gone? I don't know. Maybe I'll never come back.

The thought is fleeting but sharp, like the sting of a needle. My father's face flashes in my mind, the fragility of his body. He needs me. And I won't let him down. I'll figure it out somehow—I have to—but I can't keep living like this, not with this … monster.

Maybe I don't even have to stay married to him. There was no prenup, after all. I could just walk away and get a loan from the bank for the rest of my father's treatments. What I have in the kitty might be enough to pay for the bulk of it.

I open the closet and stare up at the suitcase perched on the shelf. It's old and familiar. Part of another life. I remember my thoughts when I packed it. Fear, confusion, but oh, so much hope for the future. I was so sure I could make this work. That our love would conquer whatever was wrong. The sight of it sends a sharp pang through me, but I push it aside. I need to leave now as quickly as possible.

Barefoot, I step onto the lower shelf, the wood pressing hard against my soles as I stretch upward. My fingertips graze the handle, but it's heavy. It's got all my books still inside it. The weight shifts as I tug at it.

"Come on," I mutter under my breath, my voice shaking with frustration. I pull harder and the edge of the suitcase tilts forward, the books inside rattle ominously. The sudden shift in weight catches me off guard. A sharp pain shoots through my arm, forcing me to release my grip.

"Shit!" The curse rips from my throat as the suitcase crashes to the floor with a loud thud. The sound echoes in the quiet room, mocking me. My pulse hammers in my ears as I climb down and crouch beside the suitcase, one of the wheels is hanging precariously by a thread, barely attached. I press my palm to my forehead, squeezing my eyes shut against the hot tears that finally spill over. My chest heaves as I sink down onto the expensive Persian rug. I sit with my knees pulled up to my chest.

I bury my face in my hands, my shoulders shaking. The dam breaks and I let it all go. All of it. The anger, the grief, the sheer helplessness. I cry for the life I thought I could build, for the woman I thought I was, for the man who carved his name next to mine only to hack it out with such ferocity he was like a man possessed by a whole legion of demons.

This isn't the way I wanted things to go. This isn't the life I envisioned. But now, sitting inside this mansion, surrounded by broken things, I truly can't see a way out.

When the tears stop, I sit with my arms wrapped around my knees, my head resting against them. My father's face swims to the forefront of my mind. The thought of him—frail and needing me—is like a lifeline in the darkness. I take a shuddering breath, grounding myself in that singular focus.

My gaze falls on the battered suitcase at my feet, one wheel barely hanging on. It's useless now, just like so much else around me. But I can't afford to dwell on it. I need another one, and the staff won't have anything suitable lying around—not without questions I can't stomach answering.

That leaves only one option. At this point, it annoys me more than it terrifies me to even consider it, but he has to know anyway. Plus, perhaps it will be good to get his reaction—a way to ensure my leaving doesn't endanger my father's health care. The hallways feel colder somehow, the walls closing in as I head toward his study where he always spends time in the morning before he leaves for work.

I pass his bedroom and find the door slightly ajar. I look in, trying to detect movement to see if he is in there, but it doesn't seem occupied. What I do see though is the sight of the perfectly made bed. The memories from last night flash through my mind—the way his hands had gripped my skin, the strength flowing from his body, the taste of his anger and desire mingled together. I look away, shame and fury burning through me. I need to focus. I have a mission.

His study. That's where he'll be.

I step back and make my way downstairs. The grand staircase spirals downward. The house is quiet, save for the faint sound of my footsteps. A thought comes in my head unbidden and unwelcome. This house needs children, lots of them.

I shake my head to clear the silly thought. I used to think this house was beautiful, back when it was Charles's father's. But as I descend the staircase now, what once felt magnificent now feels like a prison, every detail a relentless reminder of everything I've come to despise.

I can't understand where he gets these ideas about me— about what I wanted, about who I am. Wealth? Status? He keeps throwing these accusations like they're the core of my being, like they define me. It's infuriating.

Yes, I wanted a better life than what I had when I was growing up dirt poor. So what? It's good to have aspirations. Yes, I was prepared to marry Charles in exchange for saving my father's life. Charles is an adult. He knew exactly what he was getting into. I never lied to him. He was the one who lied to me about his financial circumstances and tried to trick me into marrying him. We never even had sex.

The only person I'd ever had sex with was Earl. I always knew it would never be like what it was with Earl so I didn't even bother to look for anyone else. What's wrong with wanting my children to go to Harvard like Charles and his sister did? It's a decision I don't regret and I would do it again and again. I'm not going to let Earl convince me that I'm a bad person for wanting to help my dad and wanting a better foundation than I had for my children. And I'm sick and tired of trying to defend myself to him. Enough is enough.

My mind drifts to our days together in that rundown trailer park, sneaking around under the cover of night. Those were the best moments of my life, stolen and sweet, free of judgment and the crushing weight of expectation. I'd told him, over and over, how I never wanted to be without him. Even then, when the world seemed against us, I had chosen him.

Where the hell did he get this idea that I only ever wanted money?

I shake my head, pushing the thoughts aside. Doesn't matter now. I've had enough. I'm not wasting my time chasing after ghosts anymore. If he won't tell me, I won't ask again. I reach downstairs and make my way to his study, which is tucked into the far corner of the house.

I pause outside the door, my heart thudding against my ribs. The anger that fueled me moments ago feels distant now, replaced by a simmering dread. Taking a deep breath, I knock.

"What is it?" an irritated voice calls from inside.

Of course, he is grumpy as usual, but I don't care. I square my shoulders and push the door open. To my surprise, the curtains are drawn shut and the glow from a single desk lamp casts long shadows across the walls. The scent of aged leather and faint cologne lingers in the air. Earl is seated at the desk, leaning back in his chair watching me with an air of quiet contemplation.

"What do you need?" he asks, his voice edged with wariness, as if he's bracing for another fight.

I step inside and shut the door behind me. My gaze flickers to the dark wood shelves lining the walls, the rows of books and neatly stacked papers, the multiple computer screens on his desk, their faint glow illuminating the sharp lines of his face. It's a far cry from the man I used to know— the one who never cared for material things, who used to dream of a simple life with me.

"I need to borrow a suitcase," I say flatly.

His brow furrows, his expression hardening. "What for?"

"That's none of your concern," I reply, my tone sharper than I intended.

He leans forward, resting his elbows on the desk, his gaze unrelenting. "Everything about you is my concern, Raven."

His words hang in the air, and I feel anger bubbling up inside me again, threatening to spill over. I straighten my shoulders, forcing myself to meet his gaze head-on. "Can you lend me one or not?"

For a moment, he doesn't respond, his eyes scanning me. Finally, he shifts his gaze away, his tone flat as he says, "Talk to Nora. She'll get you what you need."

That's it. No questions, no comments, not even a flicker of anything resembling emotion. I nod stiffly, unsure of what I expected. Curiosity? Understanding? Refusal? Something other than this distant, detached man who barely resembles the lover I once knew. He's going to let me go! Just like that. No questions. No objections. A crushing disappointment pools in my chest and I hate that I feel it at all.

I spin around and go outside to look for Nora, but she is

already coming towards me. She greets me with her usual brisk efficiency. "Mr. Jackson informed me that you'll be needing a suitcase," she says, her tone polite, but her eyes full of curiosity. "Please, follow me to the storeroom. You can pick a suitcase there."

I realize how strange this must seem to her. A wife borrowing a suitcase from her husband, as though I'm some guest rather than the mistress of the house.

"Thank you." I offer a small, tight smile and follow her up the stairs.

Nora steps aside to let me into the attic. I enter and notice that there are things that must have belonged to Charles's family here too. They didn't bother to take it with them. Dolls houses and rocking chairs.

A row of suitcases sits neatly in the closet. They are mostly pristine and absurdly expensive, but my fingers hover over the handle of a simple black one. I know this suitcase. I've seen it years before. Instinctively, I pick it up and go outside.

Nora waits in the landing, her expression unreadable.

"Thank you," I say again.

She nods. "You're welcome, Madam. If there is anything else I can do for you please do not hesitate to ask."

"Thank you, but there's nothing more I need, Nora," I say softly, and even I, can hear the sadness in my voice.

Then I turn away and carry the suitcase back to my room. Once inside, I shut the door, put the suitcase on my bed and stare at it. It's a blast from the past. I close my eyes and try to steady myself. The past couple of weeks have felt like a fever dream—unreal and vivid all at once. But the last two days? They've been a waking nightmare, a whirlwind of anger and longing and everything in between.

Bending forward I snap the suitcase open. It's empty. The

breath I'm holding comes out in a rush. I don't know what I expected, but there's nothing in it. Another disappointment for me.

Furious with myself for being so stupid and naïve again I drag the suitcase with me over to the closet and start pulling clothes off hangers, one after another, in a frenzy of movement. Each garment drops into the open suitcase on the floor, their colors blending together into a heap of frustration and simmering fury.

The air fills with the sound of hangers clattering and fabric rustling. My hands work mechanically, folding and shoving as much as I can into the suitcase. Dresses, shirts, jackets—they all disappear into Earl's black suitcase. The thought of having to return, even for something trivial, makes my stomach turn. No. I'll take everything of mine now.

I reach for the front pocket of the suitcase to stuff it with my socks and my fingers brush against something smooth and flat. Pulling it out, I see it's a neatly pressed man's handkerchief. Something my grandfather would have owned.

Inside is an envelope. I freeze. My gaze locks on it, my pulse quickening. The paper feels delicate in my hands, the edges yellowed and slightly curled as if it's been waiting for years to be discovered. My fingers tremble as I open it and take the folded letter inside it. The faint scent of old ink wafts up. The handwriting is unmistakably his, though a little neater than I remember—like he'd actually tried to make it perfect for once. My heart thuds painfully in my chest as I begin to read.

RAVEN BABE,

I should probably be paying attention to Mr. Winslow right now—he's going on about derivatives or something equally brain-numbing—but how can I when your seat is empty? It's weird not having you here to roll your eyes at me every five minutes or scribble sarcastic notes in my notebook.

Charles, the nosy bastard again, had the cheek to ask me about you. I ignored him, obviously—no need to start another pointless fight. I wonder when he'll get it through his head that you're mine.

Also, what the hell were you thinking about making a midnight snack from random fridge leftovers? Food poisoning is a thing, you know. People even die from it!!! One day when I'm rich, you'll only ever eat in the best restaurants.

Anyway, I was planning to skip after the first period and come over to see you, but I don't think I can without Miss Loewe making a big deal about the both of us being absent. She has a dirty mind and she'll probably tell all the churchgoers we're fornicating or something. I mean, she's not wrong, but she really should learn to mind her business.

Anyway, I hope you're feeling better. I can't stop picturing you all annoyed because your mom keeps fussing over you. You always hate being babied, but you know you secretly love it ... maybe just a little.

I miss you like crazy. I don't think I could live if you were not on this earth.

By the way, I've got our history notes. Well, my version of them. I marked the sections that'll probably show up on the test because, let's face it, we both know I'm better at guessing these things. You can thank me later by losing another bet. I'm calling it now: double or nothing, loser buys fries for a month.

Anyway, I'm going to show up at your door by lunch, but you'll only find this after I leave. It'll be under your pillow. Unless I forget to put it there—you know how just being with you makes me forget things. Not that I'm complaining.

I miss you terribly. Just wanted to write this note to make you

*smile. I've rubbed it with my scent or whatever, like you
always say.*

*GET BETTER SOON, okay? Will kiss you soon. I mean, when I come
during lunch.*

*Damn, all of this is so cheesy I might not give you this letter,
after all. I just need to write down my frustration at your absence.
The truth is all these words are really just to say, Baby Raven, I
fucking miss you. Like crazy. Even though it's only been one day
apart. I know ... I know ... I'm a big baby.*

Love u forever,

Your Earl

I READ the letter again and again, my chest contracting with
every word. It's like a window into another life—one where
he loved me with the kind of reckless crazy abandon that
made everything feel simple and obvious. I took our love for
granted. I never imagined it would not last. My fingers trace
the faint smudge of ink at the bottom of the page, and for a
moment, I let myself be pulled back to those days when his
love was so absolute, so tangible.

I fold the letter carefully and press it against my chest.
One thing is clear: this letter, hidden for so many years, is
proof that the love we shared wasn't just a figment of my
imagination. It was real, despite how near impossible it is to
believe now. I must hide it. If he finds it he will surely
destroy it with the same ferocity he hacked away his name
from the tree trunk.

I look at the suitcase. The lid is still open, clothes spilling
out like the emotions threatening to overwhelm me. My

hands tremble as I stare at the suitcase, half convinced I can simply close it and walk out.

But … I don't think I can.

The words, etched into the paper with such deep love, refuse to leave my mind. They are a thread, pulling me backward through time, unraveling the hurt and anger I've wrapped myself in these last few days. Earl isn't just angry. He's wounded. Something happened. Something I don't know about and he won't tell me.

And I can't ignore it any longer.

I kneel beside the suitcase. Just a few minutes earlier I was ready to leave, convinced that I could just walk out of this house, this marriage, and pretend none of it mattered. But as I grip the edges of the suitcase, my knuckles turning white, the truth stares back at me: I'm not ready. Not to leave. Not to give up. Not until I understand what broke us. No matter what, I will get to the bottom of his hate.

With a start, I take my clothes out of the suitcase and put them away in my closet, just the same way I put away the thought of running away.

When all my clothes are put away again, I press the letter to my chest. It's not just a letter; it's a piece of the Earl I used to know, the boy who once loved me so fiercely that it felt like we were untouchable. And maybe that love isn't dead. Maybe it's just buried, hidden under years of pain and resentment.

The idea terrifies me and fuels me all at once.

My fingers brush the corner of the envelope as I slip it back inside, safe but not forgotten. Rising to my feet, I glance around the room. The air feels charged, like the calm before a storm. I don't have a plan, but the one thing I know is that I can't run away. Not until I find the old him again. Not until I find out why he's like this—why we have become like this.

CHAPTER 28

EARL

*T*he room is quiet, save for the soft hum of the computers on my desk. The glow of their screens cast faint patterns of light across the polished wood. A few emails need replies. Some reports to review. Things that actually matter. Not her.

Definitely not her, but my fingers remain frozen over the keyboard and my mind filled with thoughts of her.

She wants a suitcase.

She wants to leave me.

I lean back in my chair, staring blankly at the rows of books on the shelves. My jaw clenches. Fuck her. If she wants to leave, she can leave. Let her go. Hell, I'd welcome the quiet. Since she walked back into my life, it has been nothing but drama.

I try to summon the hate and anger that's kept me moving all these years. The cold fury that's driven every carefully placed chess piece in this house of revenge.

But I can't.

The truth is, the thought of her walking out ruins everything.

My hand tightens into a fist on the desk. Why do I let her have so much control over me? Why does she still even matter? I've already told myself a hundred times over that she's just a gold digger and every ounce of tension, snide remark, and cold stare is justice. Justice for what she did to me.

So why can't I stop feeling like the world is coming to an end?

"Fuck," I mutter under my breath, raking a hand through my hair.

I sit upright and try to shake off the creeping unease. If she's packing, I have very little time. Once she leaves, I will have no more leverage. My fingers drum impatiently on the desktop. I need to do something drastic and I need to do it soon.

But before I can find the solution to my problem, the phone on my desk buzzes. I glance at the screen. It's not a number I recognize, but it's a local number.

I consider ignoring it. I don't have the energy for some telemarketer or misplaced business call right now, but because it's local something compels me to pick up.

"Earl? Hi, It's Annabelle."

The sound of her name stops me cold. Well, well, Charles's sister. Calling me. How surreal. My grip on the receiver tightens, and I lean forward in my chair, my attention piqued.

"Annabelle?" I repeat, more a query than a greeting. It's been years since I last heard from her—she was always composed and polite, unlike the chaos her brother embodied. Why the hell is she calling me now?

"Yes," she confirms, the faintest tremor in her voice. "It's … it's been a while."

Understatement of the year. I don't respond immediately, my mind trying to piece together the purpose of her call. The years, the silence, the sudden intrusion—it doesn't add up. A slow smile starts on my lips. It's not a good smile, but maybe, just maybe I've found the leverage I was looking for.

"Hi, how are you?" I ask silkily.

There's a soft laugh on the other end, the kind that manages to sound both amused and mildly self-deprecating. "Better than I thought I'd be … all things considered," she says, her tone casual, as if we're picking up a conversation left unfinished.

Her friendliness surprises me. She's not angry, cutting, not even guarded. I pulled the rug from under her family and her. But Annabelle was always … civil, even kind when it came to me. She was the only one who ever stood up to Charles's taunts or rolled her eyes at his provocations.

Still, it doesn't erase the fact that I took their house, their last remnant of wealth, left centuries ago by their ancestors. That truth lingers between us, unspoken but undeniably there. And yet, she doesn't seem bothered by it. Not at all.

"So," she says lightly, "it's been forever. I heard what happened between you and Charles. Charles and I grew apart many years ago and I haven't kept in touch with him. From what I gather, you have been up to quite a lot lately."

I don't know how to respond. I should feel triumphant, instead, I feel confused. Her unaffected tone makes me uneasy. What game is she playing at? I knew she didn't get on with her mother, but even so, she is taking being thrown out of her ancestral home too lightly.

"Yeah, I've been busy," I say finally, keeping it vague. "What about you?"

"Oh, me?" she laughs again, this time more genuinely. "I just got into town, actually. I moved to Los Angeles five years ago. Been teaching yoga."

Yoga? Not what I expected for someone who was going to Harvard last time I checked, but I guess she was always a bit whimsical and airy-fairy. I don't comment, I just let her continue.

"You, on the other hand …" She laughs again. "I couldn't believe my ears when I heard. Man, what an Alpha move. I don't think I've ever been so upset to miss a wedding before. You do know that Mother will never forgive you, don't you?"

"Yes, I gathered that," I reply dryly.

"I guess I'm calling to congratulate you. You've done amazing for yourself and you got the girl you always wanted. Not that I'm surprised—you've always had that spark. Something special."

I can't stand the flattery. It feels like a carefully placed bait, and I'm not biting. Besides, I think I hear sounds upstairs. No matter what happens I have to find a way to stop her leaving. Even if I have to bring up the matter of her father's medical treatments.

"Thanks," I say flatly, cutting Annabelle off. "It's really nice to hear from you, but I don't have much time to talk right now. I've something urgent to see to."

"Of course," she says smoothly, unfazed. "I was just wondering if you'd like to catch up sometime. Maybe grab a drink?"

The suggestion hangs in the air, and for a brief moment, I consider refusing. But then I push the thought aside. No. I'm playing the long game here. She could come in useful. Not now though. Not when Raven is somewhere upstairs packing, ready to leave.

"Sure. A drink will be nice. I'm not certain when I'll have the time, but I'll call and let you know when I can."

She hums softly, as if amused. "Fair enough. Though … will you at least be at the New Year's gala? You know, the charity thing at the community center?"

The invitation to the gala has been sitting on my desk for more than a week. This town and its self-important gatherings have never held any appeal for me. It's a place where people sneer at families like mine, whispering behind their champagne flutes about people less fortunate than themselves.

But there is a reason the invitation hasn't gone into the bin. The thought of walking into that event, watching those same people choke on their own judgment as they see what the son of the drunk has become—it's tempting. Too tempting.

"I haven't decided yet," I reply carefully.

"Well, I'll hope to see you there," she says brightly. "It was really nice catching up, Earl. Really."

"Yeah, it was nice," I lie smoothly. "Take care."

The call ends with a click. Maybe I'm just cynical, but her tone and her ease, doesn't quite sit right with me. Like she's fishing for something, but doesn't want me to know it. A trap, maybe. Or worse, a genuine olive branch.

I go upstairs and there is no movement. I open her door and see my old suitcase sitting on the floor. I frown. What is going on with her? And then I look out of the window and I see her in the conservatory and just like that, I suddenly feel happy and light again.

She's not leaving.

CHAPTER 29

RAVEN

*T*he greenhouse hums with a quiet kind of life, the air warm and fragrant with the smell of strawberries. I crouch low, my fingers brushing through the leaves to find the ripe ones hiding underneath. My earbuds are snug in my ears, Sunny's voice crackling slightly through the phone as she continues the conversation. I can hear the faint noises of customers in her bakery in the background.

"So, what's the game plan?" she asks, her voice laced with its usual mix of curiosity and sass. "How are you going to remind Earl that he's not a complete asshole?"

I smile despite myself, shaking my head even though she can't see me. "No game plan yet," I admit, plucking another strawberry and placing it gently into the basket at my feet. "I'm just … playing it by ear."

"Playing it by ear? That doesn't sound like you at all. You're the queen of strategies and ten-step plans."

I laugh softly, shifting my weight to reach further into the row. "Things are different now, Sunny. I'm trying something new: patience."

Sunny's scoff is audible even through the call. "Patience with Earl? That's ambitious."

I don't answer right away, focusing on the rhythmic motion of picking the berries. The repetitive task calms me and lets me think. "Well, I have to. I think he's planning to stay in town for a while. I heard him talking about renovating an office or something."

"You sound almost happy about that," Sunny says, and I can tell she's raising an eyebrow on the other end of the line.

"It's … complicated," I admit, standing up to stretch my back. The basket is nearly full now, the strawberries bright and gleaming in the sunlight streaming through the glass roof. "But I plan to be civil at least."

"Civil isn't exactly a glowing endorsement," Sunny points out.

"It's a start," I say, my tone firm. "I'm not going to be antagonistic all the time anymore. I'm going to try to make this work." A small smile tugs at my lips. "I'm going to try to figure him out all over again. I think he's—" I pause, unsure how to explain what I feel. "In the last few days, I've started to remember a lot of little things about him and his likes and dislikes that I forced myself to forget out of anger and sorrow. For example, he likes soup and we never ever have soup."

"Oh God, Raven. Please don't fall in love with him again," Sunny admonishes suddenly.

I'm silent for a while as I ponder her words. "I don't know. Did I ever fall out of love with him?"

"Raven," she calls, her tone filled with concern.

"Oh, Sunny, I've never fallen out of love with him. I pretended to the whole world and even myself, but there is no one else for me. There never was and never will be. Either way, I'm not giving up yet."

"But he's been an asshole to you," she cries.

"Yes, he's been an asshole, but if I believe that underneath that harsh exterior, he is hurting. Something happened to make him change so drastically and I'm not going to give up on him until I know what it is. And in the end, if after all my effort it still doesn't work, I won't be haunted by the fact that I didn't try hard enough."

She releases a heavy sigh. "All right. I just don't want you to get hurt."

"Wasn't it you who said getting hurt is part of life?" I remind her.

"I did, but I didn't mean it for you to use it against me."

I laugh.

"Hm …" she hums, her voice softening. "You really love him to pieces, huh?"

"Yeah," I admit, crouching back down to gather the last few berries. "Stop worrying about me. I'll be okay. My dad's going to get better. I'm handling things on that end and things will work out, you'll see."

"What's the sex like?" she asks suddenly.

I flush, glad she can't see me. "He comes to my room. We … uh … we get busy as usual."

"Just how busy?" she asks cheekily.

I chuckle.

"Answer the question," she insists.

"Look, I'll stop by soon and maybe I'll share details."

"You better because I tell you everything." Sunny goes suddenly quiet, and the silence stretches just long enough to make me glance at my phone.

"You're too good for him, you know that, right?" she says, her voice choked with emotion.

I laugh softly. "I'm not sure about that, especially now that he seems to have all the money in the world."

"Money is not part of this equation. Charles had money too, and see how much of a tool he was."

"Yeah, Charles lied to me, but somehow it doesn't hurt. I guess because I never loved him."

Sunny sighs at this. "At this point, I'm not even sure whose side I'm on. If I were in your shoes, I wouldn't even know who to choose."

"It's not a matter of choice," I reply. "Earl's always been in my heart. Even when I hated him for leaving so abruptly, he was still in my heart. If he still didn't have a dime to his name, he would still be in my heart. I truly wonder where he got the impression that this is not the case. It is so damn frustrating."

"Do you think someone told him something?" she asks. "Like someone who was jealous of you and wanted to break you both up."

I smile, grateful for her presence and ear daily. "Nah. Earl wouldn't believe anyone over me. It's something else. Thanks for being around, Sunny. You've been keeping me sane these past weeks."

"Don't worry about it. It's my job," she says. "Alright, get back to picking those strawberries. I am excited about the idea of baking a strawberry cake."

"More boxes of homegrown strawberries than you need coming up," I tell her cheerfully.

"Good. I'll be waiting."

I glance at the full basket, my chest warming at the thought of my father enjoying the fruits of my labor. "I think I'll also send some to my dad as well. He loves strawberries."

"Good idea. Ooo … there's a customer who needs me. Talk later?" she says.

"Yeah, later," I say and hang up.

I pull the earbuds out, and the greenhouse is suddenly quiet again. The sun filters through the glass, golden and warm, and for the first time since I got married, I feel a flicker of peace. I know now what I want to do.

CHAPTER 30

EARL

*T*he office has finally come together, but the process has been a blur of deadlines, decisions, and late nights that have left little room for anything else. Still, as I sit at my desk, I can't shake the nagging awareness of what she's been doing. It's in little things, subtle adjustments that she thinks I will hardly notice.

The soups.

At first, I thought it was the staff who'd changed the meals, but it's too specific—exactly the kinds of things I once gravitated toward. Come on, scrambled eggs with bits of crispy bacon in it. That's completely my thing! And she's the only one who knows it.

Where I used to not bother with food and settle for a quick coffee breakfast, I've now shifted to a rather pleasant food I actually want to eat. Her famous pancakes with strawberries and fresh cream or those blueberry muffins she gets from the bakery in town. It was satisfying in a way I hadn't expected and I finished more than I expected to.

And then there are the changes to the house. Fresh but understated scents linger in the halls. Somehow everything feels curated to suit me. It's subtle enough that I could pretend it's a coincidence, but I know better. It's her.

She's always seemed to understand and know and accept me more than even I did myself. It is perhaps why her betrayal hurt a thousand times worse. This quiet persistence with which she weaves herself into my life without asking isn't what I planned. But I understand what she is doing. She's trying to worm her way into my heart, but she doesn't realize my heart is rotten to the core. Not good to eat. She either chokes on rotting flesh or she worms her way out again.

The clock on the wall ticks steadily, each second dragging me closer to the inevitable showdown. Tonight is the gala, the kind of event I'd usually avoid like the plague. But this year, it feels important—like a statement I need to make. A reminder to this town, to everyone who ever doubted me, that I've risen far beyond the boy they used to sneer at.

Well, fuck you too, but guess what? I got the girl and fucking house.

With a sigh, I push back from the desk and head to my bedroom. The walk through the empty halls of the Belafonte ancestral home feels strange.

A mocking voice in my head whispers, "Look at you, a stranger in your own house. You don't belong here. You never will."

The idea of the evening presses down on me. Once inside my bedroom, I head straight for the bathroom, unbuttoning my shirt as I move because I'm already running late. The hot spray does little to wash away the restless energy thrumming through my body.

I push open the bathroom door and step into my closet. There, laid out neatly on a hanger, is the tuxedo Raven must have arranged for me.

The crisp shirt slides over my arms, the fabric smooth against my skin. Button by button, I fasten it, my jaw set. I tug on the sleeves, slipping on cufflinks that glint under the overhead light. Next comes the jacket. Its tailored lines fit perfectly.

The man staring back at me from the mirror is composed, every inch the sophisticated and successful man. But I know better. Beneath the polished surface, my thoughts churn with the same bitterness and frustration that's haunted me for years.

I flatten my lapels, letting my fingers linger a moment before I speak to the empty room. "So this is it," I murmur. "Time to get back on the plan."

Yeah, the fucking plan. My real intention for coming back to this backwater town. The reason I've been punishing her —punishing us—ever since I forced her back into my life. That small, traitorous voice in my head wonders sarcastically if I'm starting to slip and forget why I'm doing this. But no. I will never again allow myself to become the boy who worshipped the very ground she walked on. She was my moon, sun, stars. She was everything.

My eyes glint coldly in the mirror.

She needs to break down and admit what she did to me, admit what she truly thought of me while she claimed to love me more than life itself. Meanwhile, she was no better than the others. I want to see her face of the harm she caused, how she shattered the boy who loved her more than life itself. And I'll keep at it until she does.

Turning away from the mirror, I cross the room to my dresser, where a small velvet box waits. My mouth is a grim line as I pick it up. The necklace inside is worth more than most people make in a year—more than I made in all my time laboring at my different jobs over many months until I found it was easier to be a criminal than an honest man. Life is good for criminals. Diamonds catch the light with every subtle tilt, cold and brilliant. Perfect for the statement I want to make.

She'll wear this tonight, I decide. She'll have no choice in the matter. She will carry the sin of its worth around her neck, a glittering reminder of how low I've fallen and of how far she's fallen in my eyes.

Box in hand, I walk into the hallway. Each step echoes unnervingly in the quiet house. The polished floor reflects my silhouette, a dark figure gliding through corridors I never dreamt would be mine. I wanted a home, warm, inviting, shared. Instead, I've got a mausoleum full of corridors of cold hate and dead resentment.

I reach her door and hesitate, my hand halfway raised to knock. The faintest sliver of light glows beneath the threshold, a soft glow that suggests she's inside, maybe brushing her hair, maybe fiddling with the clasp of her dress. My stomach twists at the thought. For a heartbeat, I almost step back, almost show courtesy and wait for her permission.

But courtesy has no place in this game.

I lower my hand and curl my fingers around the doorknob. I will push it open without warning. The door will swing wide, her light will spill into the darkened hallway, silhouetting me in the frame.

And just like Dracula, I will step boldly into her bedroom.

CHAPTER 31

RAVEN

*M*y heart is thudding so hard I can feel the drumbeat in my veins, urging me to hurry. My fingers fumble at the back of the damned dress that clings to my ribcage with no mercy. The bodice cinches tight just under my breasts, then flares out into a gorgeous, calf-length silhouette. A part of me is breathless by how perfect it looks in the mirror—rich fabric catching the lamplight—but another part is convinced I'll suffocate before the night is over.

Sucking in a lungful of air I can barely pull in thanks to the dress, I push my hair away from my neck and try again to reach the clasp at the back. I should have just kept the other dress on. Now, I'm going to be late. My arms shake with nerves as I drop them in frustration. Tonight is our first real outing since … the incident with the tree. Actually, since our marriage. I'm desperate to make a good impression. I want him to be proud of me amongst all those snobs.

The door clicks behind me suddenly, a soft metallic sound that makes me freeze. I haven't finished fastening the dress, and if I let go of the front even for a second, it'll slip down, baring my breasts. My cheeks heat in a mixture of panic. I open my mouth to protest, but he's already inside, leaving me with no time to gather my wits.

"Earl," I gasp, clutching at the front of my dress.

He stands there, impeccable in his tuxedo—dark fabric fitting every contour of his broad shoulders and down tapering at his waist. For half a second, my heart skips a beat at how damned good he looks, but then I catch sight of his face: cool, unreadable. The flare of desire I imagined seeing is either gone or was never there.

I'm the first to speak, my voice brittle with nerves. "You look very fetching."

He offers nothing more than a faint grunt in acknowledgement. Instead, he moves closer, eyes sliding over my half-dressed state without a single spark of warmth. My stomach twists. I can't tell if he's just in one of his moods or if he truly doesn't care anymore.

"Turn around and …" he murmurs, nodding at my hand bunched up in the fabric over my chest. "Let go."

My heart stalls. The idea of letting go of the front of the dress and exposing myself to his cold almost hostile stare makes my entire body tighten. But I do it, my arms twitching with uncertainty as the material slips out of my hands. The bodice sags down, my breasts are laid bare to his eyes. A flush of heat crawls up my neck because both of us can see that my nipples are hard.

There is absolutely no expression at all on his face. It is completely, utterly, and frighteningly blank.

He steps behind me, but no closer than necessary. His touch is mechanical, almost impersonal, as he tugs the dress into place and fastens it with a surprising efficiency. He must have met a lot of clasps in the years since he's been gone, must have known a lot of women. If he notices my breath hitch, he doesn't show it. My skin prickles where his knuckles brush against me, but he doesn't linger.

Once the dress is secure, I shift away and catch a glimpse of my own reflection in the mirror. My face flushed, my eyes too bright, my chest rising and falling in unsteady waves. When I glance up, I see his reflection behind me: composed, distant, like a statue carved from ice. Completely detached.

I wait, hoping he'll say something, but his gaze flickers away from me. He crosses the room to the velvet box on the small table by the door.

I swallow hard, the tension in the room thick enough to choke me. He picks up the box—clearly a jewelry case—and for an instant, my heart leaps. Is he about to show a shred of warmth by offering me something? Or is this just another chess move in his ongoing game of reminding me exactly how small and powerless I am next to his wealth?

He says nothing, his shoulders stiff. As he moves under the light I see how tired he is, dark smudges under his eyes that have known too many late nights. He's been busy with renovations or expansions or something else I'm not allowed to help him with or enquire about. Maybe it's everything combined—our twisted relationship, the new office, the demands of this new life. Maybe he's just ... done.

My mouth parts, a question forming, but I clamp it shut. What good would it do? He's not in a talking mood, and I can't force him to see me the way I want him to. So I stand there, smoothing out the skirt of my dress, trying to steady my breathing as he holds the box in his hand.

He snaps open the box and on a dark blue velvet bed lays an opulent necklace of diamonds and crimson stones, probably rubies. It catches the soft light of the lamp and glitters extravagantly. The sight of it steals my breath. My first instinct is to recoil. I nearly gasp aloud, but I swallow the sound.

This is not me and he knows that too. He knows only I like pretty and delicate things. Why give me something so ostentatious? Clearly, this is not for me. This is either part of the you're nothing but a gold digger and you'll dress like one game or it is to impress the snobs at the gala.

He watches me, eyes flat, as though waiting for my reaction to his gift. My heart is breaking. Is this just another part of his plan—to see me flustered, to remind me of how little I have compared to him? I almost shake my head, almost refuse. But then I remind myself that if I want us to move beyond this endless war, I need to try to find out what caused him to become like this. And I won't do that by letting him provoke me into another pointless fight.

"Isn't this what you've always wanted?" he asks quietly, a trace of mockery lacing his tone. "Well, now you have it."

"Alright," I manage, my voice strangely calm. "Thank you."

He makes a sound, something halfway between a laugh and a scoff. Then he steps behind me. I hold my hair aside, and for a moment, the warm brush of his knuckles against my skin on the back of my neck sends a shiver through me. But it's purely perfunctory efficiency on his part; there's no tenderness in his touch.

Once the necklace is secured the weight of it feels like one of those slavery collars. Yet I force myself to nod and look down at the stones resting against my collarbone. They sparkle under the gentle light. In their own way, they are mesmerizingly beautiful. I'm sure Charles's mother will approve of them.

"You can keep it after we're done," he says, his voice low. "Consider it a gift of my ... generosity."

I open my mouth to speak, but the words dissolve on my tongue. Yes, if I am wrong and there is no way to reach him, then he has just paid for my father's medical bills. I just nod, not trusting my voice. His eyes linger on me for a second, then he turns away. My stomach twists. The hostile silence between us is unbearable.

I can't let him leave it like this. Not when we're about to face the outside world as a couple tonight, in front of everyone who matters. We will be the talk of the town tomorrow and the stories will get to my mother and cause her pain and anxiety. We can't look like two strangers forced into the same corner.

I reach out and wrap my fingers around his forearm. He halts, eyes swinging down to my hand. His brow furrows.

I snatch my hand away. "I ... I just ..." I stammer, uncertain what I'm trying to say. My pulse thunders in my ears, and then I do the only thing that comes to mind. The only way I know how to communicate with him. I rise on my tiptoes and press my lips to his. A brief, soft kiss, too short to be called passionate, but enough to lay my heart bare for a moment.

For a fleeting second, I swear I feel him respond—his body stiffens and there's a flicker of heat, of recognition. My own heart leaps at the possibility. Then, just as quickly, he pulls back. His expression is cold and unreadable, and my hope deflates like a punctured balloon.

He steps away, but I notice the faint outline in his pants, evidence that some part of him still reacts to me physically. Even so the set of his jaw, the hard line of his mouth, says everything else I need to know.

"Behave yourself tonight," he mutters, voice clipped. "You

are now the lady of the manor, not some tramp from the trailer park. I'll see you downstairs."

He yanks the door open and strides out, leaving me standing there, the stones glittering at my throat, my lips tingling from a kiss that tasted more of heartbreak than promise and the words that crush my soul.

CHAPTER 32

EARL

*T*he country club is a display of charm and affluence—hardwood flooring glowing with decades of polish. Perfect for reflecting the golden glow of the old chandeliers imported from Europe, large gilded oil paintings of the founding fathers of America, and red velvet drapes to frame the tall windows.

The ballroom on the first floor is reserved for this New Year's Eve gala, but when we arrive in the foyer it is already full of landed gentry. Camera flash and classical music floats through the air. I can't recall the last time I've seen so many glittering gowns and slick tuxedos in one place.

We've never been to this place before—neither of us... and certainly not our parents. They never invited trailer trash to events like this. Yet here we are, sweeping in as though we own the place, and in a way, I do. I could buy this place if I wanted to. At the very least I have the power to intimidate anyone who once might have sneered at my background.

Raven clings to my arm as we ascend the curving broad flight of stairs leading to the main ballroom. Every gaze in the room seems to latch onto us as we arrive at the entrance. There's a hum of curiosity, of whispered speculation. Some know my recent acquisitions in town, my business deals that have turned heads and tightened purses. The women eye Raven, taking in the expensive dress, the diamonds at her throat. I see equal measures of envy and curiosity. And I can't help but relish how they all stop to stare like we, the people they taunted and mocked, are now the star attraction at their big night of celebration.

Raven's fingers tremble slightly against the crisp fabric of my suit. I glance at her out of the corner of my eye and feel that familiar tug in my chest—the ache that treads the line between lust and something deeper. She looks breathtaking. What a shame she is so shallow and deceitful. Still, there's not a woman alive who can hold a candle to her beauty.

If she hadn't approached me all those years ago, I'd never have dared. She was too beautiful and I was too aware of my own nothingness. Now I'm far from nothing. I'm the richest man in the room, and I can practically taste the admiration and caution swirling in the air around us.

People converge on us almost instantly. Polite smiles, extended hands, murmuring congratulations about my "business acumen" and how they "always knew" I'd make something of myself. Liars, the lot of them, but I let them prattle on. I bask in it, letting Raven stand quietly at my side. This is what tonight is about—recognition, respect, and the power to shut them up with a single glare if I choose.

I spot a small cluster of vaguely familiar faces not too far away—some of Charles's old friends. Annabelle might be there too. They appear hesitant, as if wondering if they should greet me or shrink back. I almost laugh. Once upon a time, they'd have found any excuse to torment me. Now they don't even dare come up and say hello.

Raven remains poised, smiling politely at the well-wishers, but I feel her hand tense unconsciously around my arm whenever people crowd too close. No matter what she keeps that gentle expression on her face. It's almost disarming to see her handle this crowd so gracefully. As if she was born to it.

But then I remember, she would have been standing here anyway. She was going to marry Charles, after all. A flicker of anger sparks in my gut at the memory. Even penniless he will have an invite to this event. They don't eat their own. Bloodlines are everything to this lot. He is one of them. They understand him and he understands them. I am the stranger here. The odd one out.

We move along, exchanging pleasantries that mean nothing until a familiar voice calls out. "Earl Jackson? Is that really you?"

I turn and find my high school teacher, Mr. Langford and his partner, who is also another teacher in the same school. They're grinning, beaming as if they are really happy to see us.

"You look amazing, Raven!" Mr. Langford gushes, glancing at Raven. "I always knew the two of you would end up together! Didn't I say it back in senior year, dear?" he turns to his wife. "The perfect couple."

His wife nods enthusiastically, adding some remark about how we were "destined from the start."

Perfect couple, huh? I glance at Raven. She's smiling sweetly, responding to them with a genuine warmth I haven't seen in a while. That soft, sincere curve of her lips reminds me of the old days, those days I've tried to bury in shallow graves. Once her smile lit up my world. Now it just stokes a simmering rage in me. To think she was ready to give it all for Charles.

My hand clenches at my side. The night isn't even half over, and I'm already fighting the urge to snap at someone.

My arm slips away from Raven's, the movement so abrupt, that she stumbles and blinks in confusion. I can sense the questions in her eyes; what's wrong? Why are you pulling away? I pretend not to notice. I keep my gaze locked on the teacher who's still talking, going on about how we were always "destined" for each other. It's absurd how people rewrite history in their heads.

I let their inane conversation wash over me, nodding at the appropriate beats, and giving the bare minimum of polite responses. My mind is elsewhere, scanning the crowd until it lands on the familiar figure of Annabelle.

Years have passed and she's filled out in all the right places, but I would have recognized her anywhere. Her gown hugs the curves that leave no doubt she's in her prime. If I were any other man, I'd admire her outright. Instead, I feel nothing. The truth is every woman leaves me cold. When I first left town, I slept with a lot of women, but none of them ever made me feel anything for them except disgust when the sex was over. They bored me. They didn't want to have gherkins on their pizzas. It was not their fault. They were not Raven. And I was looking for Raven.

I sense Raven stiffen beside me, probably noticing the direction of my stare. Our teacher is still droning on about the multi-million-dollar project I've been orchestrating. The old mall, once a graveyard of shuttered stores and shattered skylights, is undergoing a complete transformation under my direction—a modern commercial hub that's got everyone buzzing.

I can practically feel Raven's curiosity prick at the edge of my consciousness. She's a sharp one and has already realized why I've been so preoccupied. I can see the inquisitiveness in her eyes; it's always been this way with her. She couldn't bear it if I even looked in the direction of another girl, especially if she was even passably attractive. There never was any reason for it. I had eyes for no one but her. Still, it used to make her eyes flare up and spit fire. I have to admit one truth. I've missed her raging jealousy. Oh, how I've missed her spitting and cursing and how sweet it was when I yanked her into my arms and stopped the crazy spitting and cursing with a crushing kiss.

Now, I'm counting on that jealousy. Let her burn, the way I burned for years thinking of her with Charles.

I spot Annabelle's approach from the corner of my eye, poised and assured as she glides through the crowd with unhurried grace. She looks polished and refined—exactly as I remember. Our eyes meet across the crowded room and I see it instantly. Years ago I was too naïve to see it. Now I can spot it a mile away when a woman wants me. And she wants me. Makes sense that she's always wanted me. It was why she used to roll her eyes in disgust when her brother and his friends tried to gang up on me.

Well, well.

There's only one woman in this room capable of making my blood run hot, but still … this opens interesting possibilities. A quick glance flickers between Raven and me. I look away back to Annabelle and smile slowly. Instantly, I sense a tremor of tension pass through Raven even though her face remains composed. Then Raven shifts slightly, her shoulders squaring as she feels the competition drawing closer.

The teachers as if on cue walk away.

A spike of adrenaline rushes through my veins as Annabelle arrives in front of us. Her perfume is light and floral, wafting into the space between us. Raven stands just a little taller, as if bracing for a blow. I feel the subtle shift in her demeanor, the tension coiling beneath her composed facade. It almost amuses me how easily Annabelle's presence can tilt the balance of Raven's carefully held calm.

Annabelle's painted lips bestow a graceful smile on us. Her mother has taught her well, she may be a yoga teacher, but she carries herself like a Queen. I force the corners of my mouth to widen further so she has no doubt that I am flirting with her.

Her eyes widen as she gets the message and she glances at Raven in surprise before she responds. "Hello, Earl," she drawls, her voice lilting in a way that must charm most men. She stops just shy of too close, as her arms extend out to me. I let myself be pulled into a casual hug.

Raven was expecting that.

Her reaction is immediate—a flicker of shock flits across her face, her lips parting as if to say something, but she quickly catches herself. Still, her lips tighten, and her eyes narrow just slightly, betraying the irritation she's struggling to suppress. The tension radiating off her is palpable, even as she tries to appear unaffected.

I feel an instinctive urge to pull away from Annabelle, but the sharp glint of annoyance in Raven's gaze intrigues me, stoking me. Still so possessive, are we? The realization sends a ripple of dark satisfaction through me.

There. Tonight won't be entirely tedious after all.

Instead of creating the distance I know Raven wants, I wrap my arms loosely around Annabelle's frame, leaning in to press a light kiss to her cheek. The contact is brief, but calculated to send Raven's annoyance into full bloom. From the corner of my eye, I catch her expression—a flash of pale shock, followed by a storm of barely contained fury. Her fists curl at her sides and her composure slips for the first time this evening.

"Hello, Annabelle," I say smoothly, stepping back just enough to reclaim my space but not before letting my hand linger on her elbow for a fraction of a second longer than necessary. "It's been a long time."

"It really has," Annabelle replies, her smile brightening. She doesn't seem to notice the charged atmosphere between Raven and me—or perhaps she's pretending not to. "And here you are, making waves as always." Her words are light and conversational. There is no harm in them.

But Raven remains unimpressed. Her silence is deafening. I can almost hear her biting the inside of her cheek, a habit she hasn't given up. Her jaw is tight, her eyes sharp as glass, and for a brief moment, I wonder if she's going to say something.

She doesn't.

Instead, she takes a step closer to me, subtly reasserting her place at my side. It's a small, almost imperceptible move, but it's enough to make me bite back a smirk. Oh, tonight is definitely going to be interesting.

Annabelle's eyes flick to Raven, her expression lighting up as if she's just noticed her. "Raven," she says warmly, her voice honeyed with just a trace of familiarity and something else. Something between them. It sets my teeth on edge because I know exactly what it is. Raven has secrets and Annabelle knows what they are. They both don't know that I already know.

"I have to say, you look absolutely stunning tonight," she

adds in that same fake friendly voice. "That dress is breath-taking. Earl has always had an eye for beauty, hasn't he?"

Raven blinks. She is so unsettled by jealousy it hasn't hit her yet. Her polite smile wavers ever so slightly. "Thank you," she replies, her tone measured but tight. Her gaze darts briefly to me, searching for reassurance. She shifts her weight, in the slight downward tug of her lips before she forces them back into a neutral line.

Annabelle doesn't stop there, her attention now fully on Raven. "I'll admit, I was surprised when I heard the news about you two. You must have had so many options, Earl. And yet …" She trails off, letting the implication linger in the air like smoke. Her smile widens, and it's the kind of smile that's designed to cut.

Raven's face freezes for a heartbeat, her composure cracking just enough for a hint of worry and confusion to bleed through. "I'm sorry, what do you mean?" she asks, her voice careful, but laced with a sharp edge.

"Oh, nothing," Annabelle says breezily, waving a mani-cured hand. "Just that you've always had your sights set on the highest goals, so I guess in the end you still got what you wanted. It's really interesting how things turn out. Life is full of surprises, isn't it?"

I can practically see the gears turning in Raven's mind, her brow furrowing as she tries to figure out what Annabelle is unsubtly hinting at.

And then, like a bolt of lightning, it hits her. Her eyes widen just a fraction, the realization dawning with a force that makes her inhale sharply.

Her gaze snaps to me, then back to Annabelle, and I don't miss the flash of shock in her expression. She's remembering —that thing she'd buried or forgotten—and it's rising to the surface now, raw and unfiltered. She tries to mask it, but it's too late. The damage is done. Annabelle knows and I know. But they don't know that I know.

Annabelle, for her part, remains blissfully oblivious or expertly pretends to be. She steps closer to Raven, her voice dropping slightly as if to convey sincerity.

"That dress—it's so perfect on you. But that necklace … phew. Gorgeous. Something I'd buy myself, but not really to your taste, is it?" She turns to me, her eyes sparkling with something that feels like a challenge. "Earl you have great taste. Then again … you always did. Even wearing greasy jeans."

Raven manages a smile, but it's faint and strained, her lips barely lifting at the corners. "That's very kind of you," she murmurs, her voice almost robotic, as if she's on autopilot.

I watch her closely, taking in every flicker of emotion that crosses her face—the uncertainty, the unease, the unmistakable hurt and the guilt. Unbelievable, but she actually forgot what she did. She's trying to hold it together now, but I know her too well. She's unraveling, and for a fleeting moment, I wonder if she'll admit what she did, or simply pretend it never happened. She stays rooted to the spot, her fingers clutching the edge of her purse like it's her only lifeline.

Annabelle doesn't seem to notice—or care. She turns her attention back to me, her smile softening into something more nostalgic.

"It's really nice to see you again, Earl. Hopefully, we'll get the chance to truly catch up later tonight." She glances spitefully at Raven. "I have lots of stories to tell you."

I tilt my head, meeting her gaze with an expression I hope conveys interest. "Sure, Annabelle. I'm looking forward to it."

The tension between the three of us is a living thing now, pressing in from all sides. Raven's silence stretches uncomfortably, and I enjoy every moment of it.

GEORGIA LE CARRE

"Well," Annabelle says finally, her voice light but laced with satisfaction. "I'll let you two enjoy the rest of your evening. It was lovely catching up."

She turns and walks away, her gown swishing elegantly around her as she disappears into the crowd. The moment she's gone, Raven exhales softly, her shoulders dropping as if she's been holding her breath the entire time.

I don't say anything to break the silence. She doesn't either, but the way she looks at me is like she's searching for answers.

"Something wrong?" I ask, my voice low and deliberately casual.

Her jaw tightens, and she shakes her head, but I can see it in her eyes: everything is wrong. She remembers. Finally, we are getting somewhere. The progress we have made tonight is enough to make the corner of my mouth twitch into something resembling a real smile.

CHAPTER 33

RAVEN

The moment Annabelle drifts away in a cloud of perfume, her perfectly polished smile fading into the sea of glittering gowns and sharp tuxedos, I realize I can't stand next to Earl one moment longer. My feet start moving before I make a conscious decision, carrying me toward the bar at the edge of the ballroom.

I don't look back. I can't.

The clink of crystal glasses and the soft hum of conversation rise to meet me as I approach the bar. I lean against the cool surface of the counter and signal the bartender. He pours a glass of champagne with practiced ease, sliding it toward me without a word. I take it gratefully, the flute cold against my fingertips, and take a long sip. The bubbles burn slightly, but it's a welcome distraction from the knot tightening in my chest.

The room feels both smothering and cavernous. It's all so beautiful, so opulent, and I am an imposter in a designer gown. This isn't my crowd. It never was. It never will be. I glance around the room, searching for a familiar face, someone I might connect with. But there's no one. No one I grew up with, no one who really knows me. This town was never mine. Earl was my crowd, and now even he feels unreachable—standing there among the wealthy and polished like he's always belonged.

And Annabelle …

The mere thought of her makes my jaw clench. I take another sip, fighting the bitter bile that rises up my throat. She wasn't overtly cruel. Of course not. She is too clever for that, but she was toying with me like a cat does with a mouse. Her condescending comments are disguised as compliments.

And Earl—oh, Earl had played along so effortlessly, as though he enjoyed every second of my humiliation. My pulse quickens at the memory, a mix of anger and something else— something closer to hurt. I shouldn't be surprised. Earl has a talent for turning the knife when I least expect it.

I take another drink, the champagne sliding down too quickly, almost making me cough. My hands tighten around the stem of the glass, and I try to steady my nerves. This isn't the time to lose it. I remind myself of the letter Earl wrote, of all the love we once shared. It's what's kept me going these past few days, what's kept me hoping, nurturing the fragile belief that we might find our way back to each other.

But tonight, it feels like that hope is slipping through my fingers. The way he looked at Annabelle—was it real? Or was it just another way to torture me, to remind me of everything I've done wrong? I can't tell. And that uncertainty gnaws at me, hollowing me out from the inside.

I take another sip, my third, and exhale slowly. Earl's mean streak is nothing new, but he's never cheated on me. The thought hits me like a punch to the gut—not because I suspect him now, but because I realize I don't. Despite every-thing, I've never doubted his loyalty in that way. Yeah, I used to get wildly jealous when we were younger, but I always knew at the back of my mind, I was overreacting. He was mine.

Even now, I don't believe him to be a cheat. He might be cruel, but he isn't a liar or a cheat. The realization unsettles me. Do I really believe he will still be faithful to me? Or am I fooling myself entirely? The questions swirl, each one more overwhelming than the last.

The bartender hovers nearby, and I catch his eye, signaling for another glass. Tonight isn't the night to figure this out. Tonight is about surviving. And if that means drowning my doubts in champagne, so be it.

I know I should return to his side, but I can't. Not yet. I need space to breathe. So I veer toward the buffet table instead, clutching my glass of champagne like a lifeline. The spread is extravagant, as expected, and I busy myself picking up a few bite-sized appetizers—miniature tarts with glossy fillings, delicate skewers of marinated shrimp, and tiny puff pastries that look almost too perfect to eat. I nibble on one absentmindedly, the flavors blending together on my tongue without making much of an impression.

My gaze drifts back to Earl, as it always does, no matter how hard I try to resist. He stands at the center of the room, impossibly handsome in his tailored tuxedo, the faintest smile curling at the edge of his lips as if he knows exactly how stunning he looks. There's an air of respectability about him now, a sharp contrast to the scrappy teen I fell in love with. But he's still Earl. My Earl.

The thought lodges in my chest like a thorn as I watch Annabelle make her way toward him again. At first, she's surrounded by a group of admirers, her laughter ringing out like delicate chimes, but gradually, the crowd thins. And it's just the two of them now. My stomach knots as Annabelle reaches out, her manicured hand brushing against his arm with an ease that sets my teeth on edge.

Earl doesn't pull away.

I freeze, my glass hovering mid-air. From this distance, I can't hear what they're saying, but their body language tells me enough. Annabelle leans in, laughing softly, her fingers lingering on his sleeve. Earl's expression remains guarded, but he allows it—her touch, her laughter, her proximity. And why wouldn't he? He hates me and wants to punish me. What better way? The realization cuts deeper than I expect it to.

Annabelle leans closer, whispering something into his ear. And my heart literally stops. Is she telling him what I told her all those years ago? No, she wouldn't. Knowing her she would keep that back and torture me with it for as long as she can. Earl's brows furrow, and he shakes his head, his lips forming a brief, curt reply. But then, he glances up, and our eyes meet.

I can't look away, though every instinct screams at me to. His gaze holds mine, sharp and unreadable, as though daring me to react. For a second, I think I catch the faintest flicker of amusement in his eyes. My grip on the champagne glass tightens. I feel exposed, as if he's stripped me bare with that one look, laying all my bitterness and insecurities out for him to see.

And then, he does it. His arm curves around Annabelle's waist, his movements deliberate, calculated. He leans down and murmurs something into her ear. Annabelle's eyes widen briefly before she throws her head back in laughter, her voice carrying across the room. Heads turn in their direction, curious smiles blooming as if they've just witnessed a charming little piece of gossip they can spread tomorrow at lunch with the girls.

I can feel the stares shifting to me now, pity and judgment mingling in their glances. My heart pounds in my chest, each beat echoing like a drum. I force myself to take another sip of champagne, draining the glass in one long swallow. The bubbles do little to ease the burn rising in my throat.

I can't do this. Not here, not now.

Without a word, I set the empty glass on the nearest tray and slip out of the room. The air grows colder as I run down the stairs and into the gardens. The chill bites at my exposed shoulders. But it's quiet here. Peaceful.

I take deep breaths and wrap my arms around myself, staring out at the twinkling fairy lights strung across the hedges. My breath forms soft clouds in the air. I don't want to cry. I can't, but the lump in my throat forms all the same.

He's punishing me once again, and truly, I am getting sick of it. It's one thing to do it in the privacy of our townhome, but for him to so blatantly flirt with another woman in my vicinity and in the presence of the entire town burns in a way that makes it hard for me to breathe.

CHAPTER 34

EARL

*T*he moment Raven storms out of the ballroom, hurt and anger etched into every inch of her expression, a ripple of satisfaction courses through me. Watching her simmer, watching her stew in frustration— it's a petty kind of victory, but a victory nonetheless. My gaze lingers on the door she disappeared through, but I force myself to stay rooted in place. Let her cool off. Or burn.

Either option suits me fine.

Annabelle is still beside me, laughing lightly at something one of the guests has said, but I barely hear her. Her presence, once mildly entertaining, has soured now that Raven is no longer watching. Even her laugh now grates on my nerves, each note a reminder that she doesn't belong next to me or with me.

"Earl," she says, her tone soft as she leans in closer. Her perfume is heady and floral, a stark contrast to the gentle of

Raven's scent. "You've barely been paying attention to me all night."

"I'm here, aren't I?" My response is measured and polite, but there's an edge to it that I don't bother to conceal anymore.

Her brows knit for the briefest moment, and then she smiles—forced, brittle.

The clock ticks closer to midnight, and the countdown looms like an inevitable reckoning. I check my watch again, not bothering to hide my impatience. Annabelle notices, of course. She always does.

"You're waiting for her, aren't you?" she asks, her voice tinged with something akin to resignation. "You always only had eyes for her. Even when it wasn't the same for her."

I glance at her then, finally giving her my full attention. There's a peculiar sadness in her expression, one that doesn't quite match the venom of her words.

"You know she's only using you, right?" Annabelle presses, her smile twisting into something cruel. "She's always been like this—chasing money, chasing status. That's all she's ever cared about. She'd marry anyone who could give her that."

Her words land like darts, sharp but ineffective. They don't pierce. How can they when I already know all about my darling wife and her love for the good life? I smile coolly at Annabelle.

"Nice to see you, Annabelle," I say, pressing a light kiss to her cheek before stepping away. "Enjoy the rest of your evening."

The ballroom is alive with the buzz of anticipation as the final seconds before the great bell is run to signify the beginning of the dance. A roar of excitement fills the air, voices joining together. Outside fireworks light the sky. Inside it's a scene of joy and unity, but my focus has shifted entirely. Raven isn't here, and my chest feels empty.

I make my way down the stairs toward the garden. The chilly air bites at my skin as I step outside, the noise of the party muffled but still audible. It doesn't take long to find her. She's seated on a stone bench, her silhouette framed by the glow of fireworks exploding across the sky.

She doesn't notice me at first. She's staring at the bursts of color above, her face caught between awe and melancholy. It's beautiful, really, the way the light dances across her features. I move closer, my footsteps silent against the stone path.

When she finally senses my presence, her head snaps toward me.

She stands abruptly, taking a step back. Her heel catches on the uneven cobblestones, and for a heart-stopping second, she teeters dangerously.

I'm there before she can hit the ground, my arm circling her waist as she falls forward. Her hands clutch at my shoulders, her breath hitching as she steadies herself against me.

"Careful," I murmur, my voice low.

Her cheeks flush, but she says nothing. The space between us feels impossibly charged, her body cold against mine. I should let go, step back, and put some distance between us. But I don't. Not yet. Her hands clutch at my shoulders, her chest rising and falling quickly, and for a moment, I wonder if it's the cold or the tension that has her trembling.

"Are you drunk?" I ask.

Her head tilts up, those wide eyes locking with mine. She doesn't answer, and instead, the flush in her cheeks deepens, whether from the chill or her temper, I can't tell. But I can feel it—anger radiating off her in waves. It makes me smile.

"It's freezing out here," I continue, taking my jacket off and draping it over her shoulders. "Don't you think it's a bit foolish to be sitting in the cold? You'll catch your death."

Her eyes narrow, and this time, she doesn't hold back. "Don't you think it's foolish," she shoots back, her words clipped and biting, "to so openly flirt with another woman in front of your wife?"

I freeze. Wife. The word slips from her lips like an accusation, but it lodges itself somewhere deeper inside me. It's the first time she's called herself that, and damn it, I like the sound of it more than I should. I like the way it anchors her to me, a declaration, even in anger. My lips twitch upward despite myself.

I study her. Her cheeks are flushed, her lips slightly parted as though she's waiting for me to strike back. And I realize, with a pang just how much I've missed this fire in her. Annabelle's easy laughter, her finishing school charm— none of it holds a candle to Raven's furious, messy, maddening presence. This, right here, is what I crave. What I've always craved.

"It's the day of the great dance," I murmur, my tone softer now, the weight of the night pressing against me. "Shouldn't we dance instead of arguing?"

Before she can retort, I move closer, lowering my head until our faces are inches apart. Her eyes widen, but she doesn't pull away.

"You were flirting with that bitch. How could—" she starts shakily.

But I don't let her finish. I close the distance between us and press my lips to hers. It's heat and desperation, a collision of all the things we haven't said, and won't admit. Her hands come up instinctively, palms pushing at my chest, but the effort is puny and lacking conviction. She doesn't really want me to stop. I can feel it in the way her body yields to mine, and in the way her lips part beneath the pressure of my own.

Suddenly, her resistance falters entirely, and I feel her drowning in the kiss, the same way I do. My hands move to her waist, pulling her closer, warming her in the freezing air. Fireworks explode above us, the brilliant colors lighting up the sky.

Then the world falls away.

And it's just us. No Annabelle. No party. Nothing. Just the unrelenting pull between us that neither of us can escape.

Her breath mingles with mine as her body trembles against me. Her hands, which moments ago were weakly pushing me away, now grip the fabric of my shirt as though she's afraid I'll vanish if she lets go. Her resolve crumbles like sand under the tide as she melts into me.

My hand trails down her back, feeling the soft curves that I know as well as my own heartbeat. I shouldn't. God knows I shouldn't. But every rational thought evaporates as she presses closer, her lips moving with a fervor that drives me wild. The cold air bites at our skin, but it only fuels the fire between us.

My lips travel down the curve of her jaw, finding the sensitive spot beneath her ear that makes her gasp. Her head tilts back, exposing her throat to me. Her fingers tangle in my hair, pulling me closer, and I can't help the low growl that escapes my throat. She shudders.

"I hate you," she whispers, her voice trembling with longing.

"Shh," I murmur, my lips grazing hers again.

I guide her toward a gazebo tucked into the shadows, away from prying eyes. She hesitates for a moment, glancing toward the distant lights of the ballroom.

"No," she breathes, her voice barely audible. "We can't … not here …"

But when I sit and pull her onto my lap, her protests dissolve into a sigh. She's straddling me now, her dress riding up to expose the delicate lace of her stockings. My hands find her thighs, sliding up to her hips. I grip them firmly and pull her tight against me.

My hands slide beneath her skirt, finding the thin strip of fabric that separates me from her. I hook my fingers around it and pull it to one side.

"Someone will come. We shouldn't," she mutters frenziedly.

"Then stop me," I whisper and slip a finger inside her tight wet pussy. Her response is a soft whimper and total surrender as she arches helplessly against me. With her head thrown back her hands clutch at my shoulders. I lean in, my lips brushing against the exposed curve of her throat as I suck the soft skin.

She moans and moves restlessly against me, chasing the sensation with an urgency that matches my own. My fingers thrust in and out of her drawing soft cries. She bites her lip to stop herself from crying out.

"You're so beautiful like this," I murmur, my voice thick with adoration. "Completely mine. Don't you dare forget it."

Her eyes snap open at my words, her gaze locking with mine. There's a fire there, a challenge that only fuels my desire. "In that case fucking act like it," she snarls.

I don't hesitate. My movements become brutal, almost primal.

Raven falls apart on top of me, trembling and unable to stop her cries. I capture her mouth with mine, swallowing every desperate, muffled sound. Her surrender is intoxicating, but it only feeds the fire raging inside me.

GEORGIA LE CARRE

When she finally stills and becomes limp, her breath comes in shallow gasps against my lips. Gently, I lower her onto the bench, the rough wood a stark contrast to the softness of her skin. The faint light from one of the lantern-style lamps nearby spills out into the garden, casting her in a glow that makes her look almost otherworldly.

She has tempted me again, and I don't resist. My hands move slowly, reverently, as I slide the fabric even higher, exposing the smooth curve of her thighs. I pause, letting the anticipation hang heavy between us. Her chest rises and falls, her lips part as if she can't believe what we're doing. She watches me, her eyes wide and dark, pupils blown with desire.

"Earl … we're behaving like animals," she whispers hoarsely.

"I know," I agree, and lower my head, my lips trailing down her neck, her collarbone, the delicate curve of her shoulder. I need to taste every inch of her.

"Someone will come," she warns nervously, as her fingers clutch together the edges of my jacket.

"It's freezing out here. No one will come."

She moans softly but doesn't stop me when my hands travel lower. I push her dress all the way up so her stomach and hips and pussy are all exposed to me. Her legs part instinctively, and I take a moment to admire her, the way she looks at me with a mixture of vulnerability and trust. Her body is completely at my mercy, and the realization sends a rush of possessive pride through me.

Slowly, I slide my finger beneath the thin fabric of her thong. It's completely soaked. She shivers, her desire tangible, and glances up to meet my gaze. Her cheeks are flushed, her lips swollen, her eyes half-lidded with pleasure.

"You're so beautiful like this," I tell her, my voice low and raw. I try to hold back, but the words just tumble out. "You have no idea what you do to me."

She looks at me hungrily, as though she's afraid I'll disappear if she lets me out of her sight. I lower my head, trailing kisses down her chest, stomach, her hips until my lips reach her fragrant pussy.

I don't rush. I savor every second, every sensation, as I lower my head and taste her. The taste of her is intoxicating and impossibly addictive. My tongue finds every sensitive spot that makes her writhe beneath me. She cries out, her hands flying to her mouth to stifle the sound. Her thighs tremble violently, the soft quiver turning into an uncontrollable shake as her fingers dig into the rough edges of the bench.

She's fighting to hold on, to maintain some shred of control, but it's slipping through her grasp like sand. She can't stop her body from responding to me in a way that's primal, unguarded, and breathtakingly honest. Every stroke of my tongue draws a desperate, broken gasp from her lips, the sound echoing in the cool night air.

I press deeper, my tongue tracing every sensitive curve, savoring the way she arches into me, unable to stay still. Her hands bury themselves in my hair, tugging hard enough to make my scalp sting, but it only spurs me on. Her soft moans escalate into cries, raw and unrestrained, and I have to grip her hips firmly to stop her from writhing away. She's utterly undone, her body is already spiraling into ecstasy.

"Earl ... oh, dear God ..." she gasps, her voice cracking as her nails rake across my scalp. The desperation in her tone, the way she clutches me like I'm the only thing keeping her grounded—it drives me to the edge of my own restraint. She tastes incredible, sweet and heady, and I can't get enough. I devour her like a man starved, each sound she makes fueling the hunger clawing at my chest.

Her back arches, her thighs squeezing my shoulders as she struggles against the overwhelming pleasure.

"Please ... I can't—" she chokes out, but her body tells a different story, moving against me with a frantic urgency. Until I feel the exact moment she falls apart completely. Her cry pierces the night as her body trembles violently, wave after wave of release crashing over her.

I lap at her sweet juices until she's utterly spent and her hands fall limply at her sides. I press a kiss to her inner thigh, my lips lingering there, and when I look up, the sight of her completely unraveled is enough to steal what's left of my composure.

I rise and pull her into my arms. Her body is warm, soft, and completely pliant against mine. The taste of her still lingering on my lips, is too much to resist.

"We can't stay here," I mutter, my voice thick with desire. "But I'm not done with you. Not even close."

She looks at me then, her eyes glassy but resolute. "Okay," she whispers, her voice trembling but certain. "Okay."

I help her straighten her dress and guide her back toward the ballroom, keeping to the shadows to avoid the curious eyes of the guests, but Annabelle must have been waiting for us because she calls out my name.

I turn around and she waves and starts walking towards us. Next to me, Raven stiffens.

CHAPTER 35

RAVEN

*T*he sound of her voice shattered the cocoon of delicious sensations that surrounded me. Earl's hand brushes mine, and when our eyes meet, there's a knowing look between us—a silent acknowledgment of what we've just done, what we're both still feeling. My heart races, my skin humming with an unspoken need for him to touch me again. Slowly, I turn away from him and face her.

Annabelle appears.

Her voice is light and twinkling with affability as if we're all best friends. She sidles up to Earl, her smile wide, her gaze focused solely on him. "I thought you'd snuck out to head home," she says, ignoring my presence entirely. The way she leans in, the way her body angles toward his as though I don't exist stings.

Without hesitation, I slide my hand through his, linking our fingers. "We were just about to leave," I say firmly, my voice steady despite the heat of anger bubbling inside me. I don't look at Annabelle, focusing instead on Earl. My words are more for her benefit than his. Let her see where his loyalties lie.

But Annabelle doesn't back down. "Oh, but before you go, I have a small request," she says, her tone sweet, almost cloying. She tilts her head, a picture of practiced innocence. "Earl, do you think you could spare a moment? It's important."

I feel the muscles in his arm tense under my grip, but his face remains unreadable. "If it's important, say it now," he replies, his voice clipped. "We're in a hurry."

Annabelle's smile doesn't falter, but there's a flicker of something in her eyes—hesitation, perhaps? "For Raven's sake," she says, glancing at me for the first time all evening, "it might be better if we talked privately."

My patience snaps. "Then don't bother saying it at all," I shoot back, stepping forward. My grip on Earl's hand tightens, and I glare at her. "We're leaving."

The words hang heavy in the air, and Earl turns to me, his brow furrowed. "Raven," he says, his voice lower now, warning, "perhaps I should hear what Annabelle has to say."

I freeze, astonished that he has responded to me in this way, in this tone, in front of her of all people. It's like he has dumped a bucket of ice water over my head.

Annabelle's expression shifts into delighted smugness, but I don't give her the satisfaction of an argument.

"Fine," I say as if it doesn't bother me in the least that my husband would put her before me, his wife. I release his hand.

"See you in the car," Earl says.

Wordlessly, I turn and walk away, my heels clicking sharply against the floor as I make my way toward the exit. The voices and laughter around me blur, my pulse pounding in my ears. Earl's words replay in my mind, each one cutting deep. He stood there, defending her, taking her side, acting as though I was the unreasonable one.

By the time I reach the valet station, my anger has morphed into something colder, more resolute. The attendant brings the car around, and I climb into the backseat without a word, my hands clenched in my lap.

The car idles quietly at the valet station, the faint hum of the engine doing nothing to quell the storm raging inside me. My hands remain clenched in my lap as I steal a glance back toward the grand entrance of the venue. The golden light spilling out onto the steps seems to mock me, warm and inviting, a stark contrast to the cold knot twisting tighter in my chest.

I wait.

The minutes tick by, each one slower than the last. A couple emerges, laughing as they descend the staircase, their silhouettes elegant and carefree. Another group follows, their voices carrying faintly in the night air. But there's no sign of him. No sign of Earl. My nails press into my palms as my mind drifts, unbidden, to the possibilities.

Is he still with her?

The thought surfaces, unwelcome and sharp, and I force myself to shake it off. I won't let my imagination run wild. He's probably just tying up loose ends, exchanging polite goodbyes. But then another thought creeps in—what if it's more than that? What if she is telling him what I told her? Nah. That I know for sure she is not doing. But what if he's holding her now, whispering the same low, intimate words he'd whispered to me not long ago?

My stomach churns, and I snap my gaze back to the valet in front of me. I don't care, I tell myself. This isn't jealousy. It's annoyance. That's all.

But the ache in my chest betrays me.

The clock on the dashboard glows brightly, each flickering number marking the passage of time. Ten seconds. Fifteen. Twenty. One minute. Five minutes. Seven minutes. By the time I catch sight of him, I'm teetering on the edge of leaving altogether.

Earl steps out of the building, his figure backlit by the golden glow of the foyer. He doesn't rush, his movements are calm and measured, as though he doesn't have a care in the world. My heart thuds heavily as I watch him scan the valet line, his eyes landing on his car. For a moment, I think he looks relieved, but it's gone too quickly to be certain.

I turn my head sharply away and pretend to be absorbed in the view outside the car. I hear the sound of his approaching footsteps, but I don't turn around. The door opens, and the seat dips slightly as he slides in beside me. He shuts the door quietly behind him. Still, I don't turn.

Neither of us speaks and the driver pulls away. The quiet hum of the tires on the tarmac fills the terrible space between us. I keep my gaze fixed out the window, watching the lights pass in a kaleidoscope of colors. Earl doesn't speak, but I can feel his presence like a gravitational pull, drawing every ounce of my attention despite my best efforts to resist.

"You're quiet," he notes.

My fingers tighten on the hem of my dress as I struggle to find the right words. Anger simmers beneath the surface, but it's tangled with hurt and pain.

"What do you want me to say, Earl?" I ask, finally turning around to face him. "That I'm thrilled you kept me waiting while you entertained Annabelle?"

"I'm sorry, but I think you're under the mistaken impression," Earl says, his voice smooth but laced with venom, "that you somehow have the right to dictate my actions. Or to speak to me in the way you are doing now." He shifts slightly, turning to face me fully, his expression a mask of calculated detachment. "I can talk to whoever I want. And if I wanted to take Annabelle up on her offer, go up to her hotel room, and fuck her—then I could. And you wouldn't get to say a word about it."

I feel the blood drain from my face. My chest tightens, a sharp ache blooming in my ribs as his words echo in my mind. *If I wanted to. If I wanted to.* The sheer audacity and cruelty of him makes tears burn into my eyes, but I refuse to let them fall. Not in front of him.

But Earl is not finished. His voice is low, almost mocking. "So don't sit there, bitch and whine, acting like you own me. You don't own me. I own you. Don't forget what this is, Raven. Don't forget what you are to me."

The tears spill over before I can stop them. Hot, humiliating streaks down my cheeks that hurt my heart. If the car wasn't already moving, I would have thrown the door open and walked into the night.

But instead, I sit there, silent, my hands trembling in my lap, speechless with shock, sorrow, and pain. To be so humiliated, so degraded ...

I want to tell him he's wrong, that he's cruel, that he's causing an irreparable rift between us, but the words lodge in my throat. What is the use? I've tried everything and nothing works. Sure, it's good for a tiny bit, while we're having sex, but almost immediately afterwards he morphs into a heartless monster again. I swallow the lump in my throat and stare out the window.

By the time the car pulls up to the house, my anger has hardened into something colder. If this is what he wants, if he wants this relationship to be devoid of intimacy, of even basic decency, then that's exactly what he'll get.

The chauffeur opens my door, and I step out and throw his jacket back into the back seat of the car. Rain has begun to fall. It's light but steady, the drops soaking into my hair and dress as I walk calmly toward the front door.

I've only taken a few steps when I feel it—a strong hand clamping down on my arm, spinning me around.

"Let me go!" I yell, twisting in his grip.

Earl's face is inches from mine, his expression thunderous. "Raven," he snaps, his face white with fury. "You don't just walk away from me like that."

"Leave me alone, Earl," I spit, yanking my arm free, but he's stronger. His fingers tighten, not enough to hurt, but enough to keep me there.

"Are you out of your mind?" I hiss, trying to shake him off again. "Let me go, Earl. Right now!"

Nora appears at the open doorway, her eyes widening in concern as she takes in the sight of us.

"Mrs. Jackson, are you alright?" she asks, her voice tentative.

"Well? Am I alright?" I ask Earl taunting.

Earl's gaze snaps to Nora like a whip. "Leave," he commands, his voice sharp enough to make her flinch.

But to her credit, she doesn't leave. "Mrs. Jackson," she calls again courageously. "Are you alright?"

Her voice carries distress and it makes me feel ashamed of myself for involving her. I turn my head towards her and flash her a smile.

"I'm fine," I say.

Nora hesitates, her hands clasped nervously in front of her.

"You can go now. Thanks, Nora."

She nods and disappears into the house.

His grip falters for that split second, and at that moment,

I wrench my arm free. My chest heaves as I take a step back, my eyes never leaving his. My heart pounds in my chest, a mix of anger, pain, and something dangerously close to regret. I see it now. How naïve I was to think I could make it work. It is hopeless.

I don't know if I can remain one more second in this place knowing for sure now that I've lost him. The raindrops falling on my head are getting bigger and colder, but it's my heart that feels like it is encased in ice.

Before he can stop me, I whirl around and run towards the garden. He shouts, calling my name, his voice urgent and rattled, but I don't stop. I'm terrified he will follow me, but thankfully, he doesn't. The rain suddenly starts pouring in heavy sheets of water. But I can't go back to the house. I know he is expecting me to as there is nowhere else to go, but I won't give him that satisfaction. I will do anything possible to be as far away from him as I can. I will wait until he is asleep then I will creep in and leave before dawn. I change direction and head toward the land at the back of the conservatory, towards the lake. The rain washes away my racking sobs. I wish I could go to my parents' home right now and this time around use my brain rather than my stupid emotions, and never come back.

The rain pours relentlessly, the icy drops soaking through my clothes until the chill reaches my very bones. My hair clings to my face, plastered against my skin, as I wander aimlessly through the grounds, my heels sinking into the soft, rain-soaked earth. The cold bites at me and makes me shiver, but it's nothing compared to the ache in my chest, the hollow emptiness that Earl's words have carved into me.

I'm like a mad woman weeping inconsolably, walking in circles, and wailing softly, 'How could he?' again and again. I'm glad there is no one to see my distress or how low I have fallen. My parents would be shocked to see the state I am in. How long has passed since I ran away from him? Must be no more than a few minutes, but it feels like forever. I don't think I can wait until he goes to sleep. Maybe I'll wait a little while longer and then I'll try and tiptoe in through the back door. My arms wrap around me, desperate for warmth, but the freezing wind cuts through my drenched dress, leaving me trembling and weak.

My mind spins back to the beginning—to the stolen moments when everything felt so perfect. To the way he looked at me, like I was the only thing that mattered. What changed? What the hell happened? How did it all fall apart so completely? How did we get here? His words replay in my head, over and over, each one a dagger sinking deeper into my heart.

You don't own me, I own you. The words are sharp, bitter.

I shake my head, trying to dispel the thoughts that threaten to drown me. The rain intensifies and I can barely see a few feet ahead of me, and I stumble as my heel catches on the uneven stone path. My breaths come in short, shuddering gasps as the cold sinks deeper into my body. My fingers are numb, and my toes ache from the chill seeping through my soaked shoes.

I don't know what to do. I don't know how to fix this—if it can even be fixed. The weight of it all crushes me, and I stop walking, my knees trembling beneath me. I close my eyes, letting the rain wash over me as exhaustion pulls at my limbs. I feel so small, so lost.

A voice breaks through the haze. "Mrs. Jackson!"

I blink, turning toward the sound. Through the sheets of rain, I see Nora hurrying toward me, an umbrella held high above her head, something bulky tucked under her armpit. Relief rushes through me, mingling with the fresh wave of tears that spill down my cheeks. She reaches me, her face pale with worry, and without a word, she drapes a thick blanket around my shoulders.

"It's freezing cold," she says, her voice trembling as she tugs the blanket tighter around me. "Come inside, please. You'll catch your death out here."

Her warmth and concern undo me. Unable to form words, I can only nod weakly. Kneeling down on the ground she takes my stilettos off and slips a pair of rain boots over my frozen feet. The simple gesture sends a fresh wave of gratitude coursing through me, and I let her guide me towards the house. I cling to the blanket as we make our way back toward the glow of Earl's house.

Under the shelter of the umbrella, Nora walks close beside me, shielding me from the worst of the rain. The warmth of the blanket is a stark contrast to the icy wetness of my clothes, and I feel the first stirrings of comfort seep into my frozen limbs.

When we reach the door, Nora opens it quickly, ushering me inside. The warmth of the house envelops me like a balm, and I feel my body start to thaw, though the ache in my chest remains as painful as ever.

"Everyone's gone to bed. Take that dress off and sit down by the fire," Nora urges gently, guiding me to a chair near a wood burner in the far end of the kitchen. "While I'll run a hot bath for you."

But I feel too weak to undress. I just sink into the chair, my fingers clutching the blanket tightly around me. The fire crackles softly, its warmth a stark contrast to the storm raging inside me. As the rain continues to lash against the windows, I close my eyes and let the exhaustion take over, hoping for even a moment's respite from the turmoil swirling in my heart.

CHAPTER 36

EARL

https://www.youtube.com/watch?v=sBW8Vnp8BzU
-the whole of the moon-

I lean forward and stare at the surveillance footage playing on my desktop. Raven sits on a chair, motionless, the blanket Nora gave her clutched tightly around her like a protective shell while she stares blankly into the fire. Her hair, wet and bedraggled clings to her face and neck in long black streaks. Even from here, from this one angle, I can see that her hands are shivering uncontrollably.

I jump to my feet and pace the floor of my study. Pure frustration simmers beneath my skin. She's trembling, for God's sake. The foolish girl is soaked to the bone, but stubborn enough to stay downstairs instead of going up to change.

Why? Why does she insist on punishing herself like this?

Or is it me she's punishing?

My jaw is clenched as I stop in front of my computer and fix my gaze on the screen. The firelight dances across her features, highlighting the whiteness of her cheeks. She looks small. Fragile. And yet, there's something defiant in the way she sits there, refusing to move, to give in to the cold or the discomfort.

I should go to her. Every cell in my body is screaming for me to go to her. To wrap her in my arms, carry her upstairs, strip those wet clothes off her, and get her warm the only way I know how to. But I can't move. I'm rooted to the spot, torn between the angry hate in my gut and the gnawing love that just won't die no matter what she does.

Why did she run out like that?

What was she trying to prove?

The questions tumble through my mind, unanswered and infuriating. Then the stabbing guilt. Maybe I pushed her too far tonight. Maybe I let my own frustrations, my own insecurities, get the better of me. I wanted to see her break. Wanted her to show me something real, something raw. But now, seeing her like this—broken and shivering—it feels all wrong.

I pick up my phone and call Nora. She answers on the second ring.

"Yes, Mr. Jackson?"

"Nora, I need you to get her upstairs," I say, my voice clipped, betraying none of the turmoil inside me. "She needs to get out of those wet clothes and into something warm. Make her take a bath if you have to, and brew her some coffee. Ensure it is hot."

"Of course, Mr. Jackson," Nora replies, her tone calm but tinged with concern. "I'm running a bath for her right now, and I'll see to the coffee as soon as I get her in the hot water."

I hang up without another word, my eyes returning to the

screen. Nora appears a moment later, speaking softly to Raven, coaxing her to move. It takes a few tries, but eventually, Raven stands, swaying slightly. I frown when I see that Nora has to steady her.

I watch them go up the stairs and through the corridor, into her room, and enter her bathroom. I exhale slowly, the tension in my chest easing slightly as they disappear from the frame. But the relief is fleeting. My thoughts circle back to everything that happened tonight, every sharp word, every deliberately provocative lingering glance at Annabelle. I knew they would devastate Raven, cut into her like knives. I wanted her to suffer like I have.

But what am I doing? Did I really believe there would be pleasure in seeing her suffer?

There is no pleasure in seeing her break. So what if she is a gold digger? So what if she lied to me? I have no right to damage such a beautiful creature.

I run a hand over my face, the blame settling heavy on my shoulders. If I keep this up, I'm going to destroy her. And God help me, I don't want that. I never wanted that. I just wanted to bring her to her knees. I wanted her to confess, but I see now that I don't even want that anymore. The pain I am causing myself by hurting her is too great to bear.

The hours pass slowly, the house growing quieter with each passing minute. I try to sleep, but my mind refuses to rest. Every time I close my eyes, I see her face—pale, wet, and trembling. By the time exhaustion finally drags me under, it's well past three in the morning.

A soft knock at my door jerks me awake.

I sit up abruptly, the blanket I'd thrown over myself slipping to the floor. My heart races as my mind snaps to Raven, panic surging through me.

"It's me, Mr. Jackson," someone says through the door.

"Nora?" I call out, my voice hoarse.

"Yes, Mr. Jackson. It's Nora." Her voice is muffled, but there's an urgency in her tone that sends a cold wave of dread washing over me.

I'm on my feet and crossing the room in a few quick strides. I throw the door open, and Nora stands there, her expression tight with worry.

"What is it?" I demand, my voice sharp. "What's wrong?"

Her hands are clasped tightly in front of her, the knuckles white. "It's Mrs. Jackson, Sir," she says in a frightened voice. "I think she's taken quite ill, Sir. I noticed last night she wasn't herself, but I thought the rest and warmth would do her good. Now... now, it's past her usual hour to awaken, and she still hasn't gotten out of bed. She won't eat anything. She insists she's fine, but ..." Nora hesitates, her gaze flicking to the floor before meeting mine again. "I think she's running a temperature too."

I stare at her, my chest tightening. Raven unwell? How? Raven doesn't get sick. She runs headlong into storms, thrives in chaos, and pushes through everything, even when she shouldn't. The idea of her being ill feels foreign. Impossible.

I glance down the hallway toward her room, a knot forming in my gut. My instinct is to go to her, but I hesitate. Nora is overreacting to a fever. Raven is healthy, young, and in her prime, she just needs a little time.

"She'll be fine," I say, my voice more dismissive than I intended. "It's the morning after the big dance. She deserves a lazy Sunday." I hear the words, but even as they leave my mouth, they feel hollow.

Nora doesn't move right away. For a brief moment, her gaze sharpens, her usually deferential demeanor cracking just enough to reveal something close to disapproval. It's subtle, but it's there, and it irritates me.

"Is there anything else?" I ask, my tone hardening.

"No, Mr. Jackson, Sir," she replies. She turns to leave, her steps brisk and purposeful.

"Let me know how she's doing by dinnertime," I call after her.

"Yes, Sir," she says over her shoulder before disappearing down the hall.

The tension in the air lingers even after she's gone. I stand there for a moment, rooted in place, my eyes fixed on Raven's door. Every fiber of me wants to go to her, to see for myself that she's fine, but something stops me. Pride, maybe. Or fear. Now that I know I don't want to see her suffer anymore, I have become more vulnerable. I can let her know that I'm defenseless to her charms and wiles again.

She'll be fine, I tell myself again, but the unease gnaws at me, refusing to let go.

I go into my study and pour myself a glass of whiskey. It's far too early for it, but fuck it. The burn of it down my throat does little to settle the anxiety in my chest. I pace, the glass in my hand forgotten as I run over every interaction from the night before. The words I threw at her, the coldness in her eyes when she left the car, the way she stood in the rain like she wanted to dissolve into it.

I should have handled things differently. I know that. But knowing that doesn't make it any easier.

By lunchtime, the restlessness becomes unbearable. I head back upstairs and loiter outside her door. My hand hovers over the handle, but I can't bring myself to knock. Instead, I linger there pathetically for a few minutes longer before retreating, frustrated and thoroughly irritated with myself.

Dinner comes and goes, and I hear nothing from Nora. The house is quieter than usual, the silence pressing in on me from all sides. It feels wrong, oppressively wrong.

Finally, I give in. I stride down the hallway to Raven's door and knock firmly. There's no answer. My chest tightens, and without waiting, I twist the handle and push the door open.

The room is dim, the curtains drawn. Raven is curled up on the bed, her back to me, the duvet pulled up to her shoulders. Her breathing is steady but shallow, and the faint flush on her cheeks makes my heart skip. I step closer, the creak of the floorboards breaking the silence.

"Raven," I say softly, but there's no response.

She looks too pale, too sickly. I reach out and place a hand on her forehead. Her skin is hot—too hot. The knot in my stomach tightens as I kneel by the bed, my palm against her temple.

"Raven," I call again.

Her eyelids flutter, and she shifts slightly, her lips parting as though she's about to speak, but she only manages a weary sigh.

I press my palm against her cheek, feeling the heat radiating from her. "You're burning up," I mutter. I caused this.

Panic claws at my chest, but it's as though her vision suddenly clears, and finally, she realizes I'm in her room. Instantly, her entire demeanor changes. Light seems to come back to her eyes, but not in a good way. She struggles to sit up, and it's an unbelievably painful sight to see.

"Leave," she mumbles and pushes my hand away. "Leave, I don't want you here."

The moment causes a spasm of coughs to shake her body. Heart-wrenching coughs that require her to hold her chest. I remember how she was when she got pneumonia once. It started as a simple cold before it plunged her into days in bed.

"Leave," she says when the coughing subsides. "I don't want you here."

I realize there is nothing I can do for her but call the doctor. He will know what is best for her.

I take one last look at her stubborn pale face, then turn around and exit her bedroom.

CHAPTER 37

RAVEN

The door clicks shut, and the silence that follows is so complete I can hear myself breathing. I stay under the covers, curled in on myself, the warmth of the blanket doing little to thaw the cold hollow feeling in my chest. Every muscle in my body feels locked in place, like moving would shatter me into pieces too small to ever put back together.

I hate how his presence lingers even after he's gone, like a shadow creeping into every corner of my thoughts. I hate the way my skin still burns from his touch, no matter how much I loathe it. But most of all, I hate the way I still feel tethered to him, as if his absence is more terrible than his presence.

I bury my face deeper into the pillow and try to go back to sleep, but it doesn't work. I'm too aware of everything— my heartbeat pounding in my ears, the faint occasional gurgling noise of the central heating pipes, the soft rustle of the blanket every time I move. It all feels too loud, too much.

I scrunch my eyes closed, determined to will myself to sleep, but my mind won't stop racing. Everything that happened last night keeps replaying in my head, looping endlessly until I want to scream. My throat is dry and my eyes are burning with unshed tears, but all I can think of is how much I want him back here, next to me. But I won't call him back. I won't give him the satisfaction of knowing how totally he's broken me.

Minutes pass, maybe hours, and exhaustion presses down on me. My body feels hot and aches with the kind of weariness that no amount of sleep can fix. I need to get up, shower, and have a cold drink, but the thought of moving feels insurmountable. Instead, I stay where I am, hoping that if I stay still enough, the world will stop spinning around me.

But it doesn't. It never does.

Eventually, I hear the faint buzz of my phone vibrating on the nightstand. I don't want to look at it—I know it's probably just another message from someone I don't have the energy to respond to. But the persistent sound gnaws at me until I finally reach out, my hand shaking as I grab the phone.

The screen lights up with a string of notifications— missed calls and messages. The first one is from Sunny asking me about the big dance and wanting to know if she can stop by with a cake later that day. Her enthusiasm feels misplaced, a stark contrast to the heaviness in my chest.

Then I see a message from Charles.

Charles!

I stare in disbelief at his name. His message is brief, just enough to make my stomach tighten.

Something amazing has happened
I really need to talk to you.
Let's meet soon. Love, C

The absurdity of it almost makes me laugh. Charles—the man I left at the altar, the man I thought I'd never hear from again—wants to meet. What could he possibly have to say? Part of me wants to reply, to ask him what's so important, but I can't bring myself to. Not when I feel shitty and everything in my life feels so tragic. I can't bring another unstable variable to it. More than anything now, I need stability, comfort, and peace. I need to get better and go back to Mom and Dad.

With a sigh, I swipe away from his message and put the phone down. The truth is, I don't want to see anyone. I don't have the energy to pretend I'm okay, to smile and nod, and feign excitement for my newly married life that already feels like a disaster.

My thoughts drift back to Charles's message. For a fleeting moment, I wonder what might have happened if I'd married him. I would have found out that he is no longer wealthy, far from it, and he couldn't live to his side of the bargain. Would I have left immediately after he had broken my trust, or would I have stayed? Even though he was an ass to others, he was always kind to me.

Would I have ended up in this mansion anyway, trapped in a loveless marriage? I might have stayed with him, but not with him and his mother. I was really dreading living with her. None of that matters now. I've made my choice, and there's no going back.

A sudden chill runs through me, and I realize the blanket has slipped off my shoulders. I sit up, the room spinning slightly as I do. My stomach growls a sharp reminder that I haven't eaten all day. I know I need to, but even the thought of food makes me nauseous. My limbs feel heavy, my head foggy, and for a moment, I wonder if I can muster the strength to get out of bed at all.

Eventually, I force myself to move. The bathroom feels like a mile away, but I make it, clutching my phone as I go. The light is harsh, and I squint against it, leaning against the sink for support. My reflection in the mirror is not a pretty sight. Blotchy skin, dark circles under my eyes, and hair sticking to my damp forehead.

As I stare at my sickly, unattractive countenance, my mom calls.

I answer quickly, forcing my voice to sound bright and cheerful. "Hi, Mom."

"Hello, sweetheart," she replies. "You had your big Gala last night, didn't you? How was it?"

"It was great," I lie cheerfully.

"Are you not well? You don't sound too good."

"I'm fine," I invent. "Just had a bit much to drink. Maybe I'm tired too."

She pauses, and I can tell she's debating whether to tell me something.

"What is it, Mom?"

She takes a deep breath. "Raven, I wanted to let you know... your father's not doing too well."

The words hit me like a punch to the gut. I grab the edge of the sink and hold on tight. "What do you mean? What happened?"

She hesitates, her voice trembling. "His treatment... there are complications. The doctors are concerned about his heart. They think it's related to the stress on his body from the thyroid cancer and the medication. They're adjusting his treatment plan, but..."

"But what?" I ask, my chest tightening.

"It's serious," she admits softly. "They're doing everything they can, but they've warned us to prepare for the worst, just in case."

For a moment, I can't speak. The space feels too small, the air too thin. "What?"

"I'm sorry, honey, I didn't—

"Why didn't you tell me sooner?" I whisper, my voice breaking.

"I didn't want to worry you," she says, and I can hear the guilt in her voice. "You've been through so much lately... I thought we could handle it. But now... I think you should come."

I nod, even though she can't see me. "I'll be there as soon as I can."

"Take care of yourself first, Raven," she says gently. "You don't sound well, and the last thing we need is for you to get worse."

I promise her I'll rest, but as the call ends, I know I won't. My father is all I can think about now, his stubborn pride, and his refusal to seek help until it was too late. The thought of losing him is unbearable, and for the first time in years, I feel truly helpless.

I sink to the floor, my back against the wall, tears streaming down my face. Not this too. This is just too much. The phone slips from my hand, and I bury my face in my knees, wishing I could do something to fix everything that's wrong.

Eventually, I wipe the tears from my face, the motion shaky and clumsy as I try to gather myself. My chest feels tight, each breath shallow, but I force myself to stand. Be strong, I tell myself. Be strong for him.

I wipe the tears from my face, forcing myself to stand despite the weakness in my legs. The cold bathroom tiles feel like they are freezing my feet as I quickly return to my room. My fingers tremble as I call for a taxi. I'm in luck, there is a taxi cruising back from another job and can be with me in five minutes. Grabbing my purse, I pull on a coat and rush to the door. My heart pounds in my chest, each beat a mix of desperation and exhaustion. I don't care how late it is or how weak I feel. My father needs me.

As I cross the foyer, I feel the chill of the house rush into my open coat and seep through my thin nightgown. My mind is in a haze, too frantic to think clearly, but as I reach the front door, something clicks. Something is not right. I stop in my tracks, glance down and realize with a sinking feeling that I'm still in my house slippers—no proper shoes to shield me from the wintry wind blowing outside.

For a moment, I hesitate. My fingers clutch my purse and I consider going back to grab my boots. But the thought of going all the way up those stairs again in my condition. No. Anyway, the taxi has arrived outside, and every second feels like a wasted eternity.

As I open the front door, Nora's voice stops me. "Mrs. Jackson!" she calls out.

I grip the doorknob tightly and turn to face her. "Mrs. Jackson, where are you going? You're not dressed for this weather!" Her voice is laced with concern, her eyes wide as she approaches.

"I'm fine, Nora. I'm just going to see my dad. He's not well," I say with as much bravado as I can muster, but my voice sounds hollow, unconvincing, even to my own ears.

"Mrs. Jackson, wait—"

But I don't give her a chance to finish. Pushing the door open, I step into the biting cold. The wind hits me like a slap, harsh and unrelenting. My slip and open coat do nothing to shield me, and I shiver violently as I rush down the steps. I hear Nora calling after me, but I don't stop. I can't.

The driver steps out gallantly to open the door for me. "Are you all right?" he asks, frowning at my state.

"I'm fine. Please just drive as quickly as you can to the hospital," I plead, climbing into the backseat.

The warmth of the car is a relief, but the cold has already seeped into my bones, and I can't stop trembling. I clutch my purse tightly in my lap, my fingers stiff and numb. The driver pulls away and I let out a shaky breath and try to steady myself.

I don't want to arrive in such a state that my mother starts worrying about me.

The streets are eerily quiet, the wind howling as it whips through the town. Snow flurries dance in the air. I watch them through the window with a strange detachment.

A harsh cough escapes my lips, and I press a hand to my chest, wincing at the sharp pain that follows. The cold has settled deep, each breath feeling heavier than the last. I ignore it, willing my body to cooperate. There's no room for weakness now.

The driver glances at me in the rearview mirror, his brows furrowed. "You sure, you're okay, Miss?"

"Yes, just a little cough. Don't worry it's not catching," I reply with a small smile.

But I'm not fine. The truth is, I feel worse with every passing second. The chill in my chest spreads, a suffocating feeling that makes it harder to breathe. I try to focus on the countryside flashing by, anything to distract myself from my growing physical discomfort.

I think of my poor father, his face, lined with age and worry. His hands, calloused from years of hard work. The thought of him lying in a hospital bed, fighting for his life, makes my chest tighten further.

The idea of losing my father is unbearable.

Tears blur my vision again, and this time, I don't bother to wipe them away. Let them fall. Let the cold take me if it

243

must. All that matters is getting to him. All that matters is being there.

CHAPTER 38

EARL

https://www.youtube.com/watch?v=uxk7aSCLj4g
-don't leave me this way-

I try to focus on construction plans that all seem meaningless and cannot hold my attention. The numbers blur, replaced by flashes of Raven's white face filled with hate as she lay in her bed. She hates me now. I killed any feeling she might have had for me. The thought causes an agonizing hurt in my chest. Why? Why did I do it?

I pick up my pen again. I've called the doctor and he made some noises about not doing house calls on Sundays, but I gave him such a tongue bruising he promised to come in about an hour. Until then I will force myself to do some work.

The knock on the door startles me. "Come in," I call, standing up. Maybe it's Raven. Maybe she's come to, after all.

Nora steps in hesitantly, her hands wringing together. The moment I see her face, I know something is wrong. "Mr. Jackson, Mrs. Jackson has left the house."

My pen clatters onto the desk. "What do you mean, left?" My voice is low, dangerous.

"She rushed out," Nora stammers. "Barely dressed, Mr. Jackson. In her slippers. Not even proper shoes. I—I tried to stop her, but she said she needed to see her father. She said he's not well. She wouldn't listen."

The words hit me like a punch to the chest. "No shoes?" I repeat, rising to my feet. "It's freezing outside, and she's already sick. What were you thinking, letting her go like that?"

"I tried," she says, her voice trembling. "But she wouldn't stop."

Panic rises in my chest, but I shove it down, burying it beneath a thin veneer of control. My mind races, trying to piece together her actions. She's gone to see her father? What's happened to him?

For a fleeting, bitter moment, a thought claws its way to the surface: maybe she's left me. Maybe this is her way out, but I shake it off. No. She wouldn't leave like this—frantic, unprepared. This isn't about me.

"Thanks, Nora. I'll take care of it now."

She nods and retreats quickly. The door clicks shut, leaving me alone with my spiraling thoughts.

I grab my phone and call her, but she doesn't answer. I have her parents's old number, but not since they moved. I try to think of what other numbers I could reach her on and I recall Sunny, her best friend. It's easy to find her; I know the location of her bakery and their website. A quick search and I'm able to extract Sunny's number. Instantly, I place a call, my fingers tap the screen agitatedly. It rings twice before she answers. "Muffin House, can I help you?"

"Hey, it's Earl," I say, trying to keep my voice steady despite the knot tightening in my chest.

Surprise and panic is immediately evident in her tone. "Oh, Earl! What's going on? Is something wrong with Raven?"

"She just left the house without her shoes to see her father. Has she called you? Do you know what's going on with her father?"

There's a pause on the line, the faint rustle of movement before her suspicious and accusing reply. "No, she hasn't called and as far as I know her father is supposed to be getting treatment. But why would she leave like that? Did something happen? Did you do something to her?"

"Look, Sunny, she's been lying in bed quite ill and now she's rushed out in the cold to see her father," I grit out, pacing the room. "Can you help me find out what is going on? Or at least give me her parents number."

"Let me try calling her first. Just hold the line."

She puts me on hold, the seconds stretching into an eternity. My free hand curls into a fist at my side. When Sunny comes back on the line, her voice is somber. "I couldn't reach her, but here's her mom's number."

"Thank you, that will be incredibly helpful."

She gives me the number, and I thank her before quickly hanging up and dialing Raven's mother. The phone rings several times before her soft voice answers.

"Hello?"

"Mrs. Moore, it's Earl," I say, the words tumbling out in a rush. "Raven just left the house to go over to you, but she said something about her father not being well to the housekeeper. Can you tell me what's going on?"

"Oh, dear," she breathes, her voice laced with worry. "Yes, her father experienced a severe drop in calcium levels due to the treatment. The doctors believe it's manageable with supplements and monitoring, but it caused muscle spasms and a brief loss of consciousness earlier today. I told Raven, and I think it really upset her."

"Oh, I see," I say slowly. "I'm sorry to hear that." I understand now why Raven was so panicked.

The image of Raven hearing this and rushing out into the winter weather, unprepared and vulnerable, ignites a fresh wave of worry and fear in me. "Is he stable now?"

"Not exactly," she assures me quickly. "The doctors have started him on calcium supplements, so now we just have to wait, but I imagine it must have shaken Raven to hear it. I'm at the hospital and she isn't here yet."

"Alright," I tell her. "She's feeling quite unwell and I believe she isn't dressed properly, so please monitor her as well and take care of her."

"Of course, I'll take care of her. She's my only daughter."

"Thank you, Mrs. Moore. I will call again in about an hour," I tell her and end the call.

Once I hang up I call the doctor and tell him the change of plans. I ask him to be on standby instead. He seems happier to hear the news. I toss the phone onto the desk and stare at the wall. The thought of Raven out in the freezing cold with no shoes gnaws at me. My foot taps restlessly against the floor. She's stubborn, but she's not invincible.

I push away from the desk and head upstairs, my gut twisting with worry. Her room is dark, and her bed is already cold. I brush a hand over the rumpled sheets, a mix of regret and helplessness clawing at me.

For a long while, I simply stand rooted to the spot, staring at the empty space. All that hate … where did it go? It's shocking I care this much. I pretend to hate her, but deep down, I know the truth: if something happens to her, I'll never forgive myself.

I sit on the edge of the bed and drop my head into my hands. All I can do now is wait.

CHAPTER 39

RAVEN

*T*he hospital corridor feels colder than the icy wind outside, the fluorescent lights harsh and sterile. I push open the door to my father's room after taking forever to find him, and the sight of him lying pale and still in the hospital bed squeezes the breath out of my chest. My mom is sitting in the corner, her phone in hand, concluding a call. She glances up at me, her face softening, but there's exhaustion in her eyes.

I don't say anything, my throat is tight with emotion, as I hurry to his bedside. He's asleep, his chest rising and falling with a gentle rhythm. I lean over and gently press a kiss to his forehead, the warmth of his skin a small reassurance. Tears well up in my eyes as I lean closer to him. I'm so tired and so cold, but seeing him like this reminds me how much I love him, how much I miss him, and how desperately I need him to be okay.

My mom comes to my side, her gaze sweeping over me.

Her lips press into a thin line of disapproval as she takes in my outfit—or lack thereof. "Raven," she says softly but with an edge of exasperation, "why would you come out dressed like this? It's freezing outside."

I shake my head, not trusting myself to speak.

"Sit down," she murmurs, guiding me to a chair. I obey, too drained to argue, and sink into the seat. She sighs and steps out of the room briefly, returning moments later with a blanket. She drapes it over my shoulders and tucks it around me, her hands warm against my chilled skin.

"Tell me about Dad," I manage, my voice a rasp. My chest aches with every word.

"Look at you. You're not well, Raven. I don't know why you came here like this. It's not like you can do anything for him."

I start coughing and she looks at me, her face lined with worry and exasperation. Then she leaves the room again, and when she comes back, she's holding a paper cup of steaming tea. I wrap my hands around it, the heat sinking into my fingers and chasing away some of the cold.

She perches on the edge of the bed, watching me for a moment before telling me about my father's calcium levels dropping to dangerously low levels. "It started with muscle spasms—his hands cramped so badly he couldn't move them. Then, earlier today, he collapsed. The doctors ran some tests and found his levels were critically low. They've started him on supplements and are keeping him under observation."

"Will he be okay?" I ask, my voice trembling. I need her to say yes, even if it's a lie.

"They're optimistic," she replies, coming over to me and brushing a strand of hair from my face. "His levels are improving, and they're confident he'll stabilize with the treatment. But it scared him, Raven. It scared me."

I nod, tears spilling over again. "I should've been here," I whisper, guilt clawing at my chest, not going to a stupid party.

Her hand squeezes mine. "You're here now, sweetheart. That's what matters."

I glance back at my father, his face is serene despite the machines beeping softly around him. The sight brings no comfort, only the sharp ache of fear and love tangled together. All I can think about is how fragile he looks, how close he came to... I can't even finish the thought. I won't.

"He looks so weak," I whisper.

"He is," she admits. "But he's fighting back. He's strong, Raven, and so are we."

The words are meant to reassure me, but right at this moment, I don't feel strong at all. I sip the tea, the warmth doing little to soothe the tight cold knot in my chest.

"I just want him to be okay," I say desperately, my voice breaking. I can't even begin to explain how impossible it would be for me to deal with his loss at this time in my life.

My mom's eyes shimmer with unshed tears. "He will be," she says.

And I cling to the words, fragile as they are, like a lifeline.

My mom adjusts the blanket around my shoulders as if I'm still the child she used to bundle up during snowstorms. Her lips press into a thin line as she studies me, and I know she sees past the surface.

"I just spoke to Earl," she says softly, the words making my heart jump. "He was worried about you running out the way you did."

I glance at her sharply, blinking in surprise. "Earl? You spoke to Earl?" I repeat, the name heavy in my mouth.

She nods, watching me closely. "He called to make sure you were okay."

The air between us feels charged, and I don't know what to do with it. My thoughts are too scattered, my emotions fraying at the edges. Why would he call? Why would he care? My surprise quickly gives way to anger. After last night, what right does he have to act concerned?

I shake my head sharply as if I can physically push him out of my mind. "Of course, I'm all right," I mutter, dismissing her words. "I don't want to talk about him."

Her brows knit together, her concern deepening. "Is everything okay between you two?"

"Yeah, everything is fine." My tone is clipped, leaving no room for further discussion. "I just want to focus on Dad, right now, Mom."

She doesn't look convinced but lets it drop, instead pulling a chair closer to the bed and settling in beside me. The minutes stretch on, filled with the quiet hum of machines and the occasional murmur of nurses outside. I barely register the passage of time, too consumed with watching my father's face and listening to the uneven rhythm of his breathing.

I must have fallen asleep in the chair because I'm startled awake by the dull vibration of my phone on the bedside table. My pulse quickens, and for a moment, I'm disoriented. I grab it, squinting at the screen in the dim light. Earl.

The name flashes like a beacon, and I stare at it, debating. My fingers hover over the screen, but the anger simmering in my chest holds me back. I let it ring, the sound cutting through the stillness like a reprimand.

Minutes later, another vibration—a text. I hesitate before opening it, my breath catching when I see his message.

I'm outside your father's room. I don't want to intrude on your parents' privacy. Let me know if it's okay for me to come in or if you'd rather step out.

The words sink in strangely, and I have to read them again just to be sure. He's here? My mind sluggishly tries to process what this means. He came all this way? Why? For what? The shock of it nearly eclipses my anger at him, but not entirely. I set the phone down, staring at it like it's something foreign.

I glance at the closed door, half expecting him to walk through it despite his message. The thought makes my stomach twist. I'm furious that he's here, furious that he thinks he can insert himself into this moment after everything that's happened. But I can't deny the flicker of something else beneath the anger. A small weak flicker of hope.

I pull the blanket tighter around me. My mom stirs slightly but doesn't wake. Just for a few moments, I focus on my father, on the sound of his breathing, on anything but the man waiting outside the door.

CHAPTER 40

EARL

*T*he hospital corridor is eerily quiet at this hour, the fluorescent lights casting a cold, sterile glow that only amplifies the feeling of guilt inside me. I stand just outside her father's room, peering through the narrow glass window in the door.

Raven didn't come out. She simply put the phone down and slumped deeper into the chair and almost immediately fell back to sleep. Under the blanket tight her body is curled into itself as if she's trying to shield herself from the world. Her exhaustion is palpable as her chest rises and falls slowly as she drifts in and out of a restless sleep. The dim light accentuates the shadows under her eyes.

I've never seen her like this before. She's always been a force of nature, strong-willed and defiant, even in the face of chaos. But now? Now, she looks so fragile it makes my heart ache. She's still so beautiful, even in sickness, but that only makes the guilt twist harder in my stomach.

I've done this to her.

I've been so wrapped up in my anger, my need to punish her for the past, that I've ignored what she's been carrying.

My phone vibrates softly in my pocket, but I don't look at it. My focus stays on her, on the faint furrow of her brow as she shifts slightly in her seat. My gaze shifts to her father. He's lying pale and still, the machines around him humming softly as they monitor his condition.

I've avoided her parents for so long, not out of malice but because I couldn't face them. They've always been kind to me, treating me like family. And now, seeing him like this, I'm ashamed about how I've acted. I should have been here for him, for her. I should have done more.

I step away from the door and lean against the cool wall.

She's sick. I can see it in the way she moves, sluggish and weak, but knowing her, she'll ignore and carry on as if nothing is wrong with her. This mule-headed stubbornness is usually a mixture of infuriation and endearment, but right now, it's terrifying. She won't let herself rest, not while her father is like this. She'll push herself until she breaks.

I pull my phone out and type another message, my fingers hesitating over the screen. The words feel inadequate, but it's all I can do right now.

Please take care of yourself.
Check on that cold before it gets worse.
I'll be back later for you.

I send it before I can overthink, the soft buzz in my hand signaling its delivery. I glance again through the narrow glass and see her phone vibrating on the table beside her. She stirs slightly, her eyes fluttering open for a brief moment. She looks at the screen, her expression unreadable, before letting her eyes drift closed again. She's too exhausted to even pick up the phone.

I know she knows it's a message from me, and yet she can't be bothered to even look at it. The rejection stings, but how can I blame her? I've been such a beast. Why should she trust me? Why should she let me in? I turn and walk away, my footsteps echoing softly in the empty corridor. Each step feels heavier than the last, the dark cloud of my remorse and regret pressing down on me.

I step outside, the icy unforgiving wind cuts through my jacket, but I inhale the cold air deeply. It helps to clear my head. I glance back at the hospital, the warm glow of the lights spilling onto the pavement. She's in there, fighting her own battle, and all I can do is pray I haven't pushed her past the brink.

The town is quiet, blanketed by the stillness and by the time I get home, it's late. I head straight to Raven's room, unable to shake the image of her slumped in that chair, barely holding herself together.

I push the door open, and the state of the room stops me in my tracks. Her dress from earlier is crumpled on the floor, damp and wrinkled. The bed is unmade, the blanket half-hanging off the side. A cup of tea sits abandoned on the bedside table, its contents untouched and cold. The air feels stale as if it's holding onto the exhaustion she left behind. It's a mess, a stark contrast to how she usually keeps things, and it feels like a snapshot of her state of mind—disordered, neglected, overwhelmed.

I take a deep breath and pull out my phone and call Nora. She answers after a few rings, her voice groggy but attentive. I'm already pacing as I speak, the words tumbling out too fast.

"Can you get a couple of maids to come up to my wife's

room?" I ask. "I need her room cleaned. A dress needs to be sent to the dry cleaners, and the bed made properly. Bring a heavier blanket and make sure the heating is turned up. It's freezing in here."

"Of course," she replies without hesitation, her professionalism cutting through the tension in my voice.

She arrives alone carrying a thick, folded blanket, sheets, and a basket of cleaning materials.

"I didn't bother the maids. This is easy work. I'll get on it," she says.

She moves with practiced efficiency, her presence grounding me in a way I didn't expect. She starts by tidying the bedside table, discarding the cold tea and wiping down the surface. Then she starts stripping the bed. The air in the room seems to shift, becoming lighter and more bearable.

I stand in the doorway, arms crossed, watching her work. The sight of the room being put back in order brings a strange sense of relief, and then I decide to join in, helping her tuck in the fresh sheets. It feels like such a small thing in the grand scheme of everything, but it's something tangible, something I can do for her.

Nora smiles at me. "Thank you, Mr. Jackson."

"Thank you, Nora. I'll have to see about giving you a raise next month."

She beams at me, then moves towards the bathroom. A few minutes later, she comes back out. "All done. Is there anything else, Mr. Jackson?" Nora asks. Her voice is warm and kind and it pulls me out of my thoughts.

I shake my head and smile at her. "No. That's all. Thank you."

She hesitates, her gaze lingering on me. "She'll be alright, you know," she says gently as if she can see the worry etched into my face. "She's young and strong."

I don't respond. The words stick in my throat, too heavy to form. I simply nod, and she leaves, the sound of the door closing behind her echoing in the quiet.

The room feels too empty, too quiet. I'm used to Raven's inimitable presence filling the space, her positive energy, her stubborn determination. Without her, it's like the house has lost its heartbeat.

I settle onto the sofa in the corner of the room, unable to leave. My eyes scan the now-tidy space, landing on the freshly made bed, the folded blanket at the foot. It's all ready for her, but there's no guarantee she'll come back. I lean back against the sofa, my hands gripping the edges. What if I've lost her forever? The minutes stretch into hours, each one more unbearable than the last.

Eventually, exhaustion takes over and I drag myself to my own room, collapsing on the bed without bothering to change. Sleep doesn't come easily, though. The image of her, so small and tired in that hospital chair, stays with me, haunting me as the night stretches on. And in the background the pitiful sound of her father's labored breathing—it all replays in my mind, over and over.

I glance at my phone on the nightstand, tempted to text her again. To check on her, to make sure she's okay. But I know she won't respond. Even if she was awake, she's too stubborn, too angry, and I've done too much damage for her to let me in again so easily. I just hope she is sleeping.

The hours tick by until I give up on sleep entirely. I return to her room, sitting on the edge of the bed, my head in my hands. The weight of my mistakes, my regrets and my fear of losing her for good presses down on me. I don't know how to fix this. I don't even know if I can.

But I know one thing: I'll do whatever it takes to try.

CHAPTER 41

RAVEN

I wake up to the sound of my mom's soft but firm voice. She's standing at the foot of my father's bed, her arms crossed and her face set in that determined expression I know too well. "Raven," she says, her voice brooking no argument. "You need to go home and rest. You're no good to anyone if you make yourself sick."

I shake my head, sitting up straighter in the chair beside my dad. "I'm fine," I insist, my voice hoarse and unconvincing. The truth is, my body aches, my head feels heavy, and every breath seems to scrape against my chest. But I'm not ready to leave.

She steps closer, her gaze softening as she places a hand on my shoulder. "Honey, please. Just go home, get a change of clothes, and rest for a little while. You can come back later, but right now, you're running yourself into the ground for no reason. You're not helping your father by becoming sick yourself."

I want to argue, to tell her that I need to be here for Dad, but the exhaustion is too much. Reluctantly, I nod. "Fine. I'll go home, but only for a little while."

"By the way, Earl brought you shoes and a change of warm clothes."

I stare at my mother in astonishment. "He did?"

She smiles. "Yeah. That's what husbands do for their wives."

I take a deep breath. "Yup. I guess so."

The cold air outside makes me shiver as I step out of the hospital and into the taxi. By the time I get home, I'm trembling, my breaths coming in shallow gasps. I force myself up the stairs and into the shower, hoping the hot water will help. Instead, it's the final straw. My legs feel weak, and I barely make it to the bed before collapsing, my head is spinning and my chest feels so tight it feels as if I can barely breathe.

Nora's voice pulls me from a restless haze. "You need to eat something," she says gently, placing a tray of food on the bedside table. Her concern is evident in her voice.

I manage a few bites of soup, its warmth comforting me as it slides down my throat. But even lifting the spoon feels like an effort, and eventually, I lie back down, too drained to argue when she fusses over the duvet and turns up the thermostat of the heater. The room grows warmer, but the chill in my bones refuses to leave.

A sharp knock on the door comes later, startling me out of a half-sleep. The sound feels louder than it should, reverberating in my pounding head. I open my eyes to see the local doctor stepping in.

"Hello, Raven," he says.

"Hello, Doctor," I croak. "I'm actually pretty fine. Probably just need a couple of days of bed rest."

"Well, someone looks like they are feeling poorly and it's not me."

His examination is brisk but thorough, and the look on his face when he's done confirms what I already suspect.

"You're not fine, Raven," he says firmly. "You have pneumonia. If you don't rest and let us treat you properly, this could get very serious."

"I can't," I protest weakly, my voice barely above a whisper. "I have to go back to the hospital. My dad needs me."

"Your mother told me to tell you that your dad is doing much better," another voice says from the doorway. I look around to see Earl standing there, his arms crossed and his jaw tight. His presence is imposing, as always, but there's a deep concern and anxiety in his eyes that makes me falter. "She also said he's stable and getting the treatment he needs. The person who's in danger right now is you, Raven."

Anger flares despite my fatigue. "I don't need you to tell me what to do," I snap, turning my face away from him. The sharpness of my tone doesn't mask the exhaustion behind it, and I hate how vulnerable it makes me feel.

"You're staying here," he says firmly, his tone leaving no room for argument. "You need to let yourself heal."

The doctor nods in agreement before turning to me. "He's right. Pneumonia is no laughing matter, child. You must carefully take all medications I'm prescribing. He scribbles something on his pad and gives it to Earl before leaving.

Earl doesn't move from the doorway, his eyes still fixed on me. There's something unreadable in his expression, a mixture of frustration and worry.

I turn away from him and he crosses the room and sits on the edge of the bed. For a moment, he doesn't say anything, he just watches me with an intensity that confuses me. Then, without warning, he leans down and wraps his arms around me. The gesture is unexpected, and for a moment, I stiffen, unsure of how to respond.

The warmth of his embrace seeps into me, melting the tension in my body. The exhaustion catches up to me all at once, and I let the tears I've been holding back finally fall.

"I'm scared," I whisper against his chest, my voice cracking. "What if something happens to Dad?"

"Nothing's going to happen," he says softly, his voice a low rumble that vibrates against my cheek. "Your dad is strong, and so are you. I'm going to fly in a specialist tomorrow, but you have to promise to take care of yourself too."

I nod eagerly. "Yes, I will. Help him, Earl. Help him."

"I will," he says quietly.

We stay like that for what feels like hours, the silence broken only by the sound of my ragged breathing. His arms tighten around me, grounding me and eventually, exhaustion wins, and I drift off, lulled by the steady rhythm of his heartbeat.

The nightmare comes sometime during the night.

I'm back at the hospital, but everything is wrong. The walls are on fire, the flames licking up towards the ceiling. Smoke fills the air, suffocating and blinding me. I see my dad's bed engulfed in flames, the machines around him sparking and crackling. I try to reach him, but my legs feel like they're moving through quicksand.

When I turn, Earl is there, but he's too far away. His face is twisted in pain, and before I can call out to him, a deafening crash sounds as the floor beneath him gives way. He falls into the darkness, his outstretched hand disappearing into the void.

I wake with a start, screaming, my chest heaving and my face wet with tears. The room is dark, the only light coming from the faint glow of the bedside lamp. The terror of the dream is still clawing at me and I flail wildly. Before I can fully process where I am, I feel strong arms wrap around me, pulling me close. I can't tell if they are real or part of the nightmare.

"It's okay," Earl's voice murmurs in my ear, steady and reassuring. "You're safe. I've got you."

I clutch at him desperately, my sobs shaking both of us. "Don't leave," I whisper, my voice breaking. "Please don't leave."

"I'm here and I'm not going anywhere," he promises, holding me tighter. His warmth surrounds me, and for the first time in what feels like forever, I believe him. The fear and the nightmare fade into the background, replaced by the steady comfort and safety of his strong presence.

CHAPTER 42

EARL

She feels so small in my arms, so fragile, that I'm terrified I might break her just by holding on too tightly. But I can't let go—not ever. Her body shakes as the last of her sobs fade into quiet sniffles, and when she finally relaxes against me, I settle her back into the bed and pull the soft blankets around her like a cocoon. She's too weak to protest, her head lolling against my chest as I tuck her in.

Her hair is damp from sweat, sticking to her forehead, and I brush it back gently, my fingers trembling. Watching her fight this sickness has been unbearable. She's been slipping in and out of restless sleep, her breaths labored and shallow, and I've been powerless to do anything but stay by her side. It's a kind of helplessness I've never known before, and it's shredding me from the inside out. I can't take my eyes off her; every rise and fall of her chest feels like a victory and a warning all at once.

"You need to rest," I whisper, more to myself than to her.

Her eyelids flutter, but she doesn't open them. I don't move, afraid to disturb her as I cradle her like a child. My mind races with every mistake I've made, every moment I've hurt her, and the weight of my shame feels like it might crush me. The memory of every cutting word, every instance when I pushed her away, crashes down on me now.

And all for what?

To protect my pride?

To convince myself that I can live without her?

But I can't. I never could. Even if she doesn't love me, even if she only stays with me because she needs the security my money can provide, she's still mine. My gold digger, my everything. I've always known it, deep down, but it took seeing her like this—so breakable, so close to slipping away—to admit it to myself.

Without her, nothing else matters.

The door creaks open, and Nora comes in, balancing a tray of food. She glances at me, her expression softening when she sees the way Raven is curled against me.

"The poor mite needs to eat," she says gently, setting the tray down on the bedside table.

I nod, shifting Raven slightly so she's propped up against the pillows. "Raven," I murmur, brushing my thumb across her cheek. "Wake up. You need to eat something."

Her eyes flutter open, glassy and unfocused, and she groans softly. "I'm not hungry," she mumbles.

"You have to try," I insist, lifting the bowl of soup from the tray. Nora hands me a spoon, and I hold it to Raven's lips. She resists at first, turning her face away, but eventually, she relents and takes a small, reluctant amount.

"Good," I say softly, offering her another spoonful. "Just a little more."

When the bowl is half-empty, she leans back against the

pillows, her eyes closing again. I set the tray aside and press a kiss to her forehead. "Rest now," I whisper.

* * *

THE HOURS BLUR together as I stay by her side. The light shifts outside, moving from dim gray to full dark, and from full dark to dim gray back to light, but I don't move. When Nora brings fresh clothes, I help Raven to the bathroom, supporting her trembling frame as she shuffles across the room. She's too weak to bathe herself, so I fill the tub and gently guide her in. Her cheeks flush with embarrassment as I roll up my sleeves and kneel beside the tub, but she doesn't protest.

"Just relax," I tell her, dipping a soft sponge into the soapy water. I run it over her arms and shoulders, careful not to press too hard. Her tension eases gradually, her head leaning back against the edge of the tub as I work. When I move to wash her hair, she closes her eyes, letting me massage the shampoo into her scalp.

"You're doing great," I say softly, rinsing the suds away.

She doesn't respond, but the corners of her lips twitch, almost a smile. It's a small victory, but it's enough to keep me going.

When the bath is over, I wrap her in a warm towel, dry her off, dress her and use the hairdryer on her hair. Meanwhile, Nora has already had the maids to change the sheets and air the room while she was in the bath. The heat is turned up too. Raven looks a little less pale, a little less fragile.

She sits at the small table in the corner, and I hand her the dose of medicine the doctor prescribed.

"Here you go," I say, watching as she swallows it with a grimace.

Nora sends food, enough for both of us. Raven glances at me, her brow furrowed. "What about you?" she asks quietly.

"I'll eat later," I say, but she shakes her head.

"No," she says firmly. "Eat now. Nora has clearly made for both of us. See two plates and two sets of cutlery."

We eat together quietly. It's a truce. A pleasant state of affairs. Tender, even. The occasional clink of utensils fills the room, a comforting rhythm against the backdrop of her recovery.

Nora returns a few minutes later with some kind of gooey-in-the-middle dessert. Not really my thing, but Raven seems to enjoy it. As she eats, I watch her hungrily. She seems thinner. But there is definitely more color in her cheeks.

"How's the project?" she asks suddenly, her voice still weak but curious. "The mall renovation one you're working on."

I hesitate. I don't usually talk about my work, but the way she's looking at me—earnest and attentive—makes me relent. "It's going well," I say casually. "We're ahead of schedule, and I'm happy with the progress so far."

She nods, a faint smile tugging at her lips. "That's good," she murmurs, her eyes growing heavy. "I'd never have thought you'd be involved in real estate and construction and making this little town a better place, but it suits you."

Then she sinks back into the pillows, her eyes closing. All in all, her words make me smile, and they make me feel proud. She falls asleep quickly, her breathing steady and even. I stay for a while, making sure she's deeply asleep before slipping out of the room.

I make my way to the music room and stand in front of

the portrait I commissioned, the one I'd intended to use as a weapon, a way to humiliate her. I see how she must have seen it and it makes my body convulse with shame. Only a truly ugly person could have thought to do such a thing. I have become ugly. So ugly I don't look much in the mirror anymore. Even I can't bear the sight of me.

But this painting is not her. And it's not me. It is an aberration. A season of hate did that.

I rush to the painting, rip it down from the wall, and break the frame with my bare hands until it is a heap of gilded wood and crumpled canvas. There are chips everywhere. But even throwing it away isn't enough. I need to destroy it, to burn away the anger and bitterness that have poisoned everything between us.

I take the broken heap to the backyard and chuck it near the fire pit. The match flares to life in my hand. I hold it to the edge of the canvas. The flames catch quickly, consuming the image of her with an almost beautiful ferocity. I watch it burn, the heat warming my face as the last remnants of my resentment turn to ash.

I feel lighter. The anger is gone, replaced by something raw and fragile but undeniably real. It's time to start over, to build something new from the ruins of what I've destroyed.

This time, I won't let anything come between us.

CHAPTER 43

RAVEN

https://www.youtube.com/watch?v=qLfqA2igdUI
-sweet dreams are made of this-

I wake up suddenly from the edges of a restless sleep. My eyes flutter open, and I immediately notice the dim glow of flickering light painting the walls of my bedroom. My heart quickens with panic. Something's wrong. I feel it in my chest. Even the room seems colder. I sit up and clutching a blanket tightly around me, I move toward the window, the source of the light.

Pressing my palm to the icy glass, I squint into the darkness. The yard is bathed in the orange hue of flames. My breath catches when I see Earl—tall, motionless, his face lit by the fire consuming broken bits of wood and a canvas.

The sight sends a shiver down my spine, not from the cold or the raw intensity of his stance, but because I know exactly what he is burning.

The blanket falls away from my shoulders and my knees nearly buckle. "The painting?" I whisper, trying to make sense of it.

Why is he doing this? What does it really mean?

Suddenly, he turns his head and looks up at me. He looks at me as if he's seeing a ghost. His expression is agonized. For a long moment, we stare at each other.

Then I retreat to the bed and sit on the edge, my hands clasped tightly together. My chest feels tight, my breaths come in shallow gasps. Earl, what are you letting go of?

Then the door opens, and I glance up sharply. Earl steps inside, his eyes look at me as if nothing else in the world matters to him. The faint scent of smoke clings to him, mingling with the cooler air of the room.

I don't speak. I can't. The warmth of him feels like a balm against the raw ache inside me. He moves, the light from the hallway framing him like a halo.

He walks to the fallen blanket, picks it up and approaches me. When he stops in front of me, I can feel the heat radiating from his body. Gently, he places the blanket around my shoulders. The tension is thick, almost overpowering, but I don't pull away. My fingers clutch the soft wool tightly as if bracing for something I dare not name. Dare not hope for.

"Are you alright?," he asks, his voice soft but laced with something deeper, something that stirs the air between us like a tangible thing.

I nod, my throat too tight to form words. Instead, I reach up my hand, my fingers brushing lightly against his chest. His breath hitches, and for a moment, we're both frozen, caught in the wonder of each other.

Then I rise to my feet, the blanket slipping from my shoulders to pool at my feet. The cold air brushes against my skin, but I don't care. All I can focus on is him—on the way his eyes darken as they roam over me, on the way his chest rises and falls with each unsteady breath.

I step closer, my hands finding their way to the hem of his shirt. "I never thought the smell of smoke would be such a turn-on," I whisper.

He shakes his head. "You should rest." His voice is resolute.

But he doesn't stop me as I lift his shirt over his head, revealing the lean, strong lines of his body. My hands glide over his skin, the warmth of him is beautiful.

"Raven," he warns, but his voice is a husky murmur.

I silence any further protests with a kiss. Soft and tentative at first, but the moment he responds, everything shifts. His arms wrap around me, pulling me flush against him, and the kiss deepens, igniting a fire that burns hotter than the one outside.

He tries to pull back, his hands gripping my arms as if to steady himself. "You're not well enough," he breathes, his voice strained.

"I'm well enough for this. Let's make a deal. You do all the hard work and I'll just lie back and enjoy myself," I reply, my lips brushing against his.

But he hesitates.

"I need you. Please."

Something in him snaps when he hears me beg. He scoops me up in one fluid motion and carries me to the bed. The world tilts as he lays me down gently, his body hovering over mine.

The air between us crackles with anticipation as I reach for him, my fingers trailing down his chest. He shudders under my touch, his restraint unraveling with every second.

"Raven, baby," he murmurs, his voice thick with emotion.

"It's been so long since I heard you call me that," I whisper, guiding his hands to the hem of my gown.

He hesitates for a heartbeat, his eyes searching mine, but then he gives in. The gown slips over my head, and his hands follow, exploring every inch of me with reverence.

When he leans down, pressing his lips to my collarbone, a soft gasp escapes me. His kisses are a sinner's kisses, slow, deliberate, each one a confession, a silent apology, and a promise to do better.

My hands tangle in his hair, pulling him closer as his lips trail lower. His breath against my skin sends a shiver down my spine, and I arch into him, needing more.

"Oh baby," he groans, his voice breaking as his control slips further.

And the intensity of his gaze steals the breath from my lungs, and then he kisses me again, pouring every ounce of himself into it.

His lips are firm yet tender, the heat of his mouth igniting something primal within me. I cling to him as if letting go might shatter this fragile moment, my hands threading through his smoke-scented hair, tugging him closer.

His kisses move down the curve of my neck leaving a trail of fire in their wake. His fingers trace the outline of my collarbone, his touch reverent, as though he's memorizing the lay of my skin. When his lips close around the sensitive peak of my breast, a gasp escapes me. The sensation sends a delicious shiver racing down my spine.

My body arches into him, desperate for more.

But he doesn't rush. He lingers, his tongue flicking over the hardened nub, his teeth grazing just enough to drive me wild. A whimper escapes my lips, and I feel him smile against my skin, his hands splaying across my waist as if to steady me. The warmth of his breath against my bare skin makes goosebumps rise, and I can't stop trembling.

"You're perfect," he murmurs, his voice rough with emotion. "Every inch of you."

A mixture of vulnerability and longing swells inside me. He continues his journey, his lips exploring every curve, every hollow, every freckle and scar, as though they hold stories he's desperate to learn. His hands skim the length of my thighs, parting them gently, his gaze flicking up to meet mine.

There's a question in his eyes, a silent request for permission.

I nod and he leans forward, pressing his forehead against mine for a brief, heart-stopping moment before he claims my mouth again. The weight of his body settles over me, grounding me, and I can feel his need pressing against me, undeniable and urgent.

When his hard cock finally pushes into me, the world blurs at the edges. The stretch is exquisite, a perfect ache that steals the air from my lungs. I cry out, my nails digging into his shoulders. He kisses my temple, my cheeks, murmuring soothing words I can barely hear over the pounding of my heart.

"Tell me if it's too much," he whispers, his voice shaking. "I'll stop. I don't want to hurt you."

I shake my head, tears pricking my eyes from the overwhelming intensity of it all. "It's not too much and you're not hurting me," I say, my voice trembling. "Please, don't stop."

He moves slowly at first, each thrust deliberate and measured, as though he's holding himself back. But the tension between us builds like a storm, and soon we're lost in it, our movements frantic and desperate. My legs wrap around his waist. Once he is anchored to me, I tilt my hips to meet him, each collision of our bodies sending incredible sparks of pure pleasure skittering through me.

"Raven," he groans, his voice raw with emotion. The way he says my name like it is a prayer, makes me almost climax. I cling to him, my arms wrapping around his back, my nails clawing into his back as though he is my lifeline.

The heat between us builds to a fever pitch, each thrust is a shockwave of sensations. It's overwhelming and consuming, as though I'm teetering on the edge of something infinite. He plunges deeper as his rhythm intensifies.

Every inch of me feels electrified, all my nerves are ablaze with sensation. The weight of him above me, the heat of his skin against mine, the way he fills me completely—it's too much. My body trembles uncontrollably.

"Earl," I cry, his name tumbling from my lips as the pressure inside me coils tighter and tighter. I'm so close, but I don't want this to be over. I try to hold back, but my thighs clench around him and instantly his body understands and he becomes relentless. His thrusts are deep and fast, each one hitting a spot that has me seeing stars.

"You're perfect. Every part of you." His voice, low, rough, and thick with desire.

His words unravel me completely, the coil inside me snapping with such force that I feel myself shatter around him, my body convulsing as waves of ecstasy crash over me. It's blinding, overwhelming, my back arching off the bed as I cry out, his name breaking on my lips. Every muscle in my body trembles as the pleasure floods every inch of me.

His thrusts carry on through the aftershocks, his own climax building as he drives into me one final time. Suddenly, he stills, his body shuddering against mine as he finds his release, a low, guttural sound escaping him as he buries his face in the crook of my neck. His arms tighten around me, his chest heaving.

A strange peace envelops our spent bodies. Our hearts pound in unison and it feels as if there are only two of us tangled together forever.

It is so beautiful and precious that for a long time, neither of us moves until eventually, he shifts carefully and pulls me into his arms, cradling me against his chest. The steady rise and fall of his chest under my cheek—it's everything I didn't know I needed.

I listen to the rhythm of his heartbeat as it returns to normal. His fingers trail up and down my back in lazy, soothing patterns, and I close my eyes, letting the calm of the moment wash over me.

A lump forms in my throat and I press a kiss to his chest, the taste of salt from his skin mingling with my tears.

We lie there without saying a word to the other, our bodies entwined. I think of how far we've come, of all the hurt and anger we've survived, and I feel something new blooming between us—hope. A fragile, beautiful hope that maybe, just maybe, this time will be different.

Eventually, sleep claims us, but we don't let go of each other. We stay tangled together, our bodies a testament to the love and healing we've begun to find our way back to.

CHAPTER 44

RAVEN

*T*he damp heat in the conservatory wraps around me like a cocoon, its glass walls glowing softly under the afternoon light. The air smells faintly of damp earth and blooming jasmine. I lean back in the chair, a wool blanket draped over my legs, and hold the phone to my ear as my mother's familiar voice spills through the speaker.

"He's doing so much better, Raven," she says, her voice tinged with relief. "The specialist Earl flew in was a Godsend. Your father's strength is improving daily. He even asked for his crossword puzzles this morning."

A smile spreads across my face. "That's wonderful, Mom," I say, keeping my tone light even as a pang of guilt tugs at me. I haven't been there. I've been so consumed with my own recovery, with Earl … with everything.

"I knew you'd want to hear the good news," she continues, her voice softening. "But how are you, darling? Are you taking care of yourself?"

"I am," I assure her, though I don't delve into details. It's easier to keep the conversation focused on them for now. I want to wait until I can visit them in person, to show them I'm doing better rather than just saying it.

We talk a little longer, her words filling the space with warmth. When we finally say goodbye, I feel lighter and happier. I set the phone on the small table beside me and glance toward the garden beyond the glass. There is a thick layer of snow over it now. It looks so pristine and beautiful. If I was better I would be out walking it.

Still, I have good news. Very good recent news that I want to tell my mother about, but not just yet. Until I'm absolutely sure. There's still too much uncertainty. Things between me and Earl have been improving, but I just need a bit more time to be sure, so I'm going to keep it to myself for a little while longer.

My thoughts shift fully to Earl. He'd left early this morning, his expression tight as he kissed my forehead and told me he'd be back soon. Something had happened at the construction site. A scaffolding collapsed, and there were injuries. My chest tightens just thinking about it. I know Earl is careful, but accidents can happen to anyone. I reach for my phone again, hesitating before composing a quick text.

Are you okay? Please let me know when you'll be back.

I hit send, my thumb lingering over the screen as if waiting for an immediate response. He hasn't texted all day, and the silence gnaws at me, but I understand. Some people are hurt, a few even seriously so. I shouldn't be selfish. He'll call me when he has the time.

The sound of hurried footsteps breaks my thoughts, and I glance up to see Nora standing at the door. She looks distressed and her hands twist in her apron.

"Mrs Jackson," she says, her voice trembling slightly. "There's … there's a … guest here to see you."

I sit up straighter, the tension in her voice setting me on edge. "Who is it?"

"It's … it's Mr. Belafonte. Charles Belafonte," she says and there is disapproval in her voice. "and he … well, he let himself in. He knows the house too well—he's lived here all his life so … I couldn't stop... I'm so sorry, Mrs. Jackson."

My stomach knots. Charles! I've ignored his calls, his texts, his attempts to reach me, hoping he'd get the message and leave me alone. The last thing I want is to deal with him now, but I can see the worry in Nora's eyes.

"Should I call the police?" she asks, her voice dropping to a whisper.

"No. Of course not," I say quickly, forcing my voice to remain calm despite the alarm coursing through me. "It's okay. Let him in. I'll handle it."

Nora hesitates for a moment, but she nods and disappears down the hallway. I take a deep breath and brace myself. Charles's persistence has always been unnerving, but the thought of him escalating things right now when Earl and I have just started to find each other again feels worse somehow.

Moments later, I hear his footsteps approaching. The conservatory suddenly feels smaller as I wait. When Charles steps into the room, his presence feels invasive, like a gust of cold air forcing its way inside.

"Raven," he says, his voice smooth but with an edge that sets my nerves alight. "I heard on the grapevine that you're not feeling well."

I steel myself, meeting his gaze head-on. "Charles," I say, my tone carefully neutral. "What are you doing here?"

Charles's smile doesn't falter, and something about it feels wrong, sending a ripple of unease through me. He steps closer, his polished shoes clicking softly against the tiled floor. The light filtering through the glass walls catches on his features, illuminating the intensity of his gaze.

"You know," he begins, his tone unnervingly casual, "I was livid when you wouldn't answer my calls. Weeks, Raven. It's been weeks since I've been trying to reach you, but you've refused to respond to even one message."

"Charles," I start, my voice careful and steady, because something about him feels off. "I've been … preoccupied. With my father, with everything happening in my life, and as you can see I've been unwell for more than two weeks."

He tilts his head slightly, his expression almost mocking. "I know," he says, his voice dipping lower. "But I wanted to ask you something. Something has been bothering me. Did you ever love me? Did your mother never teach you that the worst way to leave a man is to leave them at the altar? And even if you do, you're not supposed to turn around and marry someone else in the same dress?"

My heart stutters at his words, a pang of guilt shooting through me despite the steeliness I try to maintain. His eyes burn into mine, and for a moment, I can't find the words to respond.

"I … I'm sorry. I'm so sorry. I had to. You always knew I was marrying you because you promised to help my dad. When I found out you lied and you wouldn't be able to, I had no choice but to consider our contract to be null and void. It was never my intention to humiliate you, but you have to understand—"

"I do understand," Charles interrupts, his voice hardening as he takes another step closer. "At first, I was in shock. And yes, I'll admit it—ashamed. But then I started to think, to really think, and I remembered something important. I know you, Raven. I know you inside and out and I know you're no gold digger. I love you. I always have and always will."

The conviction in his tone makes my stomach twist with dread. I force myself to hold his gaze, even as every instinct tells me to run.

"Earl—" he spits the name like a curse—"that jackass might think you're some kind of whore, but I know the truth. You wanted to take care of your dad. You'd do anything for the people you love, even if it means marrying a good-for-nothing loser like him."

I feel the blood drain from my face. My hands tremble slightly, but I press them firmly against my thighs to steady myself. "Charles, you're out of line—"

"Am I?" he cuts in, his voice rising just enough to echo off the conservatory walls. He takes another step, leaning closer as his eyes flash with something I can only describe as desperation. "I've been trying to tell you, Raven. You didn't see it at the time, but I get it now. I understand now why you left me, and you know what? I love you even more for it."

A bead of cold sweat prickles at the back of my neck. His words feel like quicksand pulling me under.

Charles exhales sharply, raking a hand through his hair. "Anyway," he says, his tone shifting to something almost jubilant, "I've got good news. Really good news."

I blink at him, too stunned to respond.

He grins suddenly, the expression wide and unsettling. "I've come into money. A lot of it. My father, God bless the man's heart, planned ahead. He knew there might be financial difficulties down the line, so he allocated some extra funds—hedge funds managed by a brilliant investor. Turns out, those funds have yielded millions over the years. Millions, Raven."

My pulse thrums in my ears as he continues, his words tumbling out faster now, his excitement building.

"Do you know what that means? It means you don't need to stay with Earl anymore. You can divorce him and come back to me, Raven. I can take care of your father. I can take care of you. We can pick up right where we left off."

His words hang in the air like a storm cloud, heavy and oppressive. My mind races, trying to process his words—the audacity of his assumptions, the blatant disregard for what I might want, the sheer arrogance of thinking I'd go back to him just because he has come into money.

My stomach churns, and I force myself to stand, the motion unsteady but resolute. "Charles," I say, my voice low but firm, "I've never lied to you before and I'm not going to start now. I love Earl and I always have. I was willing to try and make a life with you, but fate intervened, and now I can't imagine a life without anyone but Earl. You need to leave before Earl comes back."

Charles's face contorts at my words, his expression a blend of disbelief and fury, as though he can't comprehend what I've just said. His lips twitch, his nostrils flare, and he takes a step forward, his voice tight with restrained anger.

"Why?" he demands, the word sharp and jagged, cutting through the air. "Why are you telling me to leave, Raven? This is what you wanted, isn't it? Money to take care of your father? Now you have it! So why won't you even give me the time of day?"

My throat dries, and I press my hands into the chair's armrests to steady myself. He's lost his mind. He doesn't want the truth. I need to placate him long enough to call for help. "Charles ..." I begin, my voice trembling slightly. "I understand what you're saying and maybe you're right, but all of this is so sudden. I just need time to … to figure it out, to come to my senses."

He laughs—a hollow, chilling sound that sends shivers racing down my spine. "Come to your senses?" he repeats, his tone mocking. "Sure. If there's one thing I've learned, Raven, it's that space gives clarity. So it's great you want to think things through. I'll make sure you have plenty of time to do that—privately."

Alarm bells ring in my head at the nasty edge in his voice. My eyes dart to the doorway, but he steps closer, his presence towering over me now. "What do you mean?" I ask, trying to keep my voice calm.

"It means," he says, his eyes narrowing into something dark and unreadable, "I'll help you. I'll take you somewhere safe. Somewhere you can think. And then, once you've had time, you'll see the truth in what I'm saying."

My heart races, panic making my heart flutter like a bird as his gaze burns into me. There's something unhinged in his eyes, a glint of ugly fury barely contained. He never showed this side of him to me, ever. Other people warned me, but I didn't heed their warning because I never saw it. Every instinct in me screams at me to get out of this room, to get away from him, but I think of the child growing inside me. I can't risk anything happening to it.

I force myself to nod, my movements slow and deliberate. "All right," I say softly, keeping my voice even despite the hammering of my heart. "But let me tell Nora where I'm going. She'll worry if I don't."

Charles's expression darkens ominously. "You don't need to," he says coldly. "Just leave. Come with me. She's just staff. You don't tell the staff where you're going. They're there to serve you, not the other way around. You need to take a few lessons from my mother."

The venom in his voice chills me, but I square my shoulders, summoning every ounce of courage I can muster. "You're right, I have to," I say firmly, reaching for my phone on the table. "But — Let me just call my mom at least and tell her you're here. She's been asking about you. They've missed you so much."

I dial Nora instead, my fingers trembling as I press the buttons. Before I can lift the phone to my ear, Charles lunges forward, snatching it from my hands. His grip is iron, his knuckles white as he clutches the device.

"What are you doing?" I stammer, panic rising in my throat. "Give it back, Charles."

His smile is gone now, replaced by a cold, terrifying calm. "Hand it over," he says, his voice low and menacing.

I try to laugh again, a feeble attempt to diffuse the tension. "Charles, stop being so ridiculous—"

The glint of metal stops my words dead in my throat. He pulls out a gun from his jacket pocket, the barrel catching the light. I freeze with shock, but my mind races with every possible escape plan, all of them useless.

"Hand. It. Over," he repeats, his voice quieter now, but far more dangerous.

I have no choice. My fingers tremble as I extend the phone toward him, my knees weak beneath me. He takes it without breaking eye contact.

"There's no need for this, Charles," I whisper, my voice breaking. "Please, put the gun away. We can talk about this. You know me. I'm not going to run away from you. We were going to get married, remember?"

His lips curl into a smile that doesn't reach his eyes. "Talking hasn't worked so far, has it?" he sneers, slipping the gun back into his pocket. "Let's not waste more time, Raven. We're leaving. Now. By the way, I saw you buying a pregnancy test at the pharmacy and, judging by your expression, the test was positive.

I stare at him aghast. Even when he pulled out the gun I did not fear him as I do now that he has casually told me he has been stalking me without my knowledge.

"Make sure you smile at the staff as we pass by them or all three of us, you, me, and baby will be leaving this world together. I always fancied the idea of a triple suicide."

Tears sting my eyes as I nod, swallowing the lump in my throat. I could lunge at him, but I could fall and harm my baby or he could make good his crazy threat. For the baby, I tell myself. For the baby's sake I will go with him and figure out how to save myself when the opportunity presents itself.

He grabs my arm, his grip firm but not bruising, and steers me toward the door. The last thing I see before stepping out of the conservatory is the faint light filtering through the glass, a fragile reminder of the peace I've just left behind.

CHAPTER 45

EARL

*T*he morning's chaos replays in my mind as I drive home. What a day it has been. My body is heavy with fatigue, but my mind is racing. In my head, my workers are yelling amongst the sickening sound of scaffolding collapsing. Liability concerns swirl with genuine worries for my crew's safety. My shirt clings to me caked with sweat and dust.

Then, I think of her.

Raven.

Her name is enough to soften the edges of the turmoil inside me. I picture her face as I left this morning, the morning sun painting her features with a soft glow. Even half-asleep, her presence was enough to ground me in a way nothing else ever has. She's become my anchor, even if I'm too stubborn to admit it outright.

I smile despite the exhaustion. I wonder how long it'll take before I can get her to completely let her guard down before the last remnants of her fear dissolve and I can finally tell her everything she means to me. I've come to terms with her need for wealth. I mean, I thought I was enough for her, but I guess I wasn't. And so what? I rather have half of her than be without her. There's so much I still need to say, but for now, I let myself bask in the thought of seeing her again.

As I pull into the driveway, the weight on my chest begins to lift. I'm home. She's home. That's all that matters. I step out of the car and stretch, brushing off the dust from my pants. My strides quicken toward the front door, eager to close the distance between us. But as soon as I enter, the energy in the house feels … wrong.

Nora is waiting in the foyer, wringing her hands, her face tight with worry. The sight stops me mid-step.

"What's wrong?" I ask, my voice sharp.

Her eyes dart toward the conservatory and back to me. "It's Mrs. Jackson," she says, hesitating. "Charles Belafonte came and took her away."

"Charles?" I thunder, disbelief giving way to red-hot fury. "What the hell was he doing here?"

"I don't know," Nora says quickly, her words tumbling out. "He just showed up, and said he needed to see her. I wanted to call the police, but Mrs. Jackson said she would take care of it. They seemed to be on good terms. She told me it was fine, but something felt off." She pauses, her brow furrowing. "She didn't say anything, but she looked at me as she was trying to speak to me with her eyes before they drove off."

My stomach twists. Speak with her eyes? I knew then that Raven wouldn't have left willingly with him, not like this. Not when we have started to fall in love with each other again. My mind races, piecing together the fragments of what I know about Charles, about his obsessive nature. Panic grips me, and without another word, I bolt upstairs, taking the steps two at a time.

"What can I do to help, Mr. Jackson?" Nora calls after me, but I can't stop. I need answers.

I burst into her bedroom, my eyes scanning the space for anything—anything—that might explain what has happened. The room is still. Too still. My gaze lands on the bathroom door, slightly ajar. My chest tightens as I step inside.

That's when I see it.

The test.

It's perched on the counter, a single object that feels like it's sucking all the air out of the room. My heart pounds as I step closer, picking it up with trembling hands. The little 3+ sign stares back at me, its meaning unmistakable. I stare at it with shock.

The indicator says 3 +.

She's pregnant. She's three weeks plus.

A rush of emotions hits me all at once. Shock. Joy. Fear. My legs feel unsteady. She's carrying my child. Our child.

But the joy is quickly overtaken by a wave of fear like I've never known. It surges through me like a fucking current. Charles has taken her. My wife and our baby—my family—are in danger. A chill creeps up my spine, and I know I can't waste another second.

I stumble out of the bathroom. My thoughts are a chaotic blur as I race back down the stairs. Nora is still standing in the foyer, her worry evident as she watches me.

"Did they say where they were going?" I demand, my voice hoarse.

"No," she replies, shaking her head. "They just left."

"Damn it," I mutter, yanking the front door open. "I'll find her."

My hands shake as I dial Annabelle's number on the way

to the car. She picks up after a few rings, her voice surprised and cautious. "Earl? Nice to hear from you. After the gala, I never thought I would again."

I cut straight to the point. "Annabelle," I say, my voice sharp. "Are you still in town? Do you know where Charles is right at this moment?"

There is a stunned pause, and then she speaks, her tone guarded. "I think so. Why? What's happening?"

"Just answer the question," I snap, starting the engine. "Is he staying anywhere nearby? Did he say anything to you?"

"No. I—I don't know," she stammers. "Earl, what the hell is going on?"

I become sick with worry and I know then that this is going to end very badly. "I need to know where he could have gone, Annabelle," I say, barely managing to keep myself from yelling at her. "He went to the house and kidnapped Raven, Annabelle. He kidnapped her. She's nowhere to be found, and her phone is switched off."

For a moment there's a silence on her end. I can almost hear her brain scrambling to process what I've just said. "Charles... he wouldn't..." Her voice falters before she groans, "That idiot. That absolute moron."

I clench my teeth, gripping the steering wheel tighter as my car zips through the streetlights. "Annabelle, listen to me. I need you to focus. Think. Where would he take her?"

"Earl, please," she pleads, her voice shaking. "No matter how stupid he is, he wouldn't hurt her. He's not—"

"Annabelle!" I bark, cutting her off impatiently. "I don't care what you think Charles's capable of. He's already crossed the line by taking her. Now focus. Where could he have gone?"

Her breath catches, and I hear the faint sound of her pacing. "I—he... it could be anywhere. He could take her anywhere. He's allowed to take her anywhere, right …" She trails off, muttering something I can't make out.

"Annabelle!" I snap again, losing all patience now. "He'll need somewhere secluded. Somewhere unexpected. Think."

There's a long pause before she whispers, almost to herself, "Nanny's old house."

"What?" I ask, leaning forward as if it will bring her answer closer.

"Our Nanny's house," she repeats, louder this time. "Our family gave it to her, but when she died and there was no money to fix it up it has been abandoned for years. It's out on the edge of town. Charles said he was fixing it up or something—just to get away from everything."

"Send me the address," I demand, already feeling a flicker of relief. This feels plausible. It feels right.

"Okay," she says quickly, and within moments my phone buzzes with the location.

"Thank you, Annabelle. Thank you," I say gratefully and cut the call short. I barely take the time to save the address before dialing the police. My voice is urgent and direct as I report the suspected abduction, providing them with the address and all the details I can think of.

As soon as the call ends, I ram my foot on the gas pedal, the car roaring as I speed toward the outskirts of town. My heart is pounding so hard it's like a drumbeat in my ears. All I can think about is Raven, pregnant and terrified.

Her face flashes in my mind—her laughter, her smile, her warmth. And then the fear. I picture her scared, alone, wondering if I'm coming for her. The thought twists my stomach, and I grit my teeth against the rising panic.

"Hold on, baby," I whisper into the silence of the car. "Just hold on, I'll be right there. I'm coming for both of you."

The roads thin out as I drive further, the town's lights

fading behind me. The address Annabelle sent is in a remote, overgrown area, and I can already feel the isolation. Every second feels like an eternity as I race towards my love.

When I finally see the faint outline of the small farm-house in the distance, my breath catches. It's shrouded in shadows, the surrounding trees casting long, eerie shapes across the property. There are no cars, and no signs of move-ment, but my gut tells me this is the place.

I kill the engine some distance away, not wanting to alert anyone inside the building of my presence. My pulse is hammering as I step out and every muscle in my body is taut with anticipation. When I get close enough, I hear faint sounds—muffled voices, Raven's voice. My heart clenches, and all my focus sharpens on getting her out of there. My hands curl into fists.

"Hold on, baby Raven" I mutter quietly. "Just hold on."

CHAPTER 46

RAVEN

*T*he basement is suffocating, every breath I take is heavy with fear and the acrid scent of Charles's sweat mixed with whiskey. The dim light from the single bulb above flickers slightly, casting ominous shadows on the dank walls. I struggle against the ropes binding my wrists to the chair, the coarse fibers biting into my skin, but they hold firm. My heart pounds erratically in my chest as Charles stands in front of me, his shirt discarded, his chest heaving with labored breaths. He sways slightly, the bottle in his hand nearly slipping through his fingers.

"You think you're too good for me, don't you?" he says, his voice slurred but venomous. His eyes are bloodshot, wild, and filled with something dark and dangerous. He takes another swig from the bottle before slamming it onto the small table nearby, the sharp clink making me flinch.

Suddenly, I realize, there is no 'good news', no millions arriving in his account. He has reached the end of his tether.

In fact, it is he who thinks I'm too good for him, otherwise he wouldn't have to drink three-quarters of a bottle of whiskey before he tries to rape me.

"Why?" he growls, stepping closer. "Why was I never enough for you?"

I shake my head, desperate to plead with him, to make him understand, but the gag in my mouth stifles my cries. Tears stream down my face, and my chest tightens with the weight of my terror. Charles crouches in front of me, his face mere inches from mine, his breath reeking of alcohol and despair.

"I've loved you since high school, Raven," he says, his tone softening in a way that's somehow more chilling. "I've done everything for you. But no matter what I did, all you ever saw was Earl."

He reaches out and brushes a strand of hair from my face, the gesture almost tender, and I do my best not to recoil. His hand lingers on my cheek, his touch burning like acid. "I could've given you everything," he whispers, his voice breaking slightly. "But you didn't even give me a chance. You still won't."

He stands abruptly, his sudden movement making me flinch again. He starts pacing, running a hand through his hair as he mutters to himself. Then, as if struck by a thought, he spins around and glares at me.

"You're going to love me," he declares, his voice rising with unhinged conviction. "Even if I have to make you."

Charles has become unhinged. Losing his money, his ancestral home and me has driven him insane. There is no talking logic with him. I have to find a way to convince him that I'm secretly in love with him. Secretly, I struggle harder against the ropes. He steps forward, leaning down so his face is level with mine. "You're mine now," he says, his tone dropping into something low and menacing. "We're going to leave this place, just you and me. Far away from everyone."

I shake my head violently, muffled protests spilling from behind the gag. His expression darkens, and he grabs my chin roughly, forcing me to look at him. Then he pulls down the gag.

"Don't fight me, Raven," he snarls. "You don't have a choice. You're mine."

Gathering every ounce of courage I have left, I look him dead in the eye and say, "I'm yours. I've always been yours. I was just playing hard to get because I didn't know how else to get you."

It is as if I unknowingly flicked a kill switch inside him. Without warning his expression twists into something monstrous. His hand snaps across my face, the sharp crack of his slap echoing in the room. Pain explodes across my cheek, and I gasp, my vision swimming.

"Stop lying. You think I'm stupid. No, you ungrateful trailer park trash, I'm not stupid," he hisses, his voice trembling with rage. "You think you can humiliate me? After everything I've done for you?"

His hand clenches into a fist, but he doesn't strike again. Instead, he steps back and reaches into his pocket, pulling out a knife. The sight of the blade sends a fresh wave of terror coursing through me. He waves it in front of me, his lips curling into a cruel smile.

"You're going to behave," he says, his tone almost mocking, "or this will end very badly for you."

The sudden sound of shattering glass from upstairs freezes us both. My breath catches, and Charles's head snaps toward the ceiling, his entire body going rigid. The knife trembles slightly in his hand as he stares at the dark hallway leading to the stairs.

"What the hell was that?" he mutters, his voice low and filled with suspicion.

Every nerve in my body is on edge as he moves toward the staircase, his footsteps cautious and deliberate. The house falls eerily silent, the only sound is my ragged breathing and the faint creak of the wooden steps under his weight.

Then, chaos erupts.

The crash of something heavy colliding with the floor reverberates through the house, followed by muffled shouts and the unmistakable sounds of a struggle. The noises grow louder, followed by the sound of bodies slamming into walls. It makes the room shake. My mind races with the worst possibilities as every second stretches into eternity.

The commotion moves closer, and then Charles's body crashes down the stairs, landing in a crumpled heap at the bottom. Blood smears the floor where he lands, his face contorted in pain and fury. My breath catches in my throat, and my eyes dart to the top of the stairs.

Earl stands there, his chest heaving, his face bruised and bloodied but alive. Relief floods through me, but it's short-lived as Charles groans and starts to stir.

"Earl, watch out!" I scream, my voice hoarse and raw.

Earl doesn't hesitate. He descends the stairs with stunning speed. Grabbing Charles by the collar, he lands a solid punch to his face. The force of the blow sends blood spraying, but Charles fights back, clawing and thrashing like a wounded animal.

"You fucking sick bastard," Earl roars, his voice echoing with fury.

The fight is brutal, with both men grappling and throwing punches with everything they have. Earl gains the upper hand, pinning Charles to the ground and delivering blow after blow until Charles is barely conscious.

When Earl stops, his chest rises and falls violently as he catches his breath. He turns to me, his eyes softening despite the blood and rage etched into his features.

"I've got you," he says, his voice hoarse as he cuts the ropes binding me.

Before I can answer, Charles lets out a low, guttural laugh. He sits up, his face a bloody mess, and pulls a gun from his waistband.

"If I can't have her," he rasps, his voice filled with malice, "no one will."

The world slows as he raises the gun, aiming it at me. Earl moves faster than I can comprehend. He throws himself in front of me just as the shot rings out.

"Earl!" I scream, as he collapses against me. Blood seeps through his shirt, staining my hands. Screaming, I press against the wound. My vision blurs with tears.

"Oh my God, no," I say, I can't say even a word again, tears pouring from my eyes. "Oh my God. Oh my God. No."

"You're going to be okay," I swear to Earl, my voice breaking. "You're going to be okay."

Charles remains slumped on the ground, his face swollen and bloodied, his breaths coming in ragged gasps. He tries to push himself up, but his arms give out, his strength failing him. His eyes are wild, darting between me and Earl, filled with equal parts fury and desperation.

The gun trembles in his hand, the metallic barrel catching the light and sending chills down my spine. I barely dare to breathe, frozen in place as the room becomes a pressure cooker of tension. Earl stirs in my arms, his face pale and his breaths shallow, but his focus remains locked on Charles.

The distant wail of sirens grows louder, slicing through

the suffocating silence. Relief should wash over me, but it doesn't. The danger isn't over—not yet. Charles's gaze shifts toward the door as the sound draws closer, his body tensing like a cornered animal. His lips curl into a twisted smirk, blood dripping from the corner of his mouth.

"You think this is over?" he rasps, his voice hoarse and broken. He lifts the gun, its barrel wavering as his hand trembles. "You can't take her from me. She was always mine."

"Charles, stop!" I scream, my voice cracking with desperation. "For fucks sake stop!"

The front door bursts open with a deafening crash, and police officers flood the room, their shouts cutting through the chaos.

"Drop the weapon!" one commands. All their guns are trained on Charles.

Charles looks around wildly, his breathing frantic, sweat and blood streaking his face. For a moment, his hand lowers, and hope flickers in my chest. But then his eyes meet mine, dark and empty, and I see his resolve harden.

"If I can't have you ..." he whispers, the words trailing off as he raises the gun—not toward us, but toward himself.

"No!" I cry, my voice raw and broken as the gunshot rings out.

The sound is deafening, a sharp crack that reverberates through the room and leaves a ringing in my ears. Charles collapses backward, his body crumpling against the wall like a broken marionette. Blood pools beneath him, staining the wooden floor in a dark, spreading shadow.

My chest heaves with sobs, but I force myself to turn away, to focus on the man in my arms. Earl's head lolls against my shoulder, his skin cold and clammy. Blood seeps through my fingers as I press against the wound in his shoulder, trying to stem the flow.

"Stay with me," I plead, my voice trembling. Tears blur my vision as I cradle his face, searching his eyes for any sign of recognition. "Please, Earl, don't leave me again."

A faint smile ghosts across his lips. "I'm not going anywhere," he murmurs, his voice weak but laced with determination. "Not without you."

A choked sob escapes me as I clutch him tighter. The police move around us, their voices distant and muted in the haze of my panic. Paramedics rush in, their equipment clattering as they begin to assess the scene. One of them crouches beside us. I instantly pull back, but Earl squeezes my hand and won't let go.

"Save him. Please save him," I beg to the paramedic.

"It's okay. I'm not leaving your side," I whisper and let go of his hand. "Let them help you."

Earl's eyes remain on mine as a silent reassurance passes between us. Then he nods and my heart breaks when I release him into their care. My hands are stained red and trembling uncontrollably. I watch them work while my insides are twisted with terror.

As the paramedics lift him onto the stretcher, my legs give out, and I sink to the floor, my chest heaving with quiet sobs. A police officer crouches down beside me. He tries to calm me down and ask me questions, but I can barely process his words.

The only thing I can focus on is Earl disappearing through the door as the paramedics rush him to the ambulance. My heart feels like it's being ripped from my chest, but amid the terror and despair, one thought anchors me.

We've survived this far. We can survive anything.

CHAPTER 47

EARL

*T*he hospital room is quiet, the sterile hum of machines the only sound breaking the stillness. I wake to the faint scent of her—soft, floral, like warmth and safety wrapped into one. My eyes open, and there she is, sitting in the chair beside my bed. My Raven.

Her hair is pulled back, wisps framing her face, and there's an exhaustion in her posture that tells me she hasn't left my side. She looks like an angel, even in her weariness. The sight of so much beauty squeezes my heart.

"Hey," I croak, my throat rough and dry as sandpaper.

Her gaze swings to mine, and relief floods her face. "Earl," she breathes, leaning closer. Her hand brushes my cheek, and I feel the warmth of her palm against my skin. "You're awake."

I smile faintly, weakly, but it's all I can manage. "Yup. Still here."

Tears brim in her eyes as she presses a soft kiss to my forehead. "Don't you dare scare me like that again."

"Didn't mean to," I murmur, my fingers twitching to reach for hers. She takes my hand without hesitation, her grip is soft and infinitely tender.

We sit like that for a moment, in comfortable silence. There's so much I want to say, but I don't know where to start. Her thumb strokes over my knuckles, her gaze dropping to our intertwined hands.

"Raven," I start. "We need to talk."

She nods, a trace of worry flickering across her face. "I know."

"First," I say, swallowing hard. "I need to apologize. For the way I've treated you. For the way I've shut you out, the way I held onto the past, I should've let go of it all a long time ago."

She shakes her head quickly. "No, Earl. You don't have to do this now. You—"

"I do," I interrupt gently. "You've been everything to me, Raven. And I've been holding onto anger because I didn't know how to deal with how much you mean to me. But you deserve the truth. All of it."

Her brow furrows, and I see her mind working, the concern etching into her features. "What truth?" she asks softly.

I take a deep breath, steeling myself. "Years ago, at that party … I heard you. I heard what you said to Annabelle."

Her eyes widen, her hand still in mine. "Earl …"

"I wasn't supposed to be there. You thought I wasn't in the room, but I was," I continue. "I heard every word."

Her face pales as the memory crashes over her. "I didn't mean—"

"You called me a grease monkey," I say, the words cutting

through the air like a blade, each syllable full of years of hurt. "A loser. Said you were only with me until you found someone better. I heard you that night, Raven. The things you said … they weren't just about me. You tore into my family, my entire life. You told Annabelle that my father was a nasty drunk and my mother—"

My voice cracks, but I press on, the flood of memory impossible to stop. "You said my mother was a drug addict who'd sent me to live with my father because she couldn't be bothered to raise me. I told you that in confidence. I've never told anyone else that. You were the only person I trusted with that information."

Her lips part to speak, to explain, but I put my finger across her lips and shake my head.

"And then I had to stand there and listen to you say I had no prospects. That I was just a fling, a good kisser … and nothing more. You'd leave me the second someone with real money came along. Do you have any idea what it felt like to hear you say all that? To hear Annabelle defend me while you … you, the love of my life, my everything, you tore me apart? She said I was the most gorgeous person she'd ever laid eyes on, and you—" My voice falters, the anger and pain surging. "You acted horrified, like the idea of being with me long-term disgusted you."

Tears spill over her cheeks as she shakes her head. "I didn't mean it, Earl. I swear. I—I was scared. Annabelle was … she was so blonde, so perfect, so confident, so wealthy, and I thought she could take you away from me. I said those things to put her off you. Obvioulsy, I didn't believe any of it. They were just lies. I didn't mean any of it. You have to believe me, Earl. You just have to."

Her voice cracks, and I see the sincerity in her eyes, the pain etched into her expression. "I hated myself for ever saying those things," she whispers. "And if I could take it back, I would. I was young. I was stupid. And I was so insanely jealous when I saw Annabelle flirting with you at the party. I was terrified of losing you. I did what I thought was my only choice. I lied to her to keep you. Do you believe me?"

"Yes," I say, my voice softer now. "I know you didn't mean it now, but that night, it broke me, and stayed with me, Raven. It shaped everything I did after that. Colored every decision I made."

She looks at me, her tears falling freely. "So that's why you left. That's why you pushed me away."

I nod. "It hurt, hearing those things. It made me feel like I wasn't good enough for you. And I thought … if I could prove you wrong, if I could make something of myself, then maybe … maybe I'd deserve you, but I was so proud, I had to dress it up as my great revenge."

Her hands fly to my face, cupping my cheeks as she leans closer. "We've always deserved each other, Earl. We're two peas in a pod, remember? I was stupid, insecure and scared when I said those things, but even after you left I never stopped loving you. Not for a moment. Never."

I close my eyes as her words wash over me, the truth I've been yearning for finally setting me free. Tears sting my eyes, and before I can stop them, they spill over. "I'm sorry," I choke out. "I've been such a monster, holding onto that anger for so long."

She wipes my tears away, her touch gentle and soothing. "There's nothing to apologize for," she whispers. "Love forgives everything, Earl. Everything."

The weight I've carried for years lifts in that moment, replaced by a deep love and warmth I haven't felt in a long time. She kisses me, soft and tender, and I let myself sink into it, into her, into us.

As she pulls back, her smile wavers, but her eyes hold nothing but love. "We'll be okay," she says, her voice trembling with conviction. "We'll figure it out. Together."

I nod, pulling her closer as my heart finally feels whole. "Together," I agree, and for the first time in years, I believe it.

CHAPTER 48

RAVEN

*H*e stares into my eyes, the intensity softening into something more profound—something that takes my breath away. A small smile begins to curve his lips, widening slowly but surely. It's a smile that knows too much, that holds an unspoken truth. My chest tightens, a flutter building inside me.

"I saw it," he says softly, his voice laced with both tenderness and certainty.

I blink, confused. "Saw what?"

His gaze flickers, his smile deepening as though the words themselves are precious. "The pregnancy test," he says simply. "In the bathroom."

The air rushes out of my lungs. I can't tell if it's panic or relief—or maybe both—that courses through me as I struggle to form words.

"I …" My voice falters, and I look down at the rough hospital blanket. Should I apologize for not telling him sooner? Explain that it wasn't planned, but I don't regret it. Or that I didn't know how to bring it up after everything that has happened?

Before I can untangle my thoughts, Earl leans forward, his hand reaching out to cup my cheek. His thumb brushes over my skin. "My darling," he says, his voice unwavering and filled with a strong emotion that makes him feel like he will forever be my rock, my port in the storm. "You've given me the greatest gift I could've ever asked for."

I stare at him, my breath catching. "You mean it?" I whisper, barely able to get the words out.

He nods, his eyes never leaving mine. "I love you," he says, his voice breaking slightly. "With all my heart, baby. And I already love the new life growing inside you too, more than I thought was possible."

Tears well up in my eyes. I can't hold it in any longer. I lean forward, capturing his lips in a kiss that speaks of everything I feel. The fear, the gratitude, the overwhelming love that has grown inside me, not just for the life we've created but for this man who has fought so hard to be with me, who has endured so much to stand by my side.

"I love you too, Earl," I whisper against his lips, my voice trembling but certain. "With all my heart. Forever. And ever."

His arms wrap around me, pulling me close as we kiss again, this time slower, deeper, as though sealing a promise we'll carry with us for the rest of our lives.

The moment stretches, the world narrowing to just the two of us. The weight of the past lifts, replaced by something that shines like stars in the night, something unbreakable. And as we hold each other, I feel it—the certainty that whatever comes next, we'll face it together.

Forever.

EPILOGUE

EARL

*T*he hallway outside Raven's hospital room feels like a liminal space—too quiet, too clean. The soft hum of monitors and faint voices from nearby rooms create an unsettling backdrop to my restless thoughts. I shift my weight from one foot to the other, my arms crossed tightly as if bracing myself for bad news. Through the small window in her door, I can see Raven sitting up in bed, her mother beside her, holding her hand. She looks so calm, so radiant. She has no idea of the turmoil still swirling inside me.

Beside me, Raven's father clears his throat. I glance at him. He's standing straighter now, a picture of health compared to the man I first met. The lines on his face are less pronounced, his color has returned, and his presence feels... steady. But his gaze is fixed on me, sharp and assessing.

"Earl," he says finally, his voice quiet but deliberate. "Can we talk?"

I nod, turning to face him fully. "Of course, Sir."

His lips press into a thin line. He glances at Raven's door, then back at me. "You've done a lot for her. I won't deny that. You've been by her side when she needed someone the most. And I can see how much she loves you." He pauses, his eyes narrowing slightly. "But I need to know something before I can fully give you my blessing."

I meet his gaze, already knowing what's coming. "You want to know about my past."

He nods, his expression unwavering. "Raven won't tell me, but I need to know the truth. Not just for her, but for the family you're about to build. What kind of man are you, Earl?"

I draw in a slow, measured breath, feeling the weight of his words. The truth isn't easy, but I owe it to him—to all of them. My fingers twitch at my sides, but I hold his gaze.

"You know my history," I begin, my voice steady but tinged with regret. "I was angry and desperate. You know my dad, how he was a drunk, and how he made sure everyone around him suffered for it. At the point he left, I knew I had to do something.

"I didn't want to end up like him, I wanted to be better and I wanted it fast. So I made bad decisions. I targeted men like Charles's father—arrogant, entitled men who thought the world owed them everything. I conned them out of their money. At the time, I told myself they deserved it, that it was justice somehow."

I see his jaw tighten, but he doesn't interrupt.

"It wasn't justice. It was theft," I admit, the words like stones on my tongue. "But I didn't just blow the money. I used it to start over. I invested it carefully, and built legitimate businesses. And after a while, I left that life behind completely. Every cent I've earned since then has been honest hard work."

There's a long silence. His gaze is piercing, and I can feel him weighing every word, every inflection. I hold my breath, waiting for the judgment to fall.

Finally, he exhales and steps closer, placing a firm hand on my shoulder. "You were young," he says, his voice surprisingly gentle. "And you made many mistakes, but you didn't stay in the gutter. You climbed out. That's more than a lot of people would've done."

His response humbles me.

"What matters now," he continues, his tone firm, "is how you treat my daughter and the life you're building with her. You've shown me thus far, Earl, the man you truly are and I have no complaints."

Relief floods through me, so overwhelming I almost laugh. "Thank you, Sir, for the trust in me," I say quietly. "I won't let you down."

He chuckles, a warm, genuine sound. "Isn't it high time you call me Dad?" he asks, his smile widening. Then, without warning, he pulls me into a quick, gruff hug.

The door to Raven's room opens then, and her mother steps out, her face alight with joy. "She's nearly ready," she says, beaming. "And she's asking for you."

Raven's father claps me on the back. "Go on, kid. She's waiting. Go deliver my grandson."

My heart swells as I step into the room, where Raven is waiting with a smile that feels like I've finally come home.

And they lived happily ever after ...

COMING NEXT...

NEIGHBOR FROM HELL

CHAPTER 1
Lauren

The barstool creaks under me as I slump forward, elbows sliding on the sticky wooden counter of O'Malley's Pub. It's a dive in the heart of Illinois, all chipped paint and flickering neon, the kind of place where the air smells of stale beer and regret. My fingers toy with the damp label of my Stella Artois, peeling it back in slow, satisfying strips.

I'm bone-tired—sales rep life is a grind, a treadmill of monotony; same journeys, same lecherous advances from area managers to handle tactfully, same bullshit quotas that make me want to claw my eyes out. I'm running and running, but I never seem to get anywhere. Twenty-eight, single, and renting a studio apartment that's one step up from a shoebox. It's not the dream I had at twenty.

I glance around. The jukebox hums a Springsteen song about glory days, and the chatter of half-drunk locals buzz like white noise. I tip my Stella Artois back, the bottle's icy glass kissing my lips, slick with condensation that beads against my fingertips. The beer hits my tongue. The cold, sharp brew slides down my throat like a temporary Band-Aid on a wound that won't stop bleeding. It's not enough though and I am beginning to worry if anything ever will.

Sandy slides onto the stool next to me, all wild brunette curls and a smile so seriously sensuous it could charm a monk into sin. She's in a black crop top and jeans, effortlessly hot in that way I've always admired. Her gin and tonic sloshes as she sets it down, ice clinking against the glass.

"Rough day, huh?" she guesses, the waft of alcohol already on her breath.

"My landlord is doubling the rent," I mutter, setting my beer down with a dull clink.

Sandy freezes mid-sip, her gin and tonic hovering an inch from her lips. The ice clinks against the glass, a tiny chime that cuts through the bar's haze—Springsteen's crooning about better days, the clatter of pool balls, the hum of slurred voices.

"What?' she explodes

"I'm done with it all, Sandy," I say, turning to her. "Men, the job, the apartment, the whole damn thing. The rent was already bleeding me dry in that cramped, shitty studio with walls so thin I can hear my neighbor's Netflix marathons. But double? Shit, I'll be eating ramen in the dark, praying the power doesn't get cut."

"You'll just have to find something else. I always thought your landlord was leach of the first degree for making you pay all that money for what is basically a double wardrobe with a toilet and a stove.

I pick at the soggy label on my bottle, peeling it back in jagged little strips. "Nah, I've really had enough, Sandy," I admit, the words tasting like defeat. "I've been spending time on Zillow and I swear, everybody's gone insane. The prices are more than double what I'm paying now."

"Yeah," she sighs. "Living in the city is becoming unbearable for sure. With these prices you'd think they come with gold toilets but no. It's the same dreary shit. What are you going to do?"

I shrug. "I'm still weighing my options."

"You need to find a sexy landlord who'll cut you a deal, you know what I mean." She waggles her brows.

"Oh, for God's sake," I say, but I laugh, the sound spilling out like a release valve popping. The tension in my chest loosens just a fraction. She's ridiculous, but I love her for it. Still, those Zillow tabs haunt me—each one a little stab of what I can't have, a reminder of my defeat. Double the rent. Double the misery. Unless I find a way out.

I take another swig of my Stella Artois, the beer's gone lukewarm now and it sits heavy in my gut. I lean my elbow on the sticky counter and stare at the defaced label on my bottle like it's got answers. It doesn't.

"Sandy," I start, my voice low, "you know my grandma died a couple months back, right?"

"Yeah," she replies. "But you weren't close, right?"

"No. I've never even met her. She cut off all contact with my mom after my mom moved to the States to marry my dad."

"Oh yes right, I know this. She disapproved of the union."

"Yeah. Anyway, it's just got me thinking, you know? That this feeling of needing a change isn't just me being bored, or being hounded out of my home by a crazy rent increase. Maybe it's sign that I need a change. A real change. Maybe I'm being nudged into the path I'm supposed to be on."

"What path are you thinking of?" she asks, and I smile. "I

know you," she says. "If you're saying this now, then you've been thinking about it for a while and you already have a direction in mind, so let's hear it."

"Well, you know, she left me this property in England. It's a small cottage on quite a generous plot of land. I haven't even seen it and my original plan was to get an estate agent over there to sell it for me. but I have been thinking about it. A lot."

"Holy shit, you're moving countries?" she exclaims.

"Not moving," I correct. "Just thinking about it."

"So you're not moving?" she asks.

"I don't know. It's a cottage in England. It probably has meadows and all that. I'm tempted, I mean why not?"

"It could also be a total dump." she says. "She must have been a nasty old lady to cut all contact with her only daughter just because she disapproved of the man her daughter wanted to marry."

"Hmmm...I keep thinking... what if I went? Just for six months. See what it's like. If it sucks, I'm back. If I love it..." I trail off, meeting her eyes.

She blinks, processing, then leans back with a sad smile. "Oh God, you're serious."

"Yeah," I mutter. I reach over, grabbing her hand, her skin warm against mine. "I'd miss you though," I say quietly. "You're my best friend, Sandy and I love you forever,. but I'm drowning here. I need to try something different or I swear I'll go insane."

She squeezes my hand back. "Yeah, okay. I can't stand in your way of a better life for you so I'll just have to hope that you'll stay for a couple of months and realize that country life is boring as shit and come right back to me. Maybe by then you'll have gotten your fill of what you need."

"Hopefully," I say.

She nods. "Fine. I can survive a few months. But you better bring me stories. Like, filthy ones. English dudes, hot accents—be my Carrie Bradshaw over there?"

I snort, pulling my hand back to cradle my bottle. What the fuck are you on about? I'm going to avoid men, remember? My life is screwed up enough. Last thing I need is another failed relationship."

She smirks, wicked and unstoppable, and lean in close. "Oh, please. An English dick might be exactly what you need to unstick yourself. I hear they're proper in all the right ways." She wiggles her eyebrows suggestively.

"Stop it," I say with a groan, but her riotous laugh pulls me in, and I start grinning. "You're deranged."

"I'm serious," she says. "You never know. They might be packing more than our lot." Her eyes light up, and she goes for her phone, nearly knocking over her glass. "Let's find out. Science, bitch. We're googling this."

I roll my eyes, but wait curiously to hear her findings.

"Okay," she says. "Average penis size UK vs US."

I try, but can't hold back the cackle that rises into my throat. "This is so dumb."

"Got it!" Sandy crows, holding her phone up like a trophy. "UK—5.6 inches hard. US—5.1. Fuck yes, they're bigger!" She's loud, too loud, and the guy next to us, an older dude in flannel, shoots us a look, but we're too far gone to care.

"No way," I say, pulling out my own phone. I make my own research and soon enough I'm scrolling through my own results, squinting at the tiny text. "Shit, you're right. And thicker, too? We're a disaster." I'm laughing now, full-on, my stomach aching as I slump against the bar, tears pricking my eyes.

"Yes, we are." She grabs her glass, raising it high, gin sloshing over the edge. "I've changed my mind now. I support you wholeheartedly so here's to England. To cottages and big dicks and you getting the hell out of this hellhole."

I lift my bottle, the clink sharp and bright against her glass. "To chances," I add, a thrill of excitement running through my veins. The beer's flat now, but I drink anyway, and it hits me like a promise. That cottage, some crumbly speck in England, might be my lifeline. Green hills, black and white cows, quiet, a reset. Maybe an Englishman with gray eyes and a thick dick —fuck, where'd that come from? I shake it off, blame it on Sandy's dirty mind leading me astray.

The bar spins on, sticky and loud, but I'm somewhere else already. This could be it. My way out. My shot.

I feel the blood rushing through my veins again, eager for what life has in store for me next. It's a wonderful feeling, one I haven't felt in forever and so I hold on to it with all of my might.

CHAPTER 2
Hugh

The engine roars beneath me as I gun my yellow Aston Martin down the winding countryside lanes, tires hugging the asphalt like a lover who won't let go. It's early April, my favorite time—spring clawing its way out of winter's grip, wildflowers popping up in messy bursts of yellow and purple along the hedgerows. The air rushing through the gap in the window, smells of new grass, rain, and damp earth.

I breathe it in deep, letting it flood my lungs, a sharp contrast to the smell of exhaust fumes and crowds of hurrying bodies in London. The city is a beast, holding opportunity and riches beyond imagination for the ruthless, but this? This is peace. I come back here at least once a month—my manor, my sanctuary—to rest, recharge, shake off the stresses of running billions in assets.

My phone buzzes in the center console, a harsh rattle against the leather. I snatch it up, thumbing the screen alive. Athena's name glows. She's my assistant, sharp as a tack and shockingly competent. I hit the speaker, keeping one hand on the wheel as the car purrs around a bend.

"Yeah?"

"Good Morning, Sir," she says in her clipped, super-efficient voice. "Good news. Barrington & Hauser have finally agreed to your terms. They sign the contract this afternoon at 2:00p.m. Hopefully you will now feel justified to thoroughly enjoy your week in the country."

"Excellent. Well done," I say with a victorious smile. This news is the icing on the cake for an idea I've been planning on.

"Thank you, Sir. The team did a brilliant job." There is pride and joy in her voice.

"I'm going to stay longer than a week this time, Athena. Can you reschedule and work on shifting most of my meetings for next two months at least to the manor. I think we can set up some kind of system here. Let's use the next two weeks to test it? I want to run things remotely, only heading to London for emergencies. Can you handle it?"

I hear the faint tap of her keyboard in the background and my gaze flicks towards the rolling pastures flashing by—

cows dotting the green, lazy and fat, chewing cud without a care in the world.

"Of course," she says moments later, smooth as ever. "I'll get started with arranging everything—video calls, secure lines, the works. Anything else?"

"Not for now. Good work with the Barrington deal. There'll be a special bonus in your paycheck this month."

"Thank you, Sir."

She cuts the call, and I lean back with a sense of great satisfaction. The team worked hard and it was not an easy deal to put together, and it's the perfect news to start my retreat. The countryside stretches out ahead, endless and gorgeous—fields stitched together with stone walls, the sky a pale blue streaked with wispy clouds. It is a balm for the soul, peace soaks into me, easing the knots in my shoulders.

Montrose Manor comes into view as the road crests—a magnificent white stone piece of history. Built in the eighteen century it has survived two world wars, five fires, and long periods of neglect and decline, but I have restored it to its former glory. The windows glint in the morning sun. Deer graze in the fields beyond, their faces turned towards the noise of my car, their tails swishing nervously. It is a fucking postcard, pristine and picturesque, and every acre is mine.

I pull up the drive, gravel crunching under the tires, and kill the engine. Silence reigns broken only by a distant whinny from the stables. I step out, boots hitting the ground, and stretch, my spine popping from the drive. The air's cool, tinged with the sweet rot of manure and hay. Home.

Then my eyes snag on it—the cottage. That damned eyesore squatting next on what should be my land, a blight on the horizon. Crumbling brick, sagging roof, overgrown with ivy and weeds. It literally looks like it's trying to claw its way back into the earth. My mood sours, a tight coil of annoyance ruining my sense of wellbeing. I've been after that patch for years—offered the grumpy old woman who lived there more than it was worth, and she still spat in my face. Now she's dead, she's willed it on to some granddaughter of hers. Never even knew the hag had family. Another stubborn fool, probably. I shove the unwelcome thoughts to the back of my mind as I head inside, but still as always it gnaws at me. It's a problem unsolved.

The warm and rich smell of coffee and bacon wafts from the dining room. I walk through the heavy oak doors and find my mother seated at the end of the long table, a plate of toast and eggs in front of her. She's all elegance—silver hair swept up, pearls at her throat—sipping tea like she's posing for a portrait. She looks up and smiles. I cross the room and kiss her offered cheek. Her skin is soft and powdery under my lips.

"Morning, darling," she greets warmly.

"You're dressed up," I comment.

"I have some errands to run in the city and I was thinking of spending the night in the flat. My flight to Paris tomorrow is quite early and I fear missing it."

"Why don't you just take the jet?" I ask curiously. "You can leave whenever you want with that option and you won't have all the hassle of flying commercial."

"Waste of resources," she says. "I have booked a seat in business class and the check in will be speedy. I'm fine."

"As you wish," I concede and drop into the chair across from her. A maid—a new girl, all nervous hands—sets a cup in front of me and pours steaming black coffee into it. I nod at her, and she scurries off. "But what's the rush? Stay a few more days. You know I like having you here."

She laughs lightly and brushes crumbs from her fingers

317

and lifts her cup of tea. "I've been closeted here for the last three months, Hugh and that is enough. This house is too quiet. When you're not here I feel like a ghost wandering around aimlessly by myself. Ever since your father... the memories... it's all a bit much. Anyway, I'm a city girl at heart. I need the noise, the bustle. Paris calls. I've been here long enough."

I sip the coffee. It's exactly how I like it: bitter and scalding hot. "Fair enough. What about the cottage next door? Any news?"

She sets her tea cup down, the porcelain clinking softly against the saucer. "The only new piece of information is; the granddaughter is American, I hear. No word from her yet. The fact she hasn't turned up is good news. Maybe she's not interested in the property at all. Maybe she'll accept your offer. We can live in hope."

I lean back, jaw tightening. "Hope? No, that's not how I run things. I want that land and I'm going to get it by hook or by crook. It's a fucking disgrace, just sitting there rotting —ruins the view, drags the look of whole estate down. You know how stunning it could be if I got my hands on it. And no neighbors for miles—complete privacy. I'm not waiting. I'm going to hire someone to work on it."

"Preston's firm will be able to sort it all out for you. They're clever. The real worry are those horrible developers, Harrington Group. They're always trying to buy up chunks of the countryside, and I hear they've been sniffing around. If that girl hears from them first and sells, it'll be lost for good. You'll never pry it back from those vultures."

My grip tightens on the cup, heat seeping into my palm. Harringtons. Greedy bastards with their glass towers and tacky resorts. The thought of them sinking their claws into the land next me makes me want to punch something.

'They'll completely devastate the whole area if she sells to them."

My mother nods, sipping her tea. "You do indeed have to move fast. If I hear anything more about the granddaughter, I'll let you know, of course."

I nod, already halfway out the room, fishing my phone from my pocket. The hall echoes with my steps—polished wood, portraits of hundreds of years worth of ancestors staring down at me. I dial my lawyer, Edward, pacing as it rings. He picks up on the second ring.

"Why the delay?' I ask. "Haven't you found her yet?'

"Rest assured, there's no delay, Sir. Everything is under control. We've got her details, and we'll send them over in the next hours so you can reach out and make an offer."

"Alright," I reply, somewhat consoled. "I'll expect these details today?"

"We'll do our very best, Sir."

CHAPTER 3
Lauren

The pilot's voice crackles over the intercom, a delightful British drawl cutting through the hum of the plane. "Ladies and gentlemen, we've just landed at Birmingham International Airport. Local time is 2:17 p.m. Welcome to England."

He informs us about the weather and finishes with 'the thanks for flying with us' spiel, but through it all I'm almost afraid to breathe. Eventually the plane lands and taxis to a halt and the cabin erupts in movement—seatbelts clicking, overhead bins snapping open—but I just sit there, frozen, my hands clenched around the armrests. My stomach is a knot, twisting tighter.

This is it. I'm here.

My adventure starts right here and now.

I shuffle off the jetway with my carry-on, a small, green beat-up suitcase. It rolls behind me, its wheels clattering against the tiled floor. The airport is gray and sterile, smelling of coffee and disinfectant. Voices bouncing off the walls in accents and languages I have never heard of. Outside the glass walls the skies are gray and it's raining steadily. I'm jet-lagged, my eyes feel gritty, and my legs are stiff from six hours crammed in economy, but there's a buzz under my skin—nerves, yeah, but the excitement too.

I told myself I'd give this a shot, one honest go. Worst case, I hate it, sell the place, pocket the cash and use it to fix my life back in the States. Best case... maybe this is the change I've been looking for. I've quit my job, burned through half my savings to get my affairs in order before leaving, and now I've got no clue what I'm walking into.

Please, God, don't let it be a nasty surprise.

The rental car is a tiny Ford Fiesta. I wrestle my suitcases into the trunk before sliding behind the wheel. Right side of the road—shit, that's gonna take some getting used to. The GPS spits out directions to Berrygrove, a name I heard of for the first time on the lawyer's paperwork, some speck in the Midlands an hour and a half from here. Google images showed a quaint market town with a cobblestone town centre, pretty and oh so English. It is surrounded by gorgeous green countryside, but at the moment the view around me is pretty dreary.

The route's a slog—motorways first, the M42 droning

with lorries and rain-slicked asphalt, wipers squeaking against the windshield. My hands grip the steering wheel, knuckles white, heart thudding as I lean forward and mutter curses at every roundabout.

"Left, no, fuck—right!" A horn blares impatiently. "Oops, sorry, sorry."

I'm a mess, second-guessing every turn, but then the rain stops and the green starts creeping in—fields, hedgerows, sheep scattered like dirty cotton balls. It's Instagram-worthy picturesque, and normally I would have been stopping to take selfies, but I'm too wired today.

The roads narrow, twisting into lanes barely wide enough for even the tin can of a car I'm in. Branches scrape the sides, and I flinch, imagining dents I can't afford. My phone signal drops to one bar, then none—great, stranded in nowhere. The GPS lags, but finally, a sign: Berryhill, 2 miles. My chest tightens, breath shallow. Google earth was useless so I've got no idea what this cottage looks like—cute little stone thing? Total wreck? The lawyer said it was "rustic". Whatever that means. I just hope it's not a money pit. I've got enough for a few months, maybe, if I'm stingy. This has to work.

The village sneaks up on me—stone cottages, a pub called The Fox & Hare, a village hall, an ancient church with a crooked steeple, and two rows of higgledy piggledy, Tudor-style white and black shops. Then the road dips, and I see it: a manor house, massive and sleek, rising out of the green like something ripped from a fairy tale. White stone, six tall Corinthian pillars, a driveway lined with trees—it's breathtaking, and my jaw drops, the car slowing as I gawk. Holy shit my GPS is saying, "You have arrived," in a British accent.

No way. This can't be it. Can it?

This is no cottage. Is it possible "cottage" is just a name, not the real deal. Was my grandmother secretly a rich snob?

Did I inherit a freaking mansion? My pulse races, a wild, stupid hope flaring up. I picture velvet curtains, chandeliers, a bathtub I could drown in—not some shack. I'm shocked, buzzing, grinning like an idiot.

But then I see it, down a rutted lane. The manor's still in sight, looming, but ahead... and there's this. A cottage. Small, squat, stone walls swallowed by ivy and weeds so tall it looks like it's trying to eat the place alive. My heart sinks to a slow, heavy thud. The cottage is a pit stop to that manor's palace— a poor cousin, crumbling and forgotten. I know it's mine before I even stop the car. Must have been lovely once, but now it looks pretty rough with its mossy stones and sagging roof, and the land around is practically a jungle, wild and overwhelming. I sit there, engine idling, reluctant to get out. This is it? This is my big escape?

I kill the ignition and hear something I almost never hear in the city. An orchestra of birds singing. Okay, that's good. I grab my suitcase, dragging it through the gravel. My boots crunch, sinking into mud as I fish the keys from my pocket— old, tarnished, mailed over by Grandma's estate lawyer.

The door creaks open, hinges groaning, and I step inside. It's an abyss. Not filthy, exactly—just... packed to the rafters. Two hundred years of junk crammed into a space slightly bigger than my old studio. Hoarder vibes hit hard. Old newspapers piled high, cans, bottles, odd bits and bobs, cracked ornaments. The faded furniture squats under dust, books and trinkets covering every inch. There are cobwebs everywhere and the is air's thick, musty, like wet paper and time.

The only clear spot is a rickety stool by the door. I drop my bag, my chest caving. Overwhelmed can't cover it—I'm drowning in this mess, and conflicted as hell. God, I can't spend the night here. Should I admit my plan had no merit, cut my losses and just turn around and go back? I can afford the ticket back to Chicago. Which is exactly what I want to do right at this moment. To get in the tin can car outside and get out of hell here because what have I fucking done? Jumped from the pan right into the fire.

Then my eyes fall upon a photo of a woman and a child hanging on a wall and a pang hits me, sharp and unexpected. Grandma and my mother. I never met her, never known her, and now I'm standing in her lonely, stubborn chaos. We could've spent weeks here, sorting out this shit, laughing over her weird crap, making it ours. My throat tightens, and I blink hard, shoving the feeling of loss and defeat down.

I should have gotten to know her and not just accepted the status quo of no contact on account of her strained relationship with my mom. My dad turned out to be a total jackass so she was right, after all. I sigh again, a resolve forming in me never again to just accept the status quo. To try to find the solution in things or the charm in them. Right. No way out now, at least today, so time to find the charm in this situation. I shove at one of the windows with both hands, the frame sticking hard, paint flaking off in little curls that dust my fingers.

It groans like it hasn't been opened in decades, wood scraping wood. I grit my teeth and push until it gives with a reluctant screech. Cold air rushes in, sharp and damp, slamming into my face. It doesn't smell of the smog of the city, but carries the scent of earth—rich, loamy—and weeds. Its bitter and wild, mingling with something faintly sweet I can't place. I suck it in, my chest expanding. There's definitely charm here. Holding that positive thought in mind I walk through the indescribable horror of the clutter and smell in the kitchen. Stoically, ignoring it all, I find the key to the back door, open it and step over the threshold onto the sagging porch. Rotten boards creak under my boots. The yard, and it looks like there is a lot of it, sprawls out in front of me, a tangled mess of green and brown. Right.

I just stand there, letting it hit me.

Sure, it's overgrown as hell—grass up to my knees, snarled with thistles and nettles that look like they could shred my jeans if I waded in. Bushes hunch along the walled edges, gnarled and choked with tall weeds, their branches clawing at the old bricks like they're trying to pull the boundary down so they can carry on their relentless march. A rusted wheelbarrow lies tipped over near a crumbling shed, half-buried in the mess, and I spot a lone daffodil in what might've been a flowerbed once, now just a graveyard of dead stalks and mud. I stare at the flower. It survived it all and stood proud. And I feel a thrill run through me. I am that flower. I will overcome too. The neglect is overwhelming, but my eyes keep moving, picking out shapes beneath the ruin. There's potential here—raw, untamed, begging for someone to give a damn.

I step off the porch, gravel crunching underfoot, and wander closer, the chill seeping through my jacket. I can see it already—flowers bursting out, vivid and messy, maybe roses or peonies, their petals spilling over the stones. Wisteria dripping from a trellis I'll build myself, purple and heavy, swaying in the breeze like something out of a painting. A veggie patch over there, near the shed—tomatoes, zucchini, chilis, and a whole bunch of herbs I could smell on my hands after picking them.

I've always wanted that, to dig into dirt and grow my own food, watch it come alive under my care. Back in my over-priced Chicago shoebox? Not a freaking chance—my landlord would probably fine me for a potted basil plant.

Here, though...

I kick at a clump of weeds, the roots stubborn, clinging to the earth, and a flicker of doubt creeps in. This will take work—weeks, months, tools I don't have, skills I' have to learn from scratch. My hands aren't soft, but they're not calloused either; they're sales-manager hands, good for typing quotas, not hauling dirt. Still, I picture it—me out here, sweaty and tanned, tearing out the junk, planting seeds, coaxing this disaster into something alive. A garden I could sit in, beer in hand, watching the sun dip behind those rolling hills. My breath catches, a stupid lump rising in my throat. Grandma must've stood here once, maybe saw the same thing before it all went to shit. Did she give up, or did it just slip away?

I feel a spark—a hope, faint but stubborn, rooting itself in me. This space is wide open, screaming for a purpose.

A thrill of excitement flows through me as the realization hits home. All of this space is mine! It is not a lease I have to bleed blood and guts for. It belongs to me. And only me.

Sure, the yard is a wreck now, but I could make it really mine. I could build something good. The thought settles in me, warm and fragile, rays of hope sneaking in through the ruin around me.

I glance up, past the tangled mess of my yard, and catch sight of the manor again—sleek and magnificent, its stone walls glowing in the late afternoon light, a fairy-tale beast dwarfing my little wreck. My chest tightens, not with defeat, but with something fiercer. Something I've never felt before in life. I decide right then, standing in those beginning rays of English sunset, and with my boots sinking in the mud, that I'll make my cottage as beautiful as that manor, or hell, even better. Not just pretty—breathtaking, alive, mine.

"One more instance where size doesn't matter," I mutter to myself, and a dry chuckle slips out. I can almost hear

Sandy laughing with me, and it's enough to prepare me to fight for my plot of chaos.

"I'll never give you up," I whisper to the wind as it blows in the direction of the manor.

Want to know more?
Pre-order the book here:
Neighbor From Hell

ABOUT THE AUTHOR

If you wish to leave a review for this book
please do so here:
Twisted Love

Please click on this link to receive news of my latest releases
and great giveaways.
<u>Georgia's Newsletter</u>

and remember
I **LOVE** hearing from readers so by all means come and say
hello here:

ALSO BY GEORGIA LE CARRE

Owned

42 Days

Besotted

Seduce Me

Love's Sacrifice

Masquerade

Pretty Wicked (novella)

Disfigured Love

Hypnotized

Crystal Jake 1,2&3

Sexy Beast

Wounded Beast

Beautiful Beast

Dirty Aristocrat

You Don't Own Me 1 & 2

You Don't Know Me

Blind Reader Wanted

Redemption

The Heir

Blackmailed By The Beast

Submitting To The Billionaire

The Bad Boy Wants Me

Nanny & The Beast

His Frozen Heart

The Man In The Mirror

A Kiss Stolen

Can't Let Her Go

Highest Bidder

Saving Della Ray

Nice Day For A White Wedding

With This Ring

With This Secret

Saint & Sinner

Bodyguard Beast

Beauty & The Beast

The Other Side of Midnight

The Russian Billionaire

CEO's Revenge

Mine To Possess

Heat Of The Moment

Boss From Hell

Sweet Poison

The Guardian

Fight Me, Little Pearl

Devil In a Suit

Made in the USA
Monee, IL
22 May 2025

17984910R00196